Letting Go

Also by Molly McAdams

Sharing You
Capturing Peace (Novella)
Deceiving Lies
Needing Her (Novella)
Forgiving Lies
Stealing Harper (Novella)
From Ashes
Taking Chances

Letting Go

MOLLY McADAMS

wm

WILLIAM MORROW
An Imprint of HarperCollins*Publishers*

LETTING GO. Copyright © 2014 by Molly Jester. All rights reserved. Printed in the United States of America. No part of this book may be used or reproduced in any manner whatsoever without written permission except in the case of brief quotations embodied in critical articles and reviews. For information address HarperCollins Publishers, 195 Broadway, New York, NY 10007.

HarperCollins books may be purchased for educational, business, or sales promotional use. For information please e-mail the Special Markets Department at SPsales@harpercollins.com.

FIRST EDITION

Library of Congress Cataloging-in-Publication Data has been applied for.

ISBN 978-0-06-235840-0

14 15 16 17 18   OV/RRD   10 9 8 7 6 5 4 3 2 1

To anyone who has lost someone: Don't ever stop moving. That doesn't mean you're moving on or forgetting, it simply means you're still living. One step at a time, and one day at a time. This is for you.

Prologue

Grey
May 10, 2012

"THEN OVER THERE is where the girls and I will be waiting before the ceremony starts," I said, pointing to the all-season tent standing just off to the side. "I think the coordinator said she'd get us in there when the photographer is taking pictures of Ben and the boys on the other side of the house so he won't see me."

I glanced behind me to my mom and soon-to-be mother-in-law talking about the gazebo, and what it would look like with the greenery and flowers, and I smiled to myself. They'd been going back and forth on whether we should keep the gazebo as it was or decorate it ever since Ben and I had decided on The Lake House as our wedding and reception site. And from the few words I was hearing now, they were still undecided. I honestly didn't care how it was decorated. I wanted to be married to Ben, and in three days, I would be.

"Grey, this place is freaking *gorgeous*. I can't believe you were able to get it on such short notice," my maid of honor and best friend, Janie, said in awe.

"I know, but it's perfect, right?"

"Absolutely perfect."

I grabbed her hand and rested my head on her shoulder as I stared at the part of the property where the reception would be held. Ben and I had promised our families that we wouldn't get married until we'd graduated from college, but that had been a much harder promise to keep than we'd thought. School had let out for summer a few days ago, and we wanted to move off campus for our junior year . . . together. That hadn't exactly gone over well with my parents. They didn't want us living together until we were married. I think in my dad's mind it helped him continue to believe I was his innocent little girl.

I'd been dating Ben since I was thirteen years old; the innocent part flew out the window over three years ago. Not that Dad needed to know that. After a long talk with both our parents, they agreed to let us get married now instead of two years from now.

That was seven weeks ago. Even though Ben had asked me to marry him last Christmas, we'd officially gotten engaged once we'd received the okay from our parents, and had started planning our wedding immediately. Seven weeks of being engaged. Seven years of being together. And in three days I would finally be Mrs. Benjamin Craft.

Given how the last few weeks had dragged by, it felt like our day would never get here.

My phone rang and I pulled it out of my pocket. My lips tilted up when I saw Jagger's name and face on the screen, but I ignored the call. Putting my phone back in my pocket, I kept my other hand firmly wrapped around Janie's and walked over to where the rest of the bridesmaids were standing around and talking. My aunts and grandma had gathered around the gazebo-debating duo, and were helping them with the pros and cons.

"So what are we going to do tonight?" I asked, hoping to get some kind of information about the bachelorette party.

"Nice try." Janie snorted. She started saying something else, but my phone rang again.

Glancing down and seeing Jagger again, I thought about answering it for a few seconds before letting out a soft laugh and ignoring the call a second time. I knew why he was calling. He was bored out of his mind and wanted me to save him from the golf day Ben and all the guys were having before the bachelor party. Normally I would have saved him from the torture of golfing, but today was about Ben. If he wanted to go golfing with all his guys, then Jagger just had to suck it up for his best friend.

Almost immediately after ignoring the call, I got a text from him. *Answer the goddamn phone, Grey!*

My head jerked back when the phone in my hand began ringing just as soon as I'd read the message, and all I could do was stare at it for a few seconds. A feeling of dread and unease formed in my chest, quickly unfurling and spreading through my arms and stomach.

Some part of my mind registered two other ring tones, but I couldn't focus on them, or make myself look away from Jagger's lopsided smile on my screen. With a shaky finger, I pressed the green button and brought the phone up to my ear.

Before I could say anything, his panicked voice filled the phone.

"Grey? Grey! Are you there? Fuck, Grey, say something so I know you're there!"

There was a siren and yelling in the background, and the feeling that had spread through my body now felt like it was choking me. I didn't know what was happening, but somehow . . . somehow I knew my entire world was about to change. My legs started shaking and my breath came out in hard rushes.

"I—what's happ—" I cut off quickly and turned to look at my mom and Ben's. Both had phones to their ears. Ben's mom was screaming, with tears falling down her cheeks; my mom looked like the ground had just been ripped out from underneath her.

Jagger was talking, I knew his voice was loud and frantic, but I was having trouble focusing on the words. It sounded like he was yelling at me from miles away.

"What?" I whispered.

Everyone around me was freaking out, trying to figure out what was going on. One of my friends was asking who I was talking to, but I couldn't even turn to look at her, or be sure who it was that had asked. I couldn't take my eyes off the only other women currently talking on a phone.

"Grey! Tell me where you are, I'm coming to get you!"

I blinked a few times and looked down at my lap. I was sitting on the ground. When had I sat down?

Janie squatted in front of me and grabbed my shoulders to shake me before grabbing my cheeks so I would look at her instead of to where my mom and Ben's were clinging to each other.

"What?" I repeated, my voice barely audible.

Just before Janie reached for my phone, I heard a noise that sounded weighted and pained. A choking sound I'd never heard from Jagger in the eleven years we'd been friends. The grief in it was enough to force a sharp cry from my own chest, and I didn't even struggle against Janie when she took the phone from me.

I didn't understand anything that was happening around me, but somehow I knew everything. A part of me had heard Jagger's words. A part of me understood what the horrified cries meant, the cries that quickly spread throughout every one of my friends. My family. Ben's family. A part of me acknowledged the sense of loss that had added to the dread, unease, and grief—and knew why it was there.

A part of me knew the wedding I'd just been envisioning would never happen.

Chapter 1

Two years later . . .

Grey
May 10, 2014

IN A FOG, I dressed, and sat down on the side of my bed when I was done. Grabbing the hard top of the graduation cap, I looked down at it in my hands until the tears filling my eyes made it impossible to see anything other than blurred shapes. I knew I had to leave, but at that moment I didn't care.

I didn't care that I'd done my makeup for the first time in two years and I was ruining it. I didn't care that I was graduating from college. I didn't care that I was already running twenty minutes late before I'd sat down.

I just didn't care.

Falling to my side, I grabbed the necklace that hadn't left my neck once in the last couple years, and pulled it out from under my shirt until I was gripping the wedding band I'd bought for Ben. The one he should be wearing but I hadn't been able to part with—almost like I'd needed to keep some part of him with me.

The last year had been easier to get through than the one before it. I hadn't needed my friends constantly trying to get me to do my schoolwork. I hadn't needed Janie pulling me out of bed every morning, forcing me to shower and dress for the day. I'd even taken off my engagement ring and put it away a few months ago. But exactly two years ago today, I'd been showing off the place where I was going to marry Ben. Completely oblivious to anything bad in the world.

And Ben had died.

At twenty years old, his heart had failed and he'd died before he'd even dropped to the ground on the golf course. He'd always seemed so active and healthy; no tests had ever picked up on the rare heart condition that had taken him too early. Doctors said it wasn't something they could test for. I didn't believe them then, and even though I'd read news articles about similar deaths in young people, I wasn't sure if I believed them now. All I knew was that he was gone.

Heavy footsteps echoed through the hall of my apartment seconds before Jagger was standing in the doorway of my bedroom, a somber look on his face.

"How did I know you wouldn't have made it out of here?" One corner of his mouth twitched up before falling again.

"I can't do it," I choked out, and tightened my hold on the

ring. "How am I supposed to celebrate anything on a day that brought so much pain?"

Jagger took in a deep breath through his nose then pushed away from the door frame. Taking the few steps over to the bed, he sat down by my feet and stared straight ahead as silence filled the room.

"I honestly don't know, Grey," he finally said with a small shrug. "The only way I made it to my car and your apartment was because I knew Ben wanted this, and would still want it for us."

"He was supposed to be here," I mumbled.

"I know."

"Our two-year anniversary would have been in a few days."

There was a long pause before Jagger breathed, "I know."

I stopped myself before I could go on. Nothing I said right now would help either of us, not when all I wanted to do was curl up in a ball on the bed that was supposed to be *our* bed, and give in to the grief. I had to remember that today wasn't hard for only me. I hadn't been the only one to lose him. Ben and Jagger had been best friends since they were six. And two years ago they'd been in the middle of a conversation when Jagger had looked over at Ben because he hadn't answered, and watched as he fell.

"Jag?" I whispered.

"Yeah, Grey?"

"How do we do it?"

The bed shifted as he leaned forward to rest his forearms on his legs, turning his head so he could look at me. "Do what?"

"Keep moving on. I thought this year was easier, I thought I was doing better until this last week. And then today . . ." I drifted off, letting the words hang in the air for a few seconds before saying, "It's like no time has passed. It's like I'm right back where I was when you picked me up and took me to the hospital. I feel like my world has ended all over again. There are still some days when I don't want to get out of bed, but not like this."

"There isn't an answer to that question. Even if there were, it would be different for you, for me, for anyone else who'd ever been in this situation. I get up and keep going because I know I have something to live for, and I know it's what he would want. I can't think about how I'll deal with the next day, I just take each day as it comes. There will always be hard days, Grey, always. We just need to take them with the good days, and keep living."

"I feel like it's cruel to his memory to move on," I admitted softly a few minutes later.

"No one ever said we had to move on, we just need to keep moving."

I met his gaze and held it as he stood up and turned, holding a hand out to me.

"You ready to move?" he asked, and the meaning in his question was clear.

"No," I replied, but still held out my hand. Slipping it into his, I let him pull me off the bed, and wrapped my arms around his waist, dropping my head onto his chest.

Jagger folded his arms around me, and brought his head down near mine to speak softly in my ear. "Don't think about next week, or tomorrow, or even tonight. Just focus on your *right now*. Right now we have to go to our graduation. Right now Ben would be flipping out because you would be making both of you late."

I choked out a laugh, and a deep laugh rumbled in his chest.

"And you would tell him . . . ?" His question drifted off, waiting for my response.

"To get over it and bet him twenty bucks that we would still beat you there."

This time his laugh was fuller, and he rubbed his hands over my back before stepping away from me. "Exactly. Then he would put an extra twenty on it, saying I would show up with fresh charcoal on my hands."

"And face," I added.

Jagger rolled his eyes. "That was one time."

"It was to your mom's wedding."

"I didn't like the guy anyway." I smiled and his eyes darted over my face before he held his hands up. "No fresh charcoal, and we'll show up at the same time. So no one wins today."

I took a deep breath in and out, and nodded my head. "I think I'm ready to move now."

"All right." He bent forward and grabbed my cap and gown off the bed before turning to leave the room.

I followed him down the hall and into the living room, pausing in the entryway only long enough to look in the mirror and wipe away the streaked makeup. Once we were in his car, I touched his forearm and waited for him to look over at me.

"Thanks, Jagger. For coming for me, for talking to me—just . . . thank you." He had no idea how thankful I was for him, and I wouldn't have known how to explain it if I tried. He was just always there to make things better, always there to help me . . . always there to be everything I needed.

He shook his head slowly once, and his green eyes stayed locked on mine. "Sometimes I need motivation to keep moving too. You don't need to thank me, just let me know when you have to talk about him, okay?"

"Yeah." Letting go of his arm, I sat back in the seat and

grabbed the long chain that held Ben's wedding band. Taking comfort in the feel of it in my palm, and the knowledge that he would be proud of Jagger and me right now.

I MADE IT through the graduation without crying again, but I never felt like I was happy that it was happening. Even though Jagger had gotten me to a point where I'd been smiling and laughing, the second he left my side when we arrived, I'd fallen back into a state where I was constantly on the verge of crumbling from the grief of what today was. Only to be made worse when Janie had hugged me longer than normal, and then I'd seen my parents and older brother, and none of them had been able to force anything more than a strained smile and "congratulations."

Lunch afterward didn't prove to be much easier for anyone. One of my uncles mentioned the date and asked how I was dealing with it, and it had turned into some awkward hush-fest where everyone started kicking the other under the table, and giving them meaningful looks as if to say: *Shut the fuck up!* For the next forty-five minutes, no one said a word. Not even a thank-you to the waitress when she'd brought the food.

As much as I hated it, and as much as I loved my family, I was relieved when we'd said our good-byes and my brother had driven me back to my apartment.

"You doing okay, kid?" he asked when he pulled into a parking space.

"Some days."

"But not today." It wasn't a question, he knew.

"Yeah . . . not today," I said softly.

"Do you want me to come up? I can hang out, crash here for the night, and head back tomorrow."

"No, it's fine. I didn't really sleep last night, so I'll probably go to bed when I get in there."

"Grey, it's four in the afternoon." He looked at me with either pity or sympathy, neither of which I wanted to see.

"Today was kind of rough, it felt like three smashed into one, and like I said, I didn't really sleep last night. I'm tired."

He was silent for a minute before he twisted in his seat to face me. "I'm worried about you."

I gritted my teeth and took calming breaths before saying, "You shouldn't be. It's been two years, I'm getting better."

"Are you?" he asked on a laugh, but there was no humor in his tone. "I knew today would be hard for you, there's no way for it not to be. But, shit, how much do you weigh?"

I jerked my head back. "What? I don't know."

"Do you look at yourself in the mirror? Do you see how you look in your clothes? You look like you're wearing someone else's clothes, and they're a size or two too big."

Glancing down at my shirt and skirt, I shook my head. "No, they—well, I'm eating! You saw me at lunch, I ate half that burger."

"No, Grey. *I* ate half your burger. You picked it up and put it down at least a dozen times before cutting it in half, and then picking up one of the halves only to put it back down. I watched you. You ate two fries. Nothing else."

I tried to think back to the restaurant, but I couldn't even remember ordering the burger, let alone cutting it. I just remembered half of it was gone when the waitress asked if I wanted a box. I'd said no. As for the clothes, today was the first time I'd actually paid attention to what I was wearing in years. I usually just put on clothes and left, not caring to see how I looked.

"Well, what do you want me to say, Graham? I'm *trying*. You have no idea how hard it is to lose someone who has been a huge part of your world for over half your life. Who has owned your heart for most of that. Who you were supposed to marry *days* before they passed! You don't understand what I've been through," I seethed, and wiped at my wet cheeks. "I finished school, I'm living, what more do you want?"

"I want you to live, Grey."

"I just said—"

"You're existing," he barked, cutting me off. "You're existing, *not* living. You're going through the motions you're supposed to without realizing that you're doing them, or why."

"That's not true!" I screamed. "You can't judge me based on what you've seen of half a day. A day that is a horrible reminder of what happened."

He grabbed my hand and squeezed, and when he spoke again, his voice was calm. "Kid, I'm not saying any of this *only* based on what I've seen today. Janie's worried about you—"

"Janie? Janie?! You're having my friends keep tabs on me, Graham?"

"Grey—"

"How often do they check in with you? Huh? Do they only see me now so they can tell you how I'm doing? Because I don't see them very much, but then again, who the hell would want to be around someone who is just *existing*?"

"Grey!" he snapped when I opened the passenger door and jumped out of his truck.

"Screw you and your *existing* bullshit, Graham! I'm fine! I'm dealing the only way I know how, and I. Am. Fine."

I didn't care that there were tears streaming down my cheeks.

I didn't care that I was overreacting. I was overreacting because I was terrified that he was right, and I didn't want him to be. I was tired of everyone looking at me with sympathy or pity. I was tired of rooms growing quiet when I walked into them . . . *still*. I was tired of the way everyone seemed to walk on eggshells around me. And I was tired of feeling like I was giving them a reason to.

I took off for my building, ignoring Graham's voice as he followed me from his truck. Grabbing my keys from my purse as I ran toward my apartment, I fumbled to find the right key so I could get in there before he could catch up with me. The keys slipped from my hand, and I reached out for them at the same time as I tripped out of my sandals and hit the concrete on my hands and knees.

Ignoring the spilled contents of my purse, I rocked back so I was sitting on my heels and let my head hang as hard sobs worked their way through my body.

Two large hands grabbed at my upper arms to help me up, and I swatted at him. "Leave me alone, Graham!" I cried.

"Shhh. It's okay," a deep voice crooned. I lifted my head enough to see Jagger before letting him pull me into his arms. "It's okay."

I pressed my forehead into his chest and shook my head back and forth. "It's not. This day won't end, and the way everyone is looking at me or talking to me is making me feel like I'm failing."

"Failing?" he asked, and tipped my head back, a soft smirk playing at his lips. "Hardly, Grey. I told you, you just gotta keep moving, and you are. You have been. You're strong, not everyone sees that because they're waiting for you to break. Just because they're expecting you to not be handling this doesn't mean you're failing."

"But they won't talk about him, they won't talk about what happened. Graham said I'm not eating, and I'm losing weight. He said Janie's telling him that she's worried about me. He said I'm just existing and going through the motions."

"Fuck Graham. He's wrong. He's not with you every day to see how you're improving." Jagger's green eyes bored into mine. "Your family hasn't seen you much this year while you've been getting better, so they don't know how to handle the situation—especially because of what today is and the fact that you are upset. He's your brother, he's going to be worried about you; but, Grey, don't let him make you feel like you're not doing better than you should be. Today is an exception. And he just happened to see you *on* an exception, all right?" His arms tightened around me, and he leaned back until he was pressed up against the wall. "You're doing fine, I promise."

He held me until I stopped crying, and released me when I pulled back.

"See? Fine."

Today was making me question everything; I didn't think I could agree with him on that. "What are you even doing here?"

"I thought you could use some company since it's an exception day, but I'm gonna go so you can spend time with your brother," he said, jerking his head at something behind me.

I looked over my shoulder to see Graham standing against the wall opposite us, his arms crossed over his chest, a strange look on his face. "How long has he been there?" I whispered to Jagger when I turned to face him again.

"The whole time."

"So he heard you . . ." I had the sudden urge to stand up for Jagger. Graham had hated him ever since we'd become friends when we were nine. But, then again, he hadn't really ever liked Ben until right before the wedding was supposed to happen, so it could have been an overprotective big-brother thing.

"Yeah, but he knows I'm right." Jagger's eyes moved to look behind me, and one eyebrow rose in silent challenge, but Graham never said anything. "Go hang out with—"

"I don't want to," I said quickly, cutting him off. "I need to either be alone, or be with someone who knows what it's like to force yourself to keep moving."

He looked down at me for a few seconds before nodding. "Okay, let's go."

"We're not staying here?" I asked when he bent down and started shoving things back into my purse.

"No. You want to keep moving, Grey. We can't do that if we sit in that apartment all night."

I took my purse from his hand and turned to follow him out of the breezeway, Graham behind us the whole time. Jagger opened the passenger door of his car and shut it behind me after I'd slid in, and I met Graham's stare from where he stood a few feet from the front of the car.

Graham's hand shot out, gripping Jagger's arm as he went to pass him, and I opened the door—ready for who knows what. It's not like I could stop them if they went at it.

"Make sure she's okay," Graham demanded, his gaze hardening when Jagger ripped his arm free.

"What do you think I've been doing for the past two years?" Jagger hissed. "She is okay, she's better than okay. Today sucks for her, but you can't treat her like she's made of porcelain because it's a bad fucking day. She needs to talk about him; she needs to talk about what happened. She doesn't need the way you all stood there at the graduation staring at her like you had no idea who she was."

"Do you see her?" Graham asked, getting closer. "Do you see how thin she is?"

"Yeah, I see her. I see her every day. She lost a lot of weight; she's also put on weight in the last few months. Give her some fucking credit, Graham. Don't just take Janie's word for it— Janie isn't around enough to give you updates on her. You want to know how your sister is doing, ask her yourself. Don't *tell* her how she is." Jagger didn't wait for him to say anything else; he stalked around the hood of the car and slid into the driver's seat.

Graham looked like he couldn't decide if he wanted to stop me from leaving with Jagger or was relieved I was leaving. When I shut my door, he put a hand over his chest in our silent *I love you,* and kept his eyes trained on mine until I put my hand over my chest as well, nodding once as Jagger backed out of the spot.

Jagger
May 10, 2014

I LET MY phone fall to the table and sighed loudly as I rubbed my hands over my face. After driving around with the music blasting and windows down for a few hours, we'd come to one of the places we used to always go to before Ben died. They had live music on the weekends and the best diner food in the area.

"Graham?" Grey guessed, and I grunted in confirmation.

"He just wanted to make sure you were okay."

"You haven't," she began, but paused for a few seconds. "Have you been giving him updates too?"

"Seriously, Grey? Your brother hates me; I didn't even know he had my number until a few minutes ago. Besides, if I had been giving him updates, he probably wouldn't have said all that shit to you, and your family wouldn't have acted like statues at the graduation."

"I heard you say something about that to him before we left. So you noticed it too, huh?"

"Wasn't hard to. My sister wanted to see you, but after we found you and saw the way they were all just staring at you, she was afraid to say anything."

"Charlie was there? Were your mom and brother there too?"

I stopped myself from rolling my eyes and just shook my head instead. "No. Mom was probably busy with her new boyfriend or husband."

Grey rolled her eyes at the mention of my mom's boyfriends, and her lips tilted up in a soft smile. "I doubt that was the reason she didn't show. But I wish Charlie had said something. I'll have to call her this summer, or something. I haven't seen her in forever." Grey's mouth fell into a frown for a second before she turned to look at the stage when everyone clapped.

I hadn't set foot in here in two years, and it felt strange, but good, to be here again. Almost like I could see Ben sitting on the opposite side of the booth, right next to Grey. But just as soon as the memory hit me, it was gone. "Do you ever feel like he's disappearing?" I asked suddenly.

Grey's head shot up, her eyes wide as she took in my words. "What?"

"Ben. Do you feel like his memory is disappearing? Everywhere, all around us."

"All the time," she murmured, and nodded absentmindedly

for a few moments. "I forced myself to stop buying his cologne, and there are times I don't remember what he smelled like. When I realize that, I panic. I'm afraid I'll forget forever, and I want to go buy another bottle. But I know I can't, I know it'll just make it harder to move on. I don't—" She cut off on a quiet sob, and covered her mouth with her hand as tears filled her eyes. "I don't remember what his laugh sounded like. I don't remember the way it felt when he held me. I'm afraid to go back to Thatch, Jag."

"What? Why?"

"I don't want to see his parents' house and know that Ben's been completely erased from it."

I sagged into the booth and blew out a heavy breath. "Yeah, I'd forgotten about that."

Six months after Ben died, his parents had moved. Not just to another house, not just out of town. They'd moved across the country to get away. They hadn't been able to handle all the memories of Ben when their only child was now gone. And in a town the size of Thatch, there were memories everywhere.

I'd felt the same, but now I was in the same spot as Grey. I was terrified of forgetting him, and now I wondered if his parents regretted leaving.

"So what are you going to do?"

She blinked a few times, like I'd just pulled her from somewhere else, and after a few seconds she shrugged. "I'm still going back. The apartment here isn't much better. He's the one who picked it out, and all I ever think about when I'm in there is that he's supposed to be in there too. It'll be hard at first, but I need to go home. What about you?" Grey's lips curved up in a rare smile, and I felt myself smiling back at her until she spoke. "I always pictured you just taking off. No one has ever been able to

hold on to you, and I feel like towns and cities are no different.
I don't see you ever finding a place where you'll want to settle
down forever."

Of course you don't. I looked down so she wouldn't see anything
she wasn't supposed to. There was truth to her words, and at the
same time she was so wrong. No one had ever been able to keep
me because I'd only ever belonged to her. I'd dated a handful of
girls in the first two years after leaving Thatch . . . if you could
call it dating, and had only ever had one girlfriend back home—
and that had been in hopes that it would get a reaction out of
Grey as much as it had been a distraction for me from the constant in-my-face relationship of Ben and Grey. If Ben hadn't died,
and if they'd gotten married, leaving is exactly what I would've
done. It was one thing to stay back, not saying anything to her,
hoping one day she would see in me what I'd seen in her since we
were kids. It was another when I had to finally acknowledge she
would never be mine.

But even though I wasn't sure she would ever get to a point
in her life where she was ready to move on, there was no way I
could leave her now. She wasn't mine, but she needed me. And I
would be there for her as long as she did.

"So where do you think you'll go?" she asked, and I looked
back up at her.

"Thatch," I said, my voice low and gravelly. "I belong in
Thatch."

Chapter 2

Jagger
May 16, 2014

FLIPPING THROUGH MY keys until I found hers, I unlocked the door to Grey's apartment and stepped in. Using my foot, I pushed aside a stack of two boxes so I could get past the entryway, and called out for her. "Grey?"

"Bedroom!" she yelled, and I made my way back there.

"How's it coming, you al—" I cut off abruptly, and a sharp laugh burst from my chest when I found her.

It'd been almost a week since graduation, and today was the day we left Pullman to go back to Thatch. We'd spent the majority of the last two days packing and putting all our furniture in a truck we'd rented so we could just load up the last of the boxes and leave today, but Grey being Grey . . . she had to do everything at the last minute. And apparently that had failed. She was sitting on the floor next to the sleeping bag she'd been sleeping in, her legs spread out as she grabbed at all of her bathroom stuff scattered on the floor around her. The biggest pout I'd seen on her face since we were in middle school.

"Did you forget to tape the bottom of the box?"

"Shut up, Jag," she huffed as she dropped more into the box.

"I'll take that as a yes. Did you tape it this time?"

Her hand paused in the air above the box, and her shoulders slumped as her head dropped back, so she was looking at the ceiling. Mumbling things too low for me to hear.

I choked back another laugh and walked into the room, bending down to help her pick up everything that had fallen. "It's okay. We'll just fill this up and tape the top, and then we'll very carefully tip it over. All right?"

"I swear to God, I can't focus on anything today. Or pack, apparently." She continued grumbling to herself, and I couldn't help but smile.

I'd been afraid today would be too hard on her—leaving the apartment that was supposed to have been her first place with Ben, but even through her annoyance with the packing and the boxes, I could tell today was a good day for her.

"Did you know—" She'd pointed at me with a box of tampons, her eyes widening when she realized what was in her hand. Dropping the tampons into the moving box, she cleared her throat, and I pretended her face wasn't as red as her hair. "*Anyway,* did you know that I packed all my clothes yesterday?"

"Yeah, Grey, I was there."

"No. I mean, *all* of them. Which means I didn't have any clothes when I got out of the shower this morning."

My eyes flashed over to her before quickly going back to the floor, and I tried to concentrate on picking up everything so I wouldn't sit there thinking about her in the shower.

"Thank God I didn't let you put all those boxes in the truck. So after finally finding a box that had my clothes in it and cutting into it, I took out some clothes and taped it back up, only to realize I'd taken out two shirts, nothing else. That is how my morning has been. All morning. I should not be allowed to drive today."

A smile spread across my face as I reached behind me for the tape sitting on top of another box. "Let me guess, no coffee this morning?"

"I packed that yesterday too!" Her horrified tone let me know she'd been kicking herself all morning over that. She fell back until she was lying on the floor, and groaned. "This is why I don't do anything until the last minute."

"We're going to pass a ton of coffee shops, we'll get you something on the way out. And you don't do anything until the last minute because you wouldn't know what to do with yourself if you were actually on time for something. Your world might implode or something."

Raising one arm to flip me off, she let it flop back to the floor before sitting up. "Okay, let's finish this."

"How much do you have left?" I asked when I slowly tilted the box, waiting for her to put her hands on the bottom so the flaps wouldn't open again.

"Just packing up the truck, this was the last box."

"Truck is full, these will have to go in your car. And look at you trying to be on time," I mumbled, and she laughed.

"You would've been so proud of me. I was running around here like mad packing up everything I saw left out."

Glancing up at her, I smirked. "And you still failed."

She made a face, but didn't say anything else.

I taped the box shut and stood up, extending an arm to help her up as well. "All right, well, let's get started and get on the road before you go into severe caffeine withdrawal."

I grabbed that box and stacked it on top of another. Lifting them both up, I walked into her living room and looked at the counter. A frown tugged at my lips, and I turned in a slow circle, seeing only boxes. "Grey, where are your keys?"

"In my purse," she called out from down the hall.

"Yeah. Where's your purse?"

"On the counter where it always—" She cut off when she turned the corner into the living room, her eyebrows pinching together as she looked at the bare counter. I watched as her mouth slowly dropped open and her eyes widened as she looked at the boxes in the living room she'd packed this morning. "Son of a bitch."

AFTER CUTTING OPEN two boxes to find her purse and keys, I finished loading up all the boxes while she went to turn in everything to the leasing office, and we were finally on our way back to Thatch. Well, after we stopped to fill up her car with gas since she'd forgotten to, and gotten her coffee. The drive only took a little over three hours, and then we were pulling into the town we'd grown up in. Small in size and population, but full of memories that hit me hard the second we'd rounded the massive lake that hid our town, and I wondered how Grey was doing now that we were here.

She'd only been able to handle being here for a little over a month last summer, and hadn't come back at all during the winter break a handful of months ago. Even though she'd already been getting so much better before that, to the point where she had been the one to bring up moving back here right after the school year had started, I couldn't help but remember how she'd said she was scared to come back here just last week. I knew if I could see her right now, she'd be gripping Ben's ring that hung on the chain around her neck. What I didn't know was if she was happy to be remembering times with him here, or if the memories were all too much.

And a few minutes later I had my answer.

At the last second, she took the exit toward the cemetery, and I cursed and hit the brakes so I could follow her. By the time I'd parked and gotten out of the rented truck, she'd already found his headstone. She stood there for a few minutes, her body swaying as she clutched at the necklace before she suddenly fell to her knees. I took a couple steps toward her before stopping myself, and ran my hands over my head as I forced myself back to lean up against the truck.

She hadn't been back here since the funeral, so I knew she needed this, and she needed to do it alone. But for her, and for me, I needed to be here for when she was ready to leave.

My throat tightened when her cries reached me, and I dropped my head to look at the ground as I fought with my own tears, her grief added to mine. I hated that he was gone. I hated that she was in pain. I hated that it felt like there was nothing I could do to help her.

My head snapped up seconds before Grey slumped against my chest, and my arms automatically went around her. I don't know how long we'd been there, but her face was red and wet with tears. Her eyes looked vacant as she took in where we were standing, and even though her breaths were shallow, they were even.

"How is he?" I asked a few minutes later, and her eyes slowly moved to look up at me.

She stared for countless moments before her lips opened enough for her to say, "He's good."

I nodded and lowered my voice to a whisper. "And how are you?"

"Broken," she answered immediately. "Broken, but moving."

"Sounds like you're right where you should be."

A faint smile played on her lips for a second before falling. "How are you?"

I'm broken too, I thought. *I break a little more every time you do. I'm torn. I've never hated myself more for wanting you than I have since Ben died. I want to make your pain go away. I want my best friend back. I would give fucking anything to take his place just so you could be whole again.* Looking into her honey-gold eyes, I shrugged. "I'm moving."

"Yeah, you are. We are," she whispered. "You didn't have to stay."

I didn't respond to that, because anything I would have said would've been too much. Instead, I stood there holding her until she was ready to leave.

Grey
May 16, 2014

JAGGER SET DOWN a box and sighed as he wiped sweat from his forehead. "That's the last of it on your end, I think. If I find something when I'm unloading, I'll just bring it by here later."

"Okay, it's not a big deal if we missed anything. Most of it is going to stay in boxes until I get an apartment . . . or figure out what I'm going to do," I mumbled, and glanced around at the bedroom I'd grown up in. "I mean, it's not like I have a lot of use for an entire apartment's worth of stuff in just one room."

The corners of his lips curved up in a smile as he looked over all the boxes. "Well, let me know if you need anything. I'm gonna go start on everything else."

I stood from where I'd been going through a box on the floor and walked toward him. "I'll go with you."

"You don't need to, Grey, I can do it."

I made a face. "So, you can help me load and unload my things, and then you're going to do the rest by yourself? All the couches, the beds . . . all of it? Because that sounds fair to you," I mumbled sarcastically.

He stopped my advance with a hand to my shoulder, and his green eyes bored into mine. "I'll be fine. Aren't you supposed to go to your brother's?"

"I told him I was coming back tonight; he's not expecting me until later."

"Grey . . ."

"Jagger." I mimicked him, and waited until he relented with a sigh.

"All right, let's go." He pushed away from the wall and turned toward my bedroom door, waiting for me to leave first.

It wouldn't have mattered to me what we were doing. I would have wanted to go with him. As much as I'd prepared to come back to Thatch, the memories I'd been blasted with had hit me harder than I could've ever expected. As good as it felt to cry and see Ben's grave today, I was terrified to be alone. I was afraid my happy feeling would leave, and I'd be left with nothing but the consuming grief.

"What are we doing here?" I asked ten minutes later when we pulled up to a building his family owned.

The outside was made up of dark bricks, and was otherwise nondescript. It didn't look old or new, just like a warehouse. Although I'd been here a few times when we were growing up, I'd never actually been inside. Jagger's grandparents had used this place for their business before retiring, and it had sat untouched for years until his mom went through one of her many phases. She'd decided to try her hand at pottery due to whatever it was her husband at that particular time did for a living, and to her credit, it was one of her longest-lasting phases and relationships. The phase had lasted a whole two and a half years—the length of her relationship—before she'd given up on it during our senior year of high school, and as far as I knew, this place hadn't been used since.

"Are you going to store all of our furniture here until we get places?"

Jagger turned to look at me; his eyes were bright and mischievous, and I knew he'd been hiding something from me. "Something like that."

"Jagger Easton, why do I have a feeling you were trying to keep me from coming with you for a reason?"

He raised one eyebrow at me, and his signature smirk crossed his face as he rested one arm on the steering wheel. "I have no idea what you mean, Grey LaRue."

"Uh-huh. I'm sure you don't."

"Well, are you going to get out and help me with everything, or are you going to sit in here and try to figure out what's going on?"

My eyes narrowed. "I don't see you moving."

He leaned in so close that my next breaths got lost in the way he seemed to fill the entire cab of the truck. "I'm always moving, Grey. I'm just waiting on you to move with me."

Before I could respond—or figure out how to get my heart started again—he was pulling away and getting out of the truck, and I just sat there staring blankly for a few seconds before I followed.

Instead of going to the back to open up the truck, he went to the door on the side of the building and pulled his car keys out of his pocket. Once he found the one he was looking for, he unlocked the door and gave me another playful look before opening the door and stepping in, flipping on the lights as he did.

"Oh my God, it's huge in here!" Shock coated my words as I looked around the massive space.

"This is just the front."

"There's a back to this?" I asked, shooting him a look.

He nodded absentmindedly as he walked over to a large kitchen, separated from the rest of the room by a long, L-shaped granite bar. There was a piece of paper propped up on the island in the middle of the kitchen, and he picked it up to read as I looked up at the second-floor loft, covering half of the view of the high ceiling.

"Charlie must've stopped by," Jagger said, pulling my attention back to where he stood in front of the refrigerator.

"Why do you say that?"

"Fridge and pantry are stocked."

My brow furrowed as I looked at the empty space, then back to him. "Are you going to tell me what's going on now?"

His mouth lifted up on one side, and he dropped his head as he walked toward me. Only lifting his eyes to meet mine, he shrugged. "*This* is my place now."

"Are you using it for a studio?"

"Uh . . . no. There are two rooms in the back, both about the same size as the upstairs loft. I'll use one for a studio and another to store the rest of our stuff for now. But I'm going to live here."

"Seriously?" My eyes widened and I looked around me again. "I didn't know you could live here."

"Back when my grandparents were using it, the upstairs was an open office so they could look out at what was going on down here. There was a small bathroom up there, but we remodeled it so it's bigger now, and has a shower and everything. There's a bathroom in the back and another in here." He gestured to a door off to the side. "We remodeled those so they look nicer. There's a laundry room hidden behind the pantry that we put in. I didn't know what to do with the floor. The back rooms and the loft had hardwood put in right before my grandma passed, so I left that, but I kind of liked the way the concrete looked for this room. So they just put the dark sealer on it, and called it a day."

I looked down at the glossy floor and nodded. "I like it, it fits with the brick walls. And the kitchen?"

"Ah, yeah, that's new," he murmured, turning to look at it.

"It's huge." Jagger made some type of agreeing noise, and I nudged his side. "You also don't cook."

"No," he said on a laugh. "But it looks nice."

I studied it for a few more seconds before turning to look at him. "Who is 'we'?"

He turned his head to face me, furrowing his brow as he did. "What?"

"You kept saying 'we' when you were telling me what had been changed. Is someone moving in with you?"

It hit me then that there might have been another reason he didn't want me coming here. I hadn't seen Jagger with a girl in years, but I also hadn't known about this place, and I'd been so focused on trying to move on with my life that it was extremely possible I didn't know about a girl he'd been talking to back here in Thatch. The thought stole my next breath and left a sinking feeling in my stomach—but I couldn't begin to understand why. I wondered for a second if he had been patching things up with his ex-girlfriend, LeAnn, and the sinking feeling grew. It morphed into something so unfamiliar and unwelcome that I tried to force thoughts of Jagger with anyone from my mind.

I swallowed roughly and took a step away from him. "That's so not my business, you don't have to answer that."

Jagger laughed and started walking toward the door. "Since when is my life not your business, Grey? You've made it your business since we were nine."

My smile was shaky when I glanced up at him before following him out. "I just realized that you might have someone moving in with you, and that may have been why you didn't want me to help you unload the truck."

I turned to look at him when I realized he'd stopped walking and I'd passed him. His lips were forming a tight line and his eyebrows were slanted down over his eyes in that way he had when something was bothering him.

"Like I said, it's not my business," I mumbled when he just kept looking at me.

He dropped his head and cocked it to the side, but not before I saw his lips quirk up—giving him a bewildered expression. "No one's moving in with me. 'We' is just me, and the guys who did the remodeling, I guess."

"Okay." I blew out a heavy breath, but I couldn't figure out if it was out of relief or hurt that Jagger had hidden something like this from me. "When did you even start this? I had no idea." I leaned up against the truck and crossed my arms over my chest as I tried to process that Jagger had been the one to have the building renovated.

"Right after fall semester started."

"Why didn't you tell me? I had no idea that you even wanted to come back to Thatch until a week ago, and this whole time you've been remodeling the warehouse so you could live here?"

Jagger didn't look up at me when he walked past me and opened up the back of the truck, and for the second time today, I knew there was something he wasn't telling me. "I just didn't think it was that big a deal. We had to focus on graduating."

By that, I could only imagine he meant that he had to keep *me* focused on graduating. I'd known I would move back to Thatch, so had Jagger, but we never really talked about it because it would unnecessarily bring up the subject of Ben. And it was with that realization that I knew I had my answer. Jagger was always trying to protect me, and that's all his secretiveness about the building was. Instead of trying to get confirmation, I kept my mouth shut as I helped him move all the furniture out of the truck and into the warehouse. He knew I was grateful for him; that had never been a question.

A FEW HOURS later, we'd successfully moved all of my furniture into the farthest room in the back and set up all of his things in the front room and bedroom. I also had a newfound hatred for the stairs that led up to the loft. I wasn't built to help carry mattresses and dressers up two flights of stairs.

"Are you alive?" Jagger asked as he came down the stairs.

"No," I groaned from where I lay sprawled out on the floor.

"Do you regret coming with me now?"

"So much. So much regret in my arms and legs at the moment." He barked out a laugh, and I ran my palms across the smooth, glossy floor before saying, "I fully approve of your decision to keep the floor like this. It's really cold and it feels amazing."

"Well, I'm glad I got your approval now that it's been done for months."

He leaned over me, a lopsided smirk on his face. He looked like the past three hours hadn't happened. Jagger wasn't skinny by any means; not to say he was ripped either, he'd always just looked naturally well built. But I knew for a fact that working out wasn't in his vocabulary, and seeing as I spent most of my time running to clear my mind, it bugged me that he was somehow still in good enough shape to make moving two apartments' worth of furniture look effortless.

"I need to drop off the moving truck, do you want to come with me? We can get lunch after, and then I'll take you home."

"I can't move!" I complained. "How do you expect me to feed myself, let alone climb up into that truck?"

"So dramatic," he drawled, and reached an arm out toward me.

I grabbed it and groaned as obnoxiously as I could when he pulled me up.

He snorted and pushed me back, laughing when I almost fell back down. "I was gonna go easy on you and let you follow me in my car, but since you apparently can't function anymore, I guess I'll just have to hook my car back up to the truck and make fun of you while you try to climb—"

"No! I'll drive your car," I offered quickly, cutting him off as we walked to the door. Anything to avoid getting back in that truck.

"That's what I . . . thought . . ." His words trailed off, his voice dropping so low I barely heard his mumbled curse before I smacked into his back.

Jagger was holding the door open, but from the way his arm flexed around the handle, I knew he would've shut it if we hadn't been blocking the doorway.

"What—hey, Mrs. Easton," I said awkwardly, and shot Jagger a look as I moved out from under his arm to give his mom a hug.

"Hi, sweetie! I'm so glad you kids are back in town for good. I hated having you all gone."

I glanced past her for a second, looking for Jagger's sister and toddler brother, before asking, "Where are Charlie and Keith?"

"Keith's napping. Charlie's at home with him while I run some errands."

"Oh. Well, we were just going to get—"

"When did you get here?" Jagger asked over me and moved so he was standing between his mom and me.

His mom gave me a look and scoffed playfully before looking up at Jagger. "Just a minute ago."

"Why—" He cut off and looked back at me. Shoving his hand into his pocket, he pulled out his keys and handed them over to me. "Go start up the car, Grey, we'll be leaving in a second."

My eyes widened, but I didn't say anything to him. "Bye, Mrs. Easton."

"Bye, honey. See you soon."

I walked to Jagger's car, and when I turned to slide in, I found them both looking at me. Jagger looked like he was trying and failing to conceal his anger, and I didn't understand it. It took a lot to piss Jagger off, and even then, he usually just gave an edgy laugh before walking away from whomever he was mad at. He'd never mentioned anything about his mom that would make him respond to her in this way anyway. I had only seen her a few times since we'd all left for college, but it'd only been in passing, and I'd never been with Jagger at those times.

Mrs. Easton looked the same as every other time I'd ever seen her. Absolutely stunning, free, and with an easy smile that never ended. Other than going through husbands and hobbies like they were underwear, she always seemed to carry an air about her like nothing could touch her, like no sadness had—or ever would—mar her world. She was definitely her own kind of person. She'd refused to change her last name even with husband number one, but had a love for changing her first name. "Today I want to be called Flower . . . Jade . . . Infinite . . . Mother Love . . . Dolphin." The list was never ending and always changing, and she refused to answer to her given name, Cindy, so I'd never called her anything other than Mrs. Easton.

She was forty going on twenty-one, and it wasn't hard to see where Jagger and Charlie got their looks. They both had her full lips and bone structure most people would kill for. Charlie had her blue eyes, but had naturally blond hair compared to Jagger's and their mom's black hair, and a lean body compared to her mom's hourglass-figured one. I hadn't seen the youngest sibling since last summer when he was about six months old, but I had no doubt when Keith got older, he'd be just as beautiful as the rest of the family.

Even with the minor differences in appearance, their personalities were what completely separated them. Where their mom was the free spirit, Charlie was the brain of the family and shy to a fault. And Jagger . . . well, Jagger was just *Jagger*. He'd always been such a contradiction. He had been the fun one, the one who was always getting Ben and me into trouble with his insane ideas—not that that ever stopped us from following up on his next idea—and yet Jagger had a protective side in him that went much deeper than just being there for those he cared for. Given how flighty his mom had always been, he'd acted like a parent to Charlie, and had been the type of friend who always pushed Ben and me to be better at everything. And even though Jagger was covered in tattoos and looked terrifying if you didn't know him, and had a wild side we all knew well, there was a part of him that was incredibly calm, artistic, passionate, and in tune with others' emotions . . . something I'd come to understand well over the past two years.

Like I said . . . contradiction.

But this? This guy who had just stepped up to his mom so he was towering over, and staring down at her . . . I'd never seen him before. Knowing him and his different moods, I laughed whenever someone met Jagger and immediately looked intimidated or scared of him. But I saw it now; this Jagger was absolutely terrifying. And yet his mom just stood there looking up at him like he was telling her that the sky was made of cupcakes.

He bent his head lower, his glare deepening as they stared each other down, and soon his mom turned and walked toward her car—no, not walking. She was dancing to her car. Definitely acting like nothing had just happened, and like she wasn't affected by or worried about the way Jagger had just treated her. Once her car pulled away, Jagger glanced at me, a sad smile pulling at his lips as he watched me for a few seconds before he moved to the back of the truck and closed it up, and then got in the front.

As soon as he dropped off the truck at the rental place and took over the driver's side of his car, he began talking about Charlie and a trip she was taking this summer, before moving on to the subject of what I planned to do in Thatch, and how long I wanted to stay at my parents' house. There was never a lull in the conversation until he was dropping me back off at their house.

"Oh, before I forget," he mumbled, and messed with the keys without taking the car key out of the ignition. "For you."

I took the key from him and started putting it on my key ring as I asked, "Warehouse?"

Jagger made an affirmative grunt. This wasn't weird for us. Ben, Jagger, and I had all had keys to each other's houses since we could drive; it had made our parents crazy. When we'd gotten our own apartments in Pullman, we hadn't even said anything as we'd exchanged keys . . . by then it had been expected. Now wasn't any different.

"Try to have fun with your brother tonight, but if it gets too hard or you need anything, call me or just come over, 'kay?"

I nodded and started to get out of the car, but stopped. Despite how he'd been making sure the conversation had never gone in that direction, I had to ask. "What's going on with your mom?"

His face tightened in well-practiced confusion. "What do you mean?"

"Don't do that," I whispered. "Don't act like you have no idea what I'm talking about." He continued to watch me, and my shoulders sagged as a strange sadness filled my chest. "You don't respond to *anyone* that way, including your mom. Then you wouldn't talk to her when I was able to hear you." I shook my head and tried to laugh, but it sounded wrong. "We tell each other everything, we've *always* told each other everything. Then today I find out about the warehouse, and you're treating your mom like that . . . and I'm sitting here trying to figure out what else I don't know, Jag. When did all of this change between us?"

The expression slipped, and those green eyes bounced around as he took in my hurt. "Nothing has changed. I wanted to surprise you with the warehouse, that's why I didn't want you to help me move, and why I'm just giving you a key. I was going to show you once I had it all set up. As for my mom . . . that's—you just don't have to worry about that right now, Grey. There's nothing going on that you need to know about, I promise."

I didn't respond. This was coming from the same guy who always called me so I could make him laugh when his mom came home announcing she was getting married *again*.

He sighed and caught my eyes with his. "I haven't heard from her in almost a year. She didn't show up for graduation, didn't tell me she wasn't coming, and then she showed up today because she found out from Charlie that I'd remodeled the warehouse. I told Charlie that you and I were back in town, she told

Mom, and now that I don't want anything to do with her, she suddenly wants to see me again."

"She's your mom, Jagger."

"Yeah," he said on a laugh. Looking away, he took a deep breath before looking at me again. "I guess I was just mad because she didn't show last week. I'll apologize to her later."

I studied his expression for a few seconds before nodding. I still didn't believe him, but the day had been long, and physically and emotionally draining, and I could've just been making his reaction out to be more than it was. "Okay."

"Have fun with Graham; if I don't see you tonight, I'll see you tomorrow."

"What, you're not tired of me yet?"

His green eyes flashed up to mine before staring straight ahead. His tone held a teasing hint, but there was no mistaking the honesty when he said, "Never."

Chapter 3

Jagger
May 22, 2014

"SOUNDS LIKE YOU'RE gonna have fun, Charlie. I'm glad you won't just be sticking around here for the summer with Mom."

I turned when she didn't respond, and watched as Charlie played with the tab on her can of soda. My brows pinched together at the sudden and weird silence in my kitchen. She'd just been going on and on about the month-and-a-half-long trip she and a few of her friends were taking in a few weeks across the country, and now she wouldn't even look at me.

"Hey." I rested my forearms on the counter and waited until she looked up at me. "What's going on?"

"Nothing."

"Bullshit. Is it Mom? Has she been saying something?" I tried to remain calm and not give too much away, but when it came to our mom, that was hard to do. I was always trying to get a feel for what Mom was pulling with Charlie, but if she wasn't doing anything, then I wasn't ready for Charlie to know all about her yet.

"No." She waved me off and rolled her eyes. "She thinks this trip will be good for me. Something about spreading my wings."

Some of the tension eased out of my shoulders when I was assured Charlie was still blind to our mom's true nature. But if it wasn't our mom, it was someone else. Cocking my head to the side, I asked, "Then what changed all of a sudden? I couldn't get you to shut up about this trip, and now I'm ready to go talk to whoever made you look like this."

Charlie snorted softly and set her blue eyes on me. "Easy there, Jag. No need to go beating anyone up. I was just thinking about . . . well, I was just thinking about something. But it's not a big deal."

"If you're thinking it, then it's a big deal. Tell me."

Her round eyes pinched with worry, and she bit down on the inside of her cheek for a minute before taking a shuddering breath. "Do you think I should go on the trip?"

My head jerked back and a strangled huff blew past my lips. I don't know what I'd been expecting her to say. She'd found someone—probable. My shy sister was pregnant—doubtful. Mom had started coming after her too—possible, even though Charlie had already shown she was still clueless about it all. But this? "Do *I* think you should go on the trip? Of course I do!"

"Really? I'm just not sure about it. I mean, I want to go. I haven't hung out with those girls much since they all left for college a couple years ago. But I just—I don't know. I feel like I'm waiting for someone to tell me it's a bad idea."

"Why would it be a bad idea, Charlie? Are you worried about something happening on the trip?"

She rolled her eyes. "No, not that. It's just, Keith is here, and someone needs to watch him."

My eyes narrowed and my hands fisted on top of the counter. "Keith is not your problem, Charlie," I growled. "Mom's the one who got knocked up again, it's her son, she can take care of him."

Charlie's eyes flashed over to mine and hardened. "But you never know when Mom's gonna just pick up and leave. She'll be gone for days, and when she goes, she leaves Keith behind!"

"You think I don't know that? I didn't have to be here for the last year and a half to know that about her. She used to leave us all the time too once she thought I was old enough to fend for both of us for a few days. The only reason she leaves Keith right now is because she knows you're home and you won't leave him there alone."

"I just don't know, Jag."

"Charlie. He is not your responsibility. You need to go on this trip, you need to get out of Thatch for a while." I laughed agitatedly and shook my head. "Shit, what you need to do is actually go to college."

"I do go to school!" she argued back.

"No. You take classes online, that's so different."

"How is that any—"

"Because you're a fucking genius, Charlie!" I yelled, cutting her off. "I know you have money to go to school. You have the test scores to go pretty much wherever you want. I *want* you to get away from here, and I don't understand why you don't want that for yourself. You're cheating yourself out of the life you deserve away from Thatch."

"You came back. Why is it so bad that I wanted to stay?"

I groaned and ran my hands over my face. "Because I want to live here. There's nothing wrong with living here, this is a great town. But I want you to have the experience that going away to school will give you. Not only are you not giving yourself that opportunity, but you're making it incredibly easy for Mom to make you raise her kid."

Charlie just stared at me for a few minutes—hurt taking the place of the hardness in her eyes. "You raised me, Jagger. Are you saying you felt like that held *you* back from your life?"

"What?" I asked on a breath. "Are you kidding me? That's so different. You're two years younger than me, you went everywhere with me anyway. Taking care of you was as easy as taking care of myself—it was not a hardship."

"Well, someone needs to take care of Keith the way you took care of me. And despite what you think about me not giving myself the opportunity of living the 'college life,' I don't want that for myself. I've never wanted that for myself. I'm smart because you made me study all the time, but that doesn't mean I like school or want to do anything that a degree from an online school can't give me. This is what I want to do, and it's so hard when you're constantly on me about doing something different— something that you think would be best for me."

I rested my hands back on the counter and hung my head. "Okay, I'm sorry. I just—I'm sorry. Yes, I think you should go on the trip. You're excited about it, it sounds fun, and I agree with Mom . . . I think it'll be good for you. Can we just talk about something else?"

"Sure," she replied softly, but didn't say anything else until I looked up at her again. "I hung out with Grey today."

"I know. She was excited to see you, that was all she talked about this morning before she left to meet up with you."

"Yeah, it was . . . fun. I've missed her, I loved hanging out with her again."

My eyebrows shot up at her tone. "Then why do you sound like a robot?"

She shrugged. "I don't. I told you it was fun. Grey seemed . . . fine."

"Yeah. First day back was rough for her, I think, but she's doing a lot better overall."

"I noticed," Charlie mumbled so softly I almost didn't catch what she said.

I pushed away from the counter and crossed my arms over my chest. "Okay, what's going on? At graduation you couldn't wait to see her, and now that you've hung out with her, you sound . . . I don't know, disappointed or something. Did something happen today?"

"No, I'm just saying she seemed fine." Her voice was still monotone, and one eyebrow was raised as she stared across the kitchen at nothing.

My head was spinning. I hated arguing with Charlie, and didn't like that we'd just gotten into it again about the whole college thing. But the way she'd looked then was completely different from how she looked now. She looked exactly how she sounded and how I'd explained it to her. Disappointed. And I wasn't sure if something had happened with her and Grey, or if Grey had broken down today. I hadn't talked to Grey after, so it was possible—and the thought was making me anxious. I needed to be able to make sure Grey was okay, but I couldn't do that when my sister was acting the way she was.

"Okay, I know something is wrong with you right now, just talk to me. Did something happen with Grey, yes or no?"

Charlie sat back in the bar stool, folding her arms over her chest to match my stance. "There's nothing wrong, and nothing happened. It's just what I said, Grey's fine," she reiterated, then whispered, "She's *just* fine."

I let my arms drop to my sides and my shoulders sag. "What am I missing? You brought up Grey, and you're acting weird as shit about her, so I know something's up!"

My sister studied me for long moments, not saying anything. Just before I asked again, she blurted out, "Grey's moving on like nothing ever happened. She's *fine* and I don't know how she can just go on acting like Ben never—like he never meant anything to her."

My mouth opened as all the air rushed out of my lungs. "What? That's what all this has been about?" When she didn't say anything, I asked, "Charlie, how can you say that? She—she lives with what happened every day. It killed her, but she's getting stronger, she's trying to continue living her life like Ben would want her to. I'm pr—" I cut off and groaned in aggravation, shaking my head as if trying to wrap my mind around what she was saying. "*You* should be proud of her. Does it bother you how I'm living? How I'm going on with *my* life?"

"No, Jagger, but that's different!"

"How is it any fucking different, Charlie?" I yelled, and threw my arms out wide. "I watched my best friend die right in front of me! We're all doing what we have to, we're all doing what Ben would want us to. It's been two—"

"She was going to marry him!" she snapped, and I took a step back. Charlie never reacted like this, but then again, I never usually yelled at her. "I just don't understand how she could go on acting like the guy who meant everything to her never existed just because he died."

I ground my jaw but didn't say anything as I stared at her, willing myself to calm down. "Grey is always struggling, Charlie. Don't hold it against her for continuing to live."

Charlie swallowed thickly and nodded as she slid off the bar stool. Grabbing her purse, she turned to leave, and just before I could ask why she was leaving, she looked back at me and said, "Is this coming from Ben's best friend, or the guy who always wanted to take Grey from him?"

"Charlie!"

"I always wanted you and Grey to be together, Jag. Always." Her eyes brightened with unshed tears, and she offered me a weak smile. "I was always waiting for the day she would see the life you wanted to give her. But she chose Ben, and now she's acting like he was never even here."

"You have no idea what you're saying. You haven't seen what she goes through every day."

"Tell me this, what would Ben say if he were here, huh? If he saw you two together all the time."

I stood there with everything in me aching, and Charlie nodded.

"That," she choked out, and cleared her throat, "that is what I'm not okay with."

I watched as she walked out of the building, and didn't try to stop her. She couldn't have been more wrong, but I didn't know what to say to make her understand. I didn't know what to say, period. I'd never seen my sister respond this way, especially to

Grey. It didn't make sense, and now I was afraid she'd said something to Grey.

Grabbing my keys, I ran out to my car and called Grey, but her phone rang until her voice mail picked up. I stopped just outside the driver's-side door, rested my elbows on top of the hood of my car, and just listened to her voice as I did every time I got her voice mail. That same happy, nothing-can-touch-me voice that had always been distinctly Grey before Ben died.

Without leaving a message, I got into my car and drove to her parents' house, but didn't stop when I didn't see her car out front. If she wasn't answering her phone and wasn't there, there were only two places I could think of where she would be.

I was just hoping it wasn't the cemetery.

Driving through town, I tried her cell one more time, and after getting her voice mail, I turned off onto an old, familiar path. I took what felt like my first real breath since Charlie had left my place, when I found Grey's car parked out near the lake and pulled up next to it. Turning off my car, I looked over at the short dock for a few minutes before stepping out and making my way down to the place we'd spent so many days and nights when we were growing up.

"I had a feeling you would show up here," she said on a teasing sigh, her voice reaching me from where she was lying down at the end of the dock.

I leaned over her and smiled when I found her smiling up at me. "How long have you been here?"

"About thirty minutes or so. How'd you know?"

I looked away and stood up, keeping my gaze on the dark water. "You didn't answer your phone."

"Ah." She laughed softly, letting the sound hang in the air

for a minute before saying, "My 'Jagger 911': not answering my phone."

My lips pulled up in a smile as I moved to lie down next to her. "I never knew why you thought I had ESP or something, it always would've been so much easier to know you needed me if you would've just called."

"But I didn't because you did have the 'or something.' You think I didn't figure out after all those years how you just knew to show up? I knew Ben would call you."

I took a deep breath in and out, and finally said, "Let's go back to thinking I had ESP."

Grey laughed and elbowed me, and as we had done so many times before, we fell into a comfortable silence just staring up at the sky. This dock had thousands of memories, and it never failed, every time I came here I was hit with them all. Every one of them included Grey, and most of them included Ben. We'd spent all our summers out here, and had bonfires near the dock when it became too cold in the winter.

I'd taught Grey how to throw a punch on this dock, and had ended up with a black eye that she'd apologized for at least a thousand times. This had been the spot where I'd caught Ben kissing her for the first time, and realized that he had snatched her up from under me. It had been the spot where Grey lost her bikini top diving off the dock during a party, which led to a night of skinny-dipping that ended up with more than a dozen of us getting busted. Ben would call me after they'd gotten into a fight, and I'd always find her here. We would spend hours here with her crying and ranting about whatever they'd fought about until I had her laughing and driving back to make up with Ben. The entire summer after Ben died, I found her here every night and would stay with her until she fell asleep from exhaustion before putting her in my car and taking her back to her parents'.

Good or bad, I would always think of this as our dock.

"Why are we here tonight?" I finally asked, and listened to her soft exhale.

"I just wanted it. I wanted the memories."

"There are memories all over this town, Grey . . ." I trailed off, the question still there.

She was quiet for a while before she whispered, "Maybe because I knew you would come. I knew you would face the memories of this place with me, and even though some are hard, they are some of my favorites of the three of us."

I turned my head toward her, waiting for her to look back at me, and noticed the wetness gathering in her eyes even through her smile.

"Some of my favorites," she repeated before looking back up toward the sky.

I continued watching her profile for a few seconds before staring up at the star-filled sky. "Tell me."

For hours we talked about our favorite times on the dock. A few times I saw her wipe at her cheeks, but even more often her laugh filled the night air. I kept looking for signs that Charlie had said something to her, but when the conversation turned to her visit with Charlie earlier today, there was nothing but the brightest smile from Grey. She adored my little sister, always had. Whatever was going on with Charlie, I would have to figure it out another time, because I didn't want to worry Grey with it. Not when she was laughing a laugh I hadn't heard in years. Not when I was smiling more than I had since Ben's death. Not when I was fighting the urge to pull Grey into my arms so I could ask her the one question I'd been wanting to ask since we were thirteen years old. A question I'd written down in a note I had been planning on giving her before I found her in Ben's arms that summer day.

I don't know why I'd never thrown the note away.

I don't know if I'd been waiting for the day Grey would leave Ben, and I could give it to her then, but I'd kept it for nine years. A note with four words on it. A note tucked into the case where I kept all my charcoals. A note I knew the girl lying next to me would never see, and a question I knew she would never read or hear—and still, a note I knew I would never be able to get rid of.

Grey
May 23, 2014

AFTER KNOCKING ON Jag's door and not getting an answer, I fumbled with my keys as I steadied the hand holding the breakfast sandwiches and stacked drinks. Shoving the key into the lock, I turned it and pushed open the door before putting the end of one of my key chains in my mouth so I could use both hands to carry everything.

Loud music met me, and I smiled around the key chain. Jagger was drawing. Letting my keys drop onto the kitchen counter, I set down everything and walked through the front room, to the hallway leading to the back rooms. I hadn't been into the room Jagger was using as a studio since we'd moved last week, and even then, I hadn't seen him put any of his stuff in here. I was excited to see a space where he displayed everything he worked on.

As I rounded the corner in the hall, my smile widened when I saw him standing there shirtless, working on a large piece. Just seeing him gave me an overwhelming feeling like I was home, and it didn't make sense. I'd seen him the night before, and if any place felt like *home,* it should've been my parents' house . . . but that knowledge didn't make the feeling lessen. Instead, I seemed to welcome it more and more with each step closer to the man in front of me.

My smile fell as soon as he bent down to wipe the charcoal off his hands onto a towel and I saw the picture. He grabbed the eraser he'd been using to create the picture on the charcoal-covered paper, and went right back to working within seconds, but those seconds had been enough. There was no mistaking the person he'd created on that paper.

Seeing my face reflected back at me this way was something in itself—it was perfect. But Jagger didn't draw people. He drew haunting landscapes, buildings, and abstract designs . . . never people. But when I tore my eyes from him and the piece he was finishing, and looked around at the dozens of drawings hanging throughout the part of the room I could see from where I was standing, I realized I was wrong. There were a handful of drawings of people—no, not people . . . person. Just one. Only me.

One of me that was so perfectly rendered that I would've sworn he'd taken a picture of me just as I'd stopped laughing. Another . . . and the only word to express the look on my face— and feel of the drawing—was "grief." Others of me in various stages over the last few years, some where I was looking directly ahead, others where I was looking away—at who knew what. Looking back to the one I'd first seen, all I could think of was passion. And why . . . why would he draw me at all, let alone draw me so that I looked like I was in love with the person staring at the drawing—the person creating the drawing.

I was so wrapped up in what I was seeing, and trying to figure out the whys, that I wasn't sure when Jagger had noticed me standing there. How long he'd been watching me silently freak out over what was directly in front of me.

My eyes finally locked on his when the music abruptly stopped, and it took me a few moments to understand that he looked terrified. He took calculated steps toward me, his mouth forming my name, but no sound was behind it—and I matched each of his steps with a couple of my own. Those drawings weren't something I was ever supposed to see, that was clear in his expression. My head shook back and forth as if I could make all this go away, as if I could try to make myself believe the minutes since I'd entered the room hadn't happened.

"Please, let me explain."

"What is that?" I asked hesitantly. "Why are you drawing me? Why *have* you been drawing me?"

"Grey, I . . ."

"You don't draw people, Jagger, you told me that! You told me you couldn't, that you were bad at it. Why would you tell me that if it wasn't true? If you've been—" Words failed me as I scrambled for an explanation, but I put my hand out, gesturing toward the large piece as if the gesture alone could finish my sentence. "I don't understand!" I finally forced out.

Jagger looked at me hopelessly for long seconds—no longer trying to get me to listen to him . . . no longer trying to even speak.

"Why are you drawing me?" I yelled, and Jagger flinched, but remained silent as he shook his head slowly back and forth.

"Answer me! I don't—I don't get it! I don't know what to think about what I'm seeing, and it's freaking me out, Jag!"

Jagger's head had stopped shaking, his eyes were still boring into mine, and the only sounds coming from his mouth were uneven breaths—like he was struggling to control his breathing.

"Please, tell me," I begged. "Tell me what I'm seeing and why I'm seeing it. You lied to me, you told me you couldn't do this," I repeated. "And then I come in and find all this? I don't know if I'm supposed to be flattered, or completely creeped out, but right now I'm leaning toward the latter because this is unexpected and beyond weird."

His eyebrows rose at my last sentence, and his deep voice rumbled softly as he said, "I don't know what you want me to say."

"Yes, you do! You told me to let you explain, and I'm waiting for you to explain this! Just tell me why I'm on that paper. Why I'm on others. Why there's no one else—only me."

His green eyes dropped to the floor before he turned his head just enough to look at the drawing behind him, but flashed back up to me when he mumbled, "Because I only wanted to draw you."

"Why, Jagger?" I pleaded when he didn't continue. "*Why* would you want to draw me?"

Jagger didn't respond, and I took two steps away from him—stopping abruptly when he admitted, "Because I couldn't have you, and this was the only way I could tell you how I felt about you."

"What?" I breathed.

A muscle ticked in his jaw as he took steady breaths in and out through his nose, and after opening his mouth only to shut it again, he huffed out a harsh breath and put his hands out to the side. "I love you. I'm pretty sure I've been in love with you since we were nine, Grey," he admitted. "I always felt like you were mine . . . I was in love with you long before I knew what it actually meant to be in love with someone."

"No, you can't. You can't be," I mumbled.

His words from last week flowed through my mind, and I inhaled audibly as I finally heard the double meaning in them. *"I'm always moving, Grey. I'm just waiting on you to move with me."*

Jagger's hands went out in front of him—as if he was reaching for me—and his face turned pleading, but I turned and sprinted toward the front of the building. Grabbing my purse and keys off the counter, I ran outside and got into my car. It wasn't until I was pulling away that I realized he could have easily caught up with me—and the fact that he hadn't meant he hadn't tried to stop me from leaving. And that made the whole situation worse than it already was.

Not because I wanted him to stop me. But because I knew I'd just hurt him bad enough for him to not even try, and that was killing me almost as much as his confession had just shocked me.

I pulled into the driveway at my parents' house and was out of my car and running toward the door within seconds of putting my car in park. Graham was standing on the stairs, like he'd been coming down them.

"There you—Grey? What happened?" he asked, his voice rising in alarm.

"I just . . . he just . . ."

"Grey, talk to me," he demanded as he met me in the entryway. "What happened?"

"Oh my God, what's wrong?" my mom asked, her steps heavy against the hardwood floor as she quickly approached us.

"Nothing," I gritted out. "Nothing, and everything."

"What—" Graham began, but I spoke over him.

"I went to Jagger's place, and h-he has pictures—drawings of me. He draws me!" I said in exasperation, pointing behind me like Jagger or the drawings would be there. "And he doesn't draw people, *he doesn't*. There were only ones of me."

"You're upset because Jagger draws you?" Mom asked awkwardly, like she was worrying she would need to have me see a therapist, and Graham snorted.

"Mom, you didn't see them! They—"

"Were they dirty?"

"What? No! But you don't understand. It—it looked like—you just couldn't understand if you didn't see them. And he . . ." I trailed off, I couldn't force out the words Jagger had told me. A huge part of me was still in denial. Telling someone else would just make this real.

"No, I think I understand," Mom said softly, her face falling into the look of sympathy I'd seen so many times from her over the past two years, but this time there was a gentle smile as well.

When I caught Graham's expectant expression that was aimed at me, and looked back to my mom, I realized they both understood. "How . . ." I trailed off, and looked to Graham again. "How could you possibly . . ."

"It's not a secret, honey." Mom shrugged and reached out to brush away some hair from my face. "That boy has—"

"No. No, he can't." Oh God. They knew and they looked like they thought it was a good thing!

"Kid," Graham said on a sigh. "Come on, think about—"

"He's my friend!"

"Grey," my mom started again.

"He was Ben's best friend!" I yelled. "He can't—I can't . . . this isn't okay!" Hard sobs tore through my chest, but no tears came. "He's supposed to be my friend, he's not—he's not . . . how can he do this? I was going to marry his *best friend*." I wasn't sure I was making sense anymore, but I couldn't seem to get a grip on what was happening. "I saw the drawings and he got nervous, and he told me he's always been in love with me! Why would he do that? Why—he can't do this to us!"

"When has Jagger ever pushed his feelings on you?" Mom asked. "You had no idea until today, and I would say you still wouldn't know if you hadn't seen the drawings. But the rest of us have known since you became friends. It wasn't hard to see the way he looked at you, or how he still looks at you."

"How can you be so okay with this?" I screamed at her. "I was *days* away from marrying Ben when he died. How can you be okay with someone else wanting to be with me? How can you do that to Ben? How can Jagger?"

"Honey, it's been two years."

"I know that, Mom! You think I don't know exactly how long it's been? But I was with Ben for seven years," I cried.

"He's gone, Grey," she said as tears filled her eyes and slipped down her cheeks. "I know it's hard, but he's gone. It's been years, and you have someone who has loved you and been there for you through everything. Someone who has taken care of you and will continue to. It's okay to let yourself love someone again. It's okay to move on."

I shook my head slowly as I stepped away from them. "No. I can't." Looking to my brother, I gestured toward him. "Why are you looking at me like you think I'm making a mistake. You hate Jagger!"

"I don't hate him, kid. I just . . ." He trailed off and shrugged his shoulders as he searched for the right words. "He was in love with my little sister. So was Ben. At that age, I wasn't okay with any guy looking at you, let alone falling for you. But I've never hated either of them, and I respect Jagger for the way he's stood back all these years, and has continued to just make sure you were okay."

"This isn't happening," I whispered.

"If you didn't like him, then that would be fine," Graham said. "This conversation could be the last of it. You didn't know how he felt, and then you find out about all of it the way you did— okay, I get it; he shocked you. But I think you're taking this so hard because deep down you're in love with him too—"

"What? No!"

"—and you don't know if that's okay. Mom's right, though. As hard as it is, Ben's gone, and it's okay to move on. It's not saying anything about you or the way you felt about Ben by letting yourself love Jagger."

"I'm not in love with him!"

Graham made a face, and my mom looked at me like she was waiting for me to realize something. But I couldn't. I refused to think about it. Because if they were right . . . no, they couldn't be. I couldn't do that to Ben. Not letting my mind go in that direction, I focused on nothing but memories of Ben as I ran up the stairs and to my room.

Jagger
May 23, 2014

LIFTING THE BOTTLE to my lips, I took a long pull of the beer before setting it down beside me, my eyes never leaving the unfinished drawing at the end of the hall as the fingers of my other hand folded and unfolded a nine-year-old note. As the pad of my thumb ran over the worn paper, the words scrawled on it played over and over in my head, as if they were mocking me. Words I'd wanted to say forever, and words I hadn't even gotten out today. If I'd thought before that they were words Grey would never hear, I knew now for a fact that if she were to hear them, they would destroy whatever remained of our friendship. Crumpling up the note, I tossed it aside and raked my hands over my head and down my face, keeping my face planted firmly in them as I wished for time to go back.

If only I hadn't been blasting my music—I would have heard her come in. If only I would have known she was coming over this morning—I wouldn't have been drawing, she wouldn't have seen it or the other drawings of her, and I wouldn't have confessed something that should have never been voiced. A dozen other if-onlys went through my mind as I sat there thinking about her horrified expression when I told her I loved her.

My phone beeped, and I grabbed it off the floor. I sighed roughly and ground my jaw when I saw the name, but opened the message anyway.

Graham: I thought you should know . . . Grey just left for Seattle. She said she's going to spend the summer with Janie. I'm sorry, man.

I read the message three times, before quickly going through my phone to call Grey. It rang until her voice mail picked up, and I hung up only to call her again—getting the same result. Without leaving a message, I called Graham.

"Hey—"

"When did she leave?" I asked quickly, cutting him off.

"Right before I texted you. I'm really sorry, Jagger, she told us about what happened this morning."

My eyes widened and I let my head fall back until it hit the wall I was sitting against. I waited for Graham to start yelling, to tell me I wasn't good enough for Grey, to hate me for being the reason she left . . . but it never came. "Why are you even telling me? Why are *you* sorry?"

There was a strange laugh on the other end of the phone, and he sighed. "Grey seemed to think I hated you too," he mused. "I don't hate you. There were times I wanted to. Times I wondered if you were going to try to mess up things for her and Ben because it wasn't hard to see how you felt about her. After he died, I kept waiting for you to make your move on her—"

"You fucking asshole," I growled, but he spoke louder before I could continue.

"She's my baby sister, dude. I wasn't around the three of you enough to know what you would do. Obviously I was wrong in thinking that. But I always kept my guard up with you, because I just never knew what to expect. I told Grey this morning, I respect you. I respect what you did for her as a friend, and what you did for Ben as his. You have no idea how much I appreciate what you've done for her in the last two years. You helped her more than any of us could, and you did it without caring that she had no fucking clue how you felt. You think I would have let her leave with just anyone after what happened the night of your graduation? Fuck no. *I* want to be able to help her; *I* want to be able to protect her from all the bad shit in the world. She should be my responsibility, but I've been here while she was finishing school. Letting her leave with you was one of the easiest decisions I've ever made, because I know you are who she needs."

I sat there, not able to say anything. I would've never expected anything like this from Graham.

"When she was a kid, she needed me and our dad. When she got older, she needed Ben. Now she needs you. I know she's in love with you too, we all do."

I forced a laugh, but it sounded pained. "No. No, she's not. You didn't see her face this morning."

"I saw her after. I don't know what happened there, but I witnessed her freaking out over here. I'm not saying she's not denying it, but I know she loves you. She's scared, Jagger, that's all."

"I don't—"

"She thinks she's not allowed to love you. Because of Ben, because of what you were to him . . . but she does, just trust us on this. She's always loved you, you've always been close, and that's changed into something more over the last two years. I want to tell you to go after her, but I think she needs this. She needs time away from this place and from you so she can see what exactly you mean to her now. Give her a couple weeks, Jagger, she'll be back."

I let the phone slide from my hand after we ended the call, and sat there for another hour until it got to be too much. Stalking through the building, I went up to my room and shrugged into a shirt before jogging out to my car. I drove to the edge of town and parked my car so the headlights were lighting my path.

Squatting down in front of the headstone, I stared at it as I tried to calm my shaking, and broke instead. I stumbled back so I was sitting, and planted my elbows on my knees as a sob tore through my chest.

"I'm sorry. I'm so fucking sorry, man," I cried. "I'm trying not to love her, but I can't, and it's killing me. She's yours; I know she's yours. You need to be here. You need to be starting a family with her. She needs you to be happy, Ben, you need to fucking be here!" Sobs tortured my body as I mourned my best friend, and hated myself for loving his girl. "You're so selfish. You can't just leave her like this, and leave me to be the one to pick up the pieces of her. Did you hear her last week? She's *still* broken, Ben! She's fucking broken! And she's not mine to fix, you need to be the one to fix her!"

Everything in me ached as I yelled at him—at nothing.

Falling back so I was staring up at the night sky, I gripped at my chest as I pleaded, "Just come back."

Chapter 4

Grey
May 30, 2014

"As much as I love having you here with me, I need to know what happened," Janie said, suddenly switching topics.

"Wait, what?"

She looked at me expectantly for a few seconds before offering me a sad smile and climbing onto her bed to lie on her stomach next to me. "I love you, Grey, and I want you to stay here as long as you want to, or need to. But I know something had to have happened, and you've been ignoring whatever it is since you got here."

I looked up at the ceiling and took some calming breaths. When I'd called Janie, all I had said was that I needed to get away. I had packed a bag and was in my car within thirty minutes of getting off the phone with her, and that had been a week ago. I'd talked to my parents a couple times, and Graham once. But after the two times Jagger called me as I got on the freeway to head to Seattle, he hadn't tried to contact me again, and I hadn't called him. I didn't know what to say to him. I felt like I didn't know him, I didn't know what in our friendship had been real, or a lie, and I hated that I was questioning him at all.

"Was going back to Thatch just too hard?" Janie asked a couple minutes later when I still hadn't said anything.

"Yes and no. The first day was hard, but it got better. I was staying with my parents and looking into getting an apartment. Jagger . . ." I paused to clear my throat. "Jagger's grandparents had this old warehouse-type studio that no one has used in years, and he turned it into an apartment and a studio. We hung out a lot that week . . ."

Janie turned and raised one eyebrow. "And how *is* Jagger?"

My eyes narrowed at the way she'd asked about him. Like she knew. Were she and Graham still talking about me? Had he told her? "Why do you ask it like that?"

"Like what?" She gave me an innocent look. "I just want to know how he is. This is the longest you two have been apart . . . pretty much ever."

She was right; other than the time my family took a trip to Europe, I'd never been away from him for this long, and it was killing me. "Have you talked to Graham lately?"

"No, not since before graduation, why?"

I studied her for a few seconds before releasing the breath I'd been holding and looking back at the ceiling. "Jagger told me he's in love with me," I whispered.

"And?"

My head whipped around to face her, shock covering my face. "And? What do you mean? This is a big fucking deal!"

Her head jerked back, and she barked out a quick laugh. "Wait, seriously? Did you—had he never told you that before?"

"No, Janie, he hadn't!"

She blinked slowly a few times, an incredulous expression covering her face. "How did you not know?"

I sat up on the bed and turned to face her. "How did *you* know? And why didn't you tell me?"

"Everyone knew. I mean, Be—" She abruptly stopped talking, her eyes wide.

"What? Tell me!"

"Grey . . . Ben even knew," she admitted, her voice so soft I thought I heard her wrong until I took in the sad look in her eyes.

"No." I shook my head and my throat tightened. "No, he couldn't have. He would have told me, he—he wouldn't have been okay with that. How did you know that Ben knew?" I yelled, and she jumped from the sudden rise in my voice.

"He told me, kind of—I mean, not exactly, but he hinted at it."

"Janie, what did he say?"

She looked away for a second before shrugging and glancing back at me. "Ben was always *all* over you. Do you remember how we would go cosmic bowling after all the parties our freshman and sophomore years?" When I nodded, she continued. "Well, on one of those nights during freshman year when we were at the alley, it just hit me. I realized he pretty much never touched you when we were at a party or bowling, and it was weird because it was so unlike you and Ben. So I waited until we were alone— you and Jagger were trying to mess each other up on your turns or something—and I asked if he was okay."

I didn't realize I was leaning toward her and holding my breath until she stopped talking, her eyes misting. "What did he say?"

"He said what he always said. 'I have my girl and my friends, why wouldn't I be?' So I told him that he was acting weird, and how it seemed like he was avoiding touching you—I also might have threatened bodily harm if he was hiding something from you. Anyway, when I said that, it was like he suddenly got what I was talking about. He looked over to where you and Jagger were, and said, 'I have the rest of my life to hold her, but I can't do that to him.'"

Her words had been choked as she fought back tears, and my chest ached when I realized that the rest of his life ended up only being another year or so.

"I had already seen how Jagger looked at you, and when Ben said that, I knew he saw it too. I don't know if they ever talked about it, but he knew."

Long minutes passed where the only sound was our hitched breathing as Janie pulled me into her arms and held me while we cried. When we pulled away from each other, she wiped at her eyes and shrugged.

"The way he looks at you, it's so obvious. I've always thought you must have known. I just thought you ignored it because the two of you were such good friends, you had Ben, and because Jagger never did anything about it. This past year, though, when you started pulling away from us and clinging to him, we all thought for sure you knew at that point. I've just been waiting for the day you call me to tell me you two were together."

"How can . . ." I shook my head and tried to swallow past the tightness in my throat. "I just don't understand how everyone seems to be so okay with this. It's like nobody cares that Ben is gone. Everyone is just expecting me to be with Jagger now that Ben died."

"Grey, no! That's not it. We just want you to be happy, and Jagger makes you happy. But no one is expecting *anything*. Ben was a huge part of your life; we all know that. But that doesn't mean you can't love someone else."

"That sounds a lot like what my family was saying," I mumbled, and she bit down on her bottom lip.

"Well, Graham and I talked about it a lot over the last year."

My eyebrows rose, but I don't know why I was even surprised anymore. "But you're all okay with it so soon."

"I think it would be different for everyone. Every situation is different. Some people, months are what they need, others, they need years. For you? It would be one thing if it had only been months. I probably would have thought you were just trying to make the pain go away. It might have even been weird around the year mark. But it's been over two years now, and that's different. And this is Jagger, he knows you, and knew Ben, better than anyone. He knows how you feel, he knows that you're hurting, and he's hurting too."

My fingers easily found the ring hanging from the long chain, and I played with it absentmindedly. I couldn't believe everyone had known, when I'd never had a clue that Jagger felt more for me than a friendly bond. I still didn't know how I felt about everyone telling me they thought I was ready to move on with someone else, or how to feel about Jagger's confession. But as I gripped that ring, a familiar twist of guilt hit me—thinking about Jagger . . . hell, thinking about *anyone* in that way felt like I was cheating on Ben.

If he hadn't died, we would be married, and I would never

have entertained the thought of someone else, just like I knew he wouldn't. The words "till death do us part" had been floating around my mind for the past week, but as they came up again, I was quick to push them back. That felt like a cop-out right now.

"You all think if I were to move on, Jagger would be the guy I'd moved on to . . . but what if I don't want Jagger?"

Janie looked at me closely, and the same sad smile my mom had given me was now playing on her lips. "Now that I don't believe."

Jagger
June 27, 2014

"OH MY GOD, Jagger?"

My hand froze on the energy drink and my entire body tightened. *Shit.*

"Is that you?"

I swallowed thickly, and slowly pulled the can out of the refrigerated section before turning around to face her. She'd been calling me three times a week since graduation, and I hadn't once answered. In a town the size of Thatch, I knew it would be impossible to avoid her forever, but I'd hoped.

"Ah!" she squealed, and launched herself at me, wrapping her arms around my neck and her legs around my waist. I stumbled back against the glass door and automatically put my arms around her.

"Hey, LeAnn," I murmured as I disentangled myself from her.

"How are you? God, you look great, Jagger!"

I took a step to the side, trying to put more distance between us; she followed me. "Uh, thanks. So do you. How've you been?"

"Oh, I'm doin' just fine. I've been working at the salon in town for about a year now."

"Yeah, Charlie said she's been going to you."

She laughed and grabbed at my forearm. "Right. God, I love that girl. Hey, have you been getting my messages? I've been calling you for a while now, hoping to get in touch with you ever since Charlie said you were about to move back from Pullman." Her hand slowly glided up my arm, her nails lightly leading the trail. It was a touch that was so familiar, and one I didn't want to feel.

"Yeah, sorry about that. I've just been busy getting settled in and everything." I moved my arm to cover my mouth as I cleared my throat and took another step back. The second my arm was down, she was touching me again.

"Charlie was telling me all about how you turned the warehouse into a place to live in, and it sounded amazing—"

"It—"

"—and it turned out great, Jagger."

I went still and my face pinched together. "I'm sorry, what?"

LeAnn shook her head in confusion, like she didn't understand why I was pissed off suddenly. "The warehouse, it looks great."

"You've seen it?" I asked darkly, each word coming out slowly.

"Yeah, I helped Charlie stock the place up on food for you!" she said on a laugh, like I should've known. And maybe if I'd actually listened to her messages, I might have.

I bit back a curse and forced a tight-lipped smile. "Ah. Well, thanks for that. It was, uh, nice to not have to go to the store first thing."

"Of course, Jag, anything for you."

Oh God. Just as I was about to make an excuse to leave, she spoke again.

"I always want to be able to take care of you."

Fucking hell. "Uh." I rubbed the back of my neck with my free hand and laughed awkwardly. "LeAnn, uh, I appreciate it. But it's . . . it's been four years."

Her determined look didn't falter as she closed the space between us. "Well, two if you count . . ." She trailed off.

If you counted the week Ben and Grey got engaged, and the week I was trying to forget that the girl I wanted more than anything was days away from getting married. That had been the last time I'd been with anyone, and I literally would have been with *any* girl just as long as I could try to forget for a few hours every day what was coming in a short time.

I looked away from her and tried to sound uninterested as I prayed to God there was someone in her life. "Still, that's a long time, LeAnn, you can't tell me you haven't found someone else in that time."

The confident look I'd always seen on this beautiful girl finally cracked, and she blinked rapidly as her head jerked back. "Wait . . . are you telling—have you found someone?"

"I'm sorry." It was all I could say in that time. I'd always belonged to Grey, whether she wanted me or not, I belonged to her still, and LeAnn was definitely someone I could never go back to.

She released my arm and took a step back. "Are you kidding me, Jagger? You *promised* me! You promised once you came back to Thatch we would be together!"

I'd said that because it was the only way she had let me break up with her after high school graduation. I looked around to see the other man in the convenience store glancing at us, and bent my head lower, dropping my voice so it wouldn't carry. "I was eighteen, LeAnn. I didn't even really know what that kind of a promise meant, and there's so much that has happened in that time. I'm sorry you thought we would still be together, but we haven't even talked in over two years."

"Who is she?" she demanded, and I blew out a heavy breath as I shook my head.

"That doesn't matter. Look, like I said, I'm sorry. But it's time you find someone—" My words were cut off when her palm connected with my cheek, and I stood there for a second, not moving or saying anything, waiting to see what she would do next.

"You will regret this. You will come crawling back to me, Jagger Easton, I have no doubt of that. You always have, you always will." She stepped so close, her chest was pressed to mine, and she looked up at me. "Because don't forget, I know exactly what you like and how you like it, and you will always compare every other girl to me. But by the time you realize you've made a mistake, I will have moved on and you will have lost your chance."

My nostrils flared as she raked her nails down my stomach, stopping just at the top of my jeans. "LeAnn," I warned.

"If you want to remember what we were like together, you know how to get ahold of me, but I'm not waiting around for you forever. I've already wasted four years."

With the hand not holding the energy drink, I grabbed both her wrists and pushed her arms away. "Don't wait for that call."

Walking away from her, I paid for the drink and lingered at the counter longer than necessary as she stormed past me and went outside.

"Don't let her fool ya," the old man behind the counter grumbled, not looking at me.

I sent him a lazy smile as I put my wallet in my back pocket. "Wasn't planning on it."

"That piece of property has had more visitors in the last year than there are single men in this town."

I barked out a laugh, and nodded my head at him. "From what I remember of her, that sounds about right."

"Not that it's my business. I just see what I see and hear what I hear."

I grabbed the drink and started walking backward toward the door. "This is Thatch, it's everyone's business. Have a good day."

I walked the few blocks back to the warehouse, and once I was inside and had the door locked—since apparently LeAnn knew where I lived—I settled down onto the couch. Pulling my phone out of my pocket, I looked at it for a while before bringing the screen to life and going through the contacts.

My thumb hovered over Grey's number for a minute before I backed out of my phone list and tossed my phone onto the other end of the couch. I'd started to call her at least fifteen times a day for the last month, but had never gone through with it, and she hadn't ever called or texted. A part of me wanted to leave Thatch, to start over the way Ben's parents had done, but I knew I couldn't. Because even though she'd been gone for far too long, I knew she would eventually come back, and I needed to be here when she did.

There was a quick knock before my front door opened, and I shot up off the couch. Only three other people had keys to this place. Charlie was still traveling across the country, Grey was in Seattle as far as I knew, and . . . fuck.

"Hey, honey," Mom said in a singsong voice as she walked over to where I was standing and made herself comfortable on one of the couches. "How are you doing?"

"Fine," I gritted, my eyes never leaving her. When she just looked around at the space, I slowly sat back down on the couch. "What are you doing here?"

She widened her eyes at me. "What? Can't I come visit my son? Besides, this *is* my place. If I wanted to be a bitch and treat you the way you're treating me, I could ask what you're doing here."

"No. Grandma left *me* this shop, but I was too young to do anything with it, so you used it until I left for college and you got out of your pottery phase."

She rolled her eyes. "I like what you did with the place, though."

I waited. I knew what was coming.

"These couches look expensive."

"They're not."

"Do not lie to me, Jagger," she sneered.

"Why don't we cut through the bullshit, and you can tell me why you're actually here so you can leave that much faster?"

She sniffed, like what I'd said had wounded her, but the look faded, and soon she was just my heartless mom again. "I just need a little bit."

My eyebrows pinched together, and my lips formed a hard line. "Define 'a little bit.'"

"Couple thousand."

I shot up off the couch, my voice rising and bouncing off the walls of the building. "A couple thousand dollars, Mom? For what!"

"That's for me to know!"

"Well, considering I've been buying everything that Keith needs, I know it sure as shit isn't for him! And do you really think I have that kind of money?"

"I know how much they left you! You and Charlie weren't their children, you didn't deserve everything they left you!"

"I don't have it anymore! I used the money to pay for school, same as Charlie is doing. And I swear to God, if you hit her up for money, I will ruin you! It's not our job to give you money or continue caring for your son. You're a grown fucking woman, get a job that isn't finding a new husband, and pay for your own life. And don't try to keep bullshitting me. I *know* they left you money. It's not Charlie's fault or mine that you blew it on husband number three. Or was it four?"

"You ungrateful little shit," she hissed, and stood up to try to be eye level with me. "If you don't have it, how are you paying for your bills? How are you sending everything for Keith? I know you don't have a job. Are you dealing?"

"Are you fucking kidding me?" I roared.

"No kid of mine is gonna deal, Jagger, I'll call the cops—"

"Call them! Fucking call them, Mom! Let them come and check the whole place, they won't find anything here."

"Tell me how you're paying your bills," she demanded.

We stared each other down as I tried to calm myself again, but my entire body was vibrating. I still had money left over from my grandparents, even after college and the renovations. Mom was smart enough to figure I hadn't used all of it. But it was in savings, and I wasn't touching it, nor was I about to give some of it to her. No one knew I sold my drawings, and if Mom found out, I knew the amount of times she came to me for money would triple. I watched her scheming expression, and a little bit of the tension left me as I realized there was no way she had any idea about the drawings.

"That's none of your business," I finally replied. "Now, unless *you're* about to die because you can't afford to feed *yourself,* don't ask me for money again. And if I see you around here again, the cops will be called, only it will be on you."

"How can you be so cold to your own mother?" she cried, and I scoffed at her fake tears.

"You wanna know how? Because I had to raise Charlie even though she's barely two years younger than me. I had to make sure she was clothed, fed, taken care of . . . everything *you* should have been doing. All the while you were bringing guys into the house like it was a fucking whorehouse. Marrying any of them who gave you more than a night, spending money we didn't have on them when they had these crazy ideas, only for them to split as soon as they had the cash. And now you have a baby and you don't even know which one of your many guys is the father, and what do you do? Come to me over and over again for money. I paid you long enough until I found out that none of that money was even going to Keith, and now once again I'm doing your job and making sure your child is fed and clothed while Charlie's watching him for you. *That* is how I can be so 'cold,' as you put it."

"Don't act like you do so much for him, you don't even see him," she spat out.

"I barely see him because I've been in a different city, and now that I'm home I don't want to risk seeing you. But if you really believe that, just ask Charlie. I'm there whenever I'm sure you're not going to be around, which is a hell of a lot more often than it should be."

"Screw you, Jagger."

"Nice, Mom. It's time for you to go." Not waiting for her to say anything else, I walked over to the door and opened it, doing a double take when I looked outside. "Are you kidding me? Is this yours?" I asked, pointing to the brand-new Escalade.

She straightened her back, and walked toward me without actually looking at me.

"You're gonna come in here and ask for a couple grand, when you have that? You're going to force me to keep buying clothes, food, and diapers for Keith, and you fucking have *that*!" Before she could say anything or pass me, I shot my arm straight out in front of her. "Key."

Mom looked at me like I was nothing. Nothing to her, nothing to Charlie, nothing to Keith . . . just nothing. With jerky motions, she took the key off her key ring and slapped it into my hand. "It was a gift," she snarled as she passed me.

"Yeah, I bet it was. If it's from soon-to-be husband number seven, don't bother telling Charlie and me about the wedding. We won't be there."

Without a look back in my direction, she climbed into the SUV and took off.

I slammed the door and locked it and stalked back to the couches, when my phone started ringing.

Grabbing it just before voice mail picked up, I answered without looking at the screen, and growled, "What?"

There was a pause before: "Wow. You're doing worse than I thought you were."

I glanced at the screen for a second and tried to talk normally as I began pacing. "Have you heard from her, Graham?"

"No, but Mom talked to her yesterday."

"And?" I prompted when he didn't continue. But from his dejected tone, I wasn't expecting good news, and my anger quickly faded into the pain I had become so used to over the past month.

"She's not coming home yet, but Mom said she sounded good. Actually her words were: 'Grey sounded great, happy even.' So there's that."

"Good," I mumbled, nodding and dropping my head until I was staring at the floor. "That's good."

"You don't sound like it's a good thing."

"No, it is. I want her happy. That's all I've ever wanted."

"I know it is. I think if she's doing good, and it's been this long but she doesn't have plans to come back, it's time you go to her," he said.

I wanted to. I wanted to so damn bad that it took everything in me to force myself over to sit on a couch rather than grab my keys and leave for Seattle. But she was happy. "I can't, Graham. You heard your mom, she's happy. A month away from here and me, and she's happy. I can't take that away from her. When she's ready to come back, she will."

Graham sighed. "I had a feeling you would say that."

"Then why call?"

"Do you still love my sister?" he asked after a few silent moments.

"Of course I do."

"Tell me something: if she found someone else and you missed your chance because you were waiting for her to come back, how would you feel?"

I froze. Everything in me just stopped for tortured moments

before I forced out, "What are you—did she—are you—Graham, is she with someone?"

"I don't know. Honestly, I don't. All I know is that she's happy, and she doesn't have any plans to come back yet. Whether that means she's found someone already or not, she *will* eventually find someone. And if you want to be that guy, you need to go get her."

"I will, I gotta go."

After hanging up, I ran to my studio as I scrolled through the contact list on my phone. I had calls to make, and I needed to get to Seattle.

Grey
July 12, 2014

AT THE SOUND of the front door slamming, I jumped back from where I was standing in the kitchen making breakfast for Janie, her roommate, Heather, and me. I glanced over at Heather, and she shrugged as she leaned away from the bar to look toward the entryway.

"Grey, Grey, Grey, Grey, Grey!" Janie yelled as she ran through the apartment to the kitchen. She was out of breath as she set down the three coffees.

"Jesus, did you run to the coffee shop?" I asked, giving her a weird look before going back to the food.

She shook her head as she tried to catch her breath. "There was—I found—hold on!" Grabbing her purse, she dug through it for a few seconds before slamming what looked like a nice-looking brochure onto the bar.

"What is it?"

"It's for some art gallery place," Heather mumbled as she looked over it. "Huh. Random."

Janie snatched it away from her and pointed it at me. "There was a stack of them at the shop, and I grabbed it because the picture on the front is all pretty, see?" She waved it in my direction for half a second before dropping it.

All I had seen was that the brochure was black.

"So I'm looking at it and decide I'm going to go see where this place is to see if it's close so we could all go, since I love art, you know?"

"You love art?" Heather and I said at the same time.

"Since when?" I asked.

She looked at me for a few seconds before gesturing wildly with her hands. "Since always! That doesn't matter! So I'm driving, and I find this place, and of course it's closed since it's, like, the ass crack of dawn right now. But there are windows, and there was an art piece in the window!"

"It's an art gallery, you'd figure there—"

"It was of *you,* Grey!" she said excitedly, cutting me off.

I kept absentmindedly moving around the scrambled eggs, staring at her like she'd gone insane, until it hit me. I inhaled audibly and dropped the spatula. "Jagger," I breathed.

"Yes! Jagger!"

"Oh my God."

"I know!" she screeched, and bounced up and down a few times. "He's having a thing at the gallery place this weekend! We have to go!"

"Wait," Heather said, grabbing the brochure and looking at it again. "What? What is a jagger?"

"Not a what," I said, my eyes not focused on anything in the apartment.

"Definitely not a what," Janie confirmed. "More like a who."

"Holy shit! Mick Jagger is in Seattle?" Heather yelled.

My lips curved up in a smile, but I still wasn't able to focus on Heather or Janie. "No, his name is Jagger Easton."

"Who names their kid Jagger?"

I glanced at Heather and laughed softly. "His mom is kind of obsessed with the Rolling Stones. He even has a sister named Charlie after the drummer, Charlie Watts, and a little brother named after Keith Richards."

"Okay, so who is he?"

I turned off the stove, and shrugged as my eyes darted over to Janie. "Jagger's just . . . Jagger."

Janie was still smiling like it was Christmas, and Heather was now giving me a weird look. "For some reason I don't think he's 'just Jagger' to you. You're all smiley and you're blushing."

My face fell, and I turned to get plates when Heather turned her stare on Janie.

"And what was this you said? *He's* the one with the art show, and there was a picture of Grey in the window? Now that definitely doesn't seem like a 'just Jagger' kind of situation."

"He's my friend," I explained without looking at them.

"Who has pictures of you in an art show?" Heather asked in disbelief.

"Drawings. He does charcoal drawings, he's really good, actually." *And he has an art show in Seattle this weekend. Does that mean he's here?* A smile slowly tugged at my lips at the same time as the pain in my chest spread.

I hadn't talked to him since the morning he'd told me he loved me. That'd been almost a month and a half ago, and I missed him. I missed my friend. I missed everything about him. I just didn't know how to talk to him after what had happened, after I'd run away from him.

"Is he cute?" Heather asked, and Janie snorted.

"Cute is an understatement for him. Hot, rough, rugged, tatted-up-amazing-body-take-me-home is a better description."

Something I'd never felt when it came to Jagger moved into my stomach, overriding the pain for the moment as I listened to Janie. We'd never talked about the way Jagger looked, so I'd never heard her describe him to anyone. And the way she had . . . I didn't know how to feel about someone else saying that.

"Well then, *I* am definitely going just so I can meet him," Heather said loudly. "God, I haven't gotten laid in months."

"What?!" I whirled around, my eyes and mouth wide in horror. Before I could say something stupid—like lay claim to Jagger—I noted both their expressions.

Janie's smile had turned into some beyond-happy smile that looked painful, and Heather looked like she'd just won something.

A knowing smile crossed Heather's face. "Do you maybe want to reconsider that whole 'just Jagger' bit now?"

Chapter 5

Grey

July 12, 2014

MY STOMACH WAS churning as we walked down the block to where the gallery was. After going back and forth with Heather and Janie for two hours this morning, they'd somehow gotten me into a salon. For the first time in over two years, I'd gotten my nails and hair done while they had gone shopping for me.

That alone should have tipped me off that tonight was going to be too much.

I don't think I'd been in anything other than leggings or sweats since graduation, and they wanted to make sure I looked completely opposite how I normally did.

Mission accomplished. I wanted to put my hair up in a messy bun and get into comfortable clothes already. I had more makeup

on than I'd worn to graduation, four-inch-heel boots, and an
outfit I'd expect someone like Janie to wear.

Well, I guess I know who picked it out.

"Stop messing with your shirt," Janie chastised for the twen-
tieth time tonight.

"It feels like I'm not wearing anything!" I hissed. "It's awkward!"

I shoved my clutch at her and looked down at myself as
I moved the shirt around, making sure I was covered. The
tank was already low cut to the point where I was showing
more cleavage than was necessary, but the material was too
thin, and loose enough that any breeze made even just by
walking had it feeling like the shirt had evaporated. The only
saving grace of this outfit was that I was wearing jeans—
unfortunately for me and my poor legs, they were constricting
the life out of me.

"Who wears this stuff?" I groaned, and turned around to look
at myself in the window of a store. I refused to admit I was happy
with the way I looked tonight . . . I was *that* uncomfortable.

"Better question, who *doesn't*?" Janie asked. "You used to too.
You just seemed to replace your entire wardrobe with sweat-
pants."

"Much more comfortable than skinny jeans."

Heather snorted. "No one ever said you were supposed to be
comfortable. Let's go before you find somewhere you can buy
something else."

I snatched the clutch back from Janie and made a face at them
before walking in the direction of the gallery again. "At least
then I would be sure I'd have full use of my legs after tonight. I
swear, there is no blood flow down there."

"Get over it, you look hot. Jagger's not going to know what to do with himself when he sees you."

"I don't care what Jagger thinks, Janie," I mumbled.

Both girls laughed, but there was a part of me that was trying so hard to cling to the idea that Jagger and I could never be anything more than friends. As the last six weeks had come and gone, and the pain of being away from him had only grown, I'd fought with what I'd thought I'd known, and what I was slowly coming to terms with. That my family might have been right, that in the last two years my love for Jagger had grown from a love that could only be formed when you'd been friends as long as we had, to something so much more. And it had changed without my ever realizing it.

They say you don't know what you have until it's gone. Whether Jagger was *gone* or not would probably be determined tonight, because up until now, I'd been the one hiding . . . I'd been the one who was *gone*. But that hadn't changed the truth of those words. I was very much aware of what I had left behind in Thatch.

But I'd also had a love that I'd known could withstand anything. Time, separation, death . . .

I just hadn't known the death would come so soon, or how hard it would be to try to live my life apart from Ben when my world had revolved around him for so long. I knew I couldn't live my life grieving over him forever. I knew that. Ben wouldn't want that for me, and if the roles had been reversed, I would want him to be happy. I would want him to love again.

But knowing he would want that for me as well was so much easier to accept than actually allowing it for myself. It's hard to continue on in life when the person holding your heart can't.

I stopped walking and stumbled back when Heather yanked on my hand, and I turned around to look at them.

"Uh, where are you going?" Heather pointed to the brightly lit gallery we'd just passed, and my lips parted on a heavy exhalation.

"Oh my God." I took a few shaky steps toward the windows, my chest tightening as I looked at the drawing Janie had been talking about. It was the one Jagger had been finishing when I'd walked into his studio that morning.

"Isn't it amazing?" Janie squealed, and grabbed my other hand.

"Jesus Christ, it looks just like you." Heather stared with open amazement. "You said he was good, but . . . damn."

"I know," I breathed.

"Well, are you ready to go in? See if your guy is here?" Heather asked.

I looked at Janie, and she must have seen the panic on my face, because she squeezed my hand once. "It's okay, Grey. Whatever happens tonight, it's okay. Just see if he's here. Talk to him. He's your closest friend if nothing else; you can't hide from him forever."

No. But in that moment, I really wanted to try. Releasing Heather's hand, I grabbed the delicate chain around my neck, searching for the ring that had been nestled between my breasts. Holding it tightly in my fist, I stared for a few more seconds at the drawing that had started all of this before slowly walking toward the entrance.

The open gallery wasn't crowded, but there were definitely a lot more people than I'd been expecting. Then again, I hadn't really known what to expect. I'd had a dozen different scenarios playing through my mind all day. Janie had just been driving too fast when she saw the drawing and that's why she thought it was of me . . . so this was all for nothing. The drawing would be the one and only piece of Jagger's in the gallery, so, again, this would all have been for nothing. The gallery would be too crowded to get in. No one would be here at all. Jagger would be here with someone . . .

My stomach clenched, and my grip on the ring tightened. If he was here at all, and he was with someone . . . I didn't think I could handle seeing it. And that sick, jealous feeling sitting at the bottom of my stomach made no sense to me. Because again, I reminded myself that I had run from him. That even though he hadn't tried to get ahold of me since the night I'd left, I hadn't tried to call him either. And most importantly, my heart still belonged to his best friend.

Janie, Heather, and I had been inside for close to twenty minutes, and I'd been staring at another drawing of me—the one that portrayed all of my grief—for countless minutes without realizing that the other two had left my side. I pressed the ring to my lips as I stared, and a jolt went through my body when I heard a deep voice directly behind me.

"This is the hardest one to look at of you."

"Jagger," I breathed. From the corner of my eye, I watched as he stepped up next to me. Close enough so our voices wouldn't carry, but far enough that I'd have to reach to touch him. Keeping my eyes on the drawing, I shakily asked, "If it's hard for you, then why is it here? Why do you keep it?"

"I don't know," he murmured. "Probably because of what you said to me that night."

My brow furrowed, and I turned to look up at him, but his eyes never left the piece in front of us. "What night was it?"

"Night of Ben's funeral."

I nodded slowly as I looked back at the canvas. "I came to your house, but I don't remember what I said."

"I opened the door, and you said, 'Make it so that this is a dream. Wake me up, Jagger.' And I remember thinking that was exactly what I wanted. To wake up. I couldn't wake us up, but while I drew this that night, I knew I would do anything to keep us moving."

And he had. He'd always been there to talk about Ben, never treated me like I was too fragile, and had always pushed me to keep going. Everything I'd needed, and everything I'd pushed away.

"I'm so sorry, Jag," I whispered a minute later.

He exhaled slowly, and when he spoke, there was a hint of the pain he'd been in since I'd left. "I never should have told you."

"Why?" I looked at him again, and when he still wouldn't look at me, I reached out for him.

"Because you ran away from me, Grey." The pain in his voice tore through me, and my arm fell limply at my side. "You ran, and you stayed gone. But I get it, Grey, I swear to God I do. I understand why that upset you, why you aren't okay with it. I thought—I thought if I gave you time, you would change your mind. I came here hoping enough time had passed, and I don't know what I would've said to make you change your mind. But after seeing you come in . . . seeing how much better you look now that I'm not in your life . . . I can't stand the thought of watching you go back to how you were. I can't do it now."

"Jagger . . ." The plea in that one word was clear, but in that moment, I still wasn't positive what I was begging of him. To forgive me? To understand why I was trying so hard to not let anyone else touch my heart? To know that I needed him more than he realized . . . more than even I had realized?

"I just needed you to know that I understand, Grey."

Before I could ask *what* he understood, he turned around and walked away from me. In our short conversation, he'd never once looked at me. My eyes went back to the drawing of me, and I listened as his heavy footfalls drifted away. I could feel each step like it was another nail in the coffin of my relationship with Jagger, as friends or something more. I knew what I did right then would forever change Jagger and me.

If I continued to look at this drawing for another minute before walking away from the gallery, then that would be it. We could never go back to the way we had been, because we couldn't go back to being as close as we were now that I knew how he felt. I couldn't do that to him; I couldn't give him hope that there would someday be an us when I knew that I would never allow it. He would eventually find someone else, and I . . . I would just focus on moving.

But if I stopped him, then the dynamics of our relationship would change in a way everyone had already been expecting them to. A way Jagger wanted them to. A way *I* wanted them to.

That thought shook me as I finally admitted what I'd been trying so hard to deny. I wanted this. I wanted him.

"Jagger," I mumbled, and turned to look for him in the gallery. He was twenty feet away from me, shaking a man's hand, with his back to me. "Jagger," I said louder when he began walking again.

He glanced over his shoulder for a second, before pausing and turning to face me. His face went blank in an attempt to mask his emotions. I walked toward him, each step feeling a little easier than the last—as if my decision was solidifying with every step closer. He didn't move toward me, and didn't say anything when I stopped directly in front of him, just looked at me with those green eyes . . . waiting.

"I'm sorry that I ran," I whispered, and a muscle ticked in his jaw from the strain he was putting on it. "I was scared, and I think I still am. But I'm not better without you. It hurts to be away from you. This?" I gestured to the side and shrugged. "Seattle? I needed to think about what you said, what my family said . . . I just needed to think. I can think here with Janie, but that doesn't mean I'm better here. And all of this"—I gestured toward myself—"was only because of tonight. Janie and Heather did this because they thought I would see you. I miss you every day, Jagger. I don't know how long I would've stayed gone, but please . . . don't stay away from me *for* me."

Taking a step forward, I leaned into his chest as I had done so many times in my life, and I knew that this was right—this was where I needed to be now. His arms automatically came up around my waist to hold me, and I sighed against his chest.

"I'm scared."

"Why? If you're scared to lose me, you won't. I'll always be here for you." His voice was low, and the way it rumbled through his chest and against my cheek was something so familiar and so calming. When had I started craving this?

"Not that. I just . . . I don't know how to let myself love you too," I confessed, and felt his body tighten against mine.

Lifting my head to look at him, I paused when I found his face inches from mine—closer than it had ever been. I let myself take in everything about him that I never had before. His green eyes that seemed to look straight through me, the bridge of his strong nose leading down to full lips that were usually in a playful smirk. But now that my gaze was on them, they slowly parted as his breathing deepened, his chest moving harder against mine. When I looked up again, his eyes were dark with want.

"Loving you scares me," I whispered, "but I know I can't keep telling myself that I'm not in love with you, Jagger."

"Excuse me." A voice called out from next to us, but neither of us moved until I was tapped on the shoulder. I turned and took a step away from Jagger when I saw an older woman standing there. Her pondering expression turned excited when I was facing her. "It *is* you."

"I'm sorry?"

"You're the muse for the pieces, are you not?" she asked, turning enough to point at the drawing I'd just been in front of.

I looked to Jagger for help, but he was still staring at me with an intensity I felt in my core. My mouth opened, and I looked back to the woman helplessly.

"Oh gosh, I'm so sorry. I didn't mean to bother you, you just look so much like her."

"I—I . . . they are—"

"She is," Jagger said quickly, stepping forward to put an arm around my waist and extending a hand to the woman. "Enjoy looking around, but I hope you don't mind me stealing my muse away."

"Of course not." The woman smiled at him, and sent me a knowing look as Jagger pulled me to his side and walked us quickly through the building and down a dark hall.

When we reached the end of the hall, he turned me so my back was pressed against the wall and his body was caging me in. He slowly brought his hands up to my face, the tips of his fingers trailing along my jaw and cheeks until he was cradling my face in his large hands. For minutes, there was only the distant sound of the music playing in the gallery and our breathing as our eyes adjusted to the dark, and we just watched each other.

"I've been waiting to hear those words from you for a long time, Grey LaRue."

My lips parted as his head dipped closer to mine, and soon Jagger was the only thing in my immediate world.

He paused a breath away, and my eyes fluttered shut when he slowly trailed his nose down mine. His lips faintly brushed against mine as he spoke. "I don't want to be Ben, and I don't want to take what the two of you had away from you. I'm not going to try to replace him, Grey, because I don't want to forget him either. I just want to love you the way I always have, and hope that one day you'll love me half as much as you love him."

Slowly moving up, he passed his lips softly across one cheek, my forehead, and nose before settling back into the place that had me straining not to reach up to press my mouth to his.

"Don't be scared. I will always take care of you, I will always put your heart before my own, and I will never push you for more than you're willing to give me," he promised. "I have no expectations, and being mine doesn't change the fact that you can talk to me about anything—including him."

I nodded my head, my nose and lips brushing against his as I did, and he leaned impossibly closer without completely closing the distance between us.

"Don't be scared, Grey," he repeated, his voice now barely above a whisper.

His mouth pressed against mine, the touch so tender, something so opposite Jagger, and yet something so *completely* Jagger when it came to the two of us. Both of our lips moved against the other's in slow, synchronized movements before he slowly pulled away. Running a hand through my hair to brush it away, he left his hand cradling the side of my head as he stared down at me.

"You know what I want. Tell me what you want from me. Whether it's everything or nothing, I'll always be here for you."

I swallowed past the tightness in my throat and brought my hand up to cover the one he was still holding against my cheek. Slowly letting my fingers glide down his arm until I was gripping the top of his forearm, I whispered, "I want you to kiss me again."

That lopsided smile crossed his face for a brief second before his lips were pressed against mine. My hands dropped to his waist when he tilted my head back, and his tongue lightly teased my lips. My body sagged into his when I opened my mouth to him, want and need for him surging through my body as the tips of his fingers barely brushed down my neck.

"Grey," he whispered into my mouth, and a shiver worked through my body.

Leaning back enough to break the kiss, I looked up into his eyes and his brow furrowed when he saw the wetness gathering in mine. His mouth opened, but I spoke first. "You deserve someone who can give you as much of them as you're giving."

Pain briefly crossed his face as he shook his head. "Tell me what you want."

I moved one of my hands up to his chest and dropped my eyes to stare at it. "I want to be selfish enough to ask you to give me everything while I try to figure this out. Figure out how to be okay, how to not be scared, how to completely give myself to you. But I—"

"You're not the only one who's struggling, Grey," he promised. "I've felt like I was betraying him for a long time, and I won't lie to you, a part of me still feels that way. It's hard knowing what is and isn't right even though he's not here anymore, because he was my best friend for most of my life. I've hated myself the last two years for not being able to stop loving you when I knew you were in so much pain. But I—I can't. I can't stop. I want you, and I want you forever."

I looked up into his darkened eyes at his words, my mind and heart equally torn. I knew a future with Ben was impossible, and I knew I'd just been blinding myself to what I'd felt for Jagger for who knew how long. But it was also hard to see myself doing this with him; it felt like I was letting Ben go, and that had a panicked feeling battling with my need for the man holding me. The love I'd always had for Jagger, mixed with the love I'd been denying . . . I could easily feel them now that I'd acknowledged my feelings and was here in front of him. But the love was terrifying me, like even my heart knew I wasn't allowed to love someone the way I'd loved Ben.

Jagger tightened his arms around me when he noticed the battle I was fighting. "You wouldn't be the only one trying to figure out how to go into this, Grey. I told you I'll be there for you, and I swear I will. Through every hard time, through every unsure moment, I'll be there . . . I just want you to be mine."

I nodded slowly, and a few tears slipped down my cheeks. "I want this. I know that I want you," I whispered. The words were true, reaffirmed by the warming feeling in my chest, but that didn't stop a tiny crack from forming in the same place for Ben. "I just hate that after you waited so long I still need to ask you to be patient with me."

He smiled softly and brushed his thumb across my cheek. "Don't. I would've waited forever for you. I hadn't been planning on telling you, and I would've left you here in Seattle as long as you needed if it weren't for your brother."

My eyebrows pulled together. "What did Graham do?"

"He said that you were doing really good here, and asked how I would feel if you found someone else. I knew I had to get here and try to talk to you. I just hadn't known how much better you would look. I'd already talked to Janie, so I knew you weren't seeing someone, but when I saw you walk in tonight I just didn't know how to fight for you when you looked so happy."

"I told you this was because of you. I haven't changed that much since I left. They picked out the outfit, made me go to a salon . . . and it was all with the hope that I would see you tonight."

Jagger's signature lopsided smile crossed his face, and he looked away for a second. "Yeah, I get that now. I should've known what Janie would do when I put her in charge."

I laughed softly and shook my head in amazement. "You really came here and did all this because you were afraid I would find another guy?"

He didn't respond, but the slight rise of one eyebrow gave me the confirmation I'd been looking for.

"No one else," I said softly. "As unfair and horrible as it is for me to say it, I know it would kill me to see you with someone else. I don't know when I fell in love with you. I can't look back and remember when exactly it changed for me, only that it has."

"I don't care about the when, Grey." He smiled as he leaned in and placed another deceptively soft kiss on my lips. What seemed so innocent had my legs weakening and my eyelids fluttering shut as I clung to his shirt. "What's next?" he breathed against my lips when he pulled back.

I blinked slowly, trying to come out of the daze of the kiss. "What do you mean?"

"Are you ready to come back to Thatch, or do you need to stay here longer? Or do you not want to go back at all?"

"No, I want to go back. I just didn't know how to before. It was easier to run away from it all and then stay gone when I knew everyone had been right. Like I told you, I'm scared. But I'm ready now . . . I'm ready to move."

"Then let's move."

LATER THAT NIGHT, after the gallery had closed, I said good night to Jagger and went back with Janie and Heather to their apartment. They both demanded details as soon as Jagger had gotten us into Janie's car and walked away, and with all their questions and pleas for me to give them *every* detail of my reunion with Jagger, I'd still been explaining everything by the time I'd started packing.

"I can't believe you didn't go back to his hotel with him!" Heather said in exasperation when I finished, and I shot her a look.

"Uh, why would I have?"

Her eyes widened like I'd missed something huge. "Have you seen that guy? And after you both declared your love and everything, how could you not want to go and explore the rest of what you've been missing?"

My hands paused above my bag, and I stared at her in shock. I'd only ever been with Ben, and up until sometime over the last six weeks, I'd been sure I would stay single for the rest of my life. Letting myself admit my feelings to Jagger had been hard enough; sleeping with him . . . well, that just wasn't something I could think of yet. He and I both knew we had to go slow, we couldn't . . . I couldn't . . .

"Grey, it's okay! Calm down, just focus on taking deep breaths in and out," Janie said quickly as she moved in front of me.

I hadn't even realized I'd started hyperventilating until I'd heard her talking. "I can't yet," I managed to get out, horrified.

"I know, it's okay. It's fine. Jagger knows that too."

"Shit, Grey, I'm sorry," Heather said. "I wasn't thinking. Janie's right; Jagger knows that. From what you said he isn't going to rush you into anything. I was just being me and . . . well, it was stupid. I'm sorry."

"Don't be, I just . . . I hadn't even thought about that. I— God, it's ridiculous to be scared over that, right?" I laughed, but it sounded off.

"It's not," Janie assured me. "All of this is a lot, and it's happened fast. You're totally allowed to freak out over things. You made a huge decision tonight, and you don't have to make the rest of them anytime soon, okay? Just go back to Thatch with him and be yourself. Let everything happen one day at a time, just like how you've been taking the last two years, all right?"

I nodded quickly. "Yeah, you're right."

One day at a time. I just needed to keep moving.

Chapter 6

Jagger
July 13, 2014

MY PHONE STARTED ringing just before Grey and I came up on the lake separating our town from another, and I slapped my hand around on my passenger seat until I found it. If Grey and I hadn't already spent the last few hours talking as I followed behind her on the way back to Thatch, I would've thought it was her.

"Hello?" I answered without looking at the screen.

"Hey! Miss me yet?"

I rolled my eyes and switched the phone over to my other hand. "I'm pretty sure I've been telling you I missed you for the last month, Charlie."

"Well, I have to make sure you don't forget about me," she said teasingly.

"Don't think that's possible, sis. How's the trip?"

"It's good! We're having fun, but I think we're all starting to get tired of cars."

"I can't imagine. Grey can barely pull off this three-and-a-half-hour trip without getting bored out of her mind. I don't know how you all can stand driving across the country and back again."

There was a pause before Charlie spoke again, this time her voice was hushed. "Grey's with you?"

"No, she's in front of me. We're just about to pull into Thatch."

"I thought you said she was in Seattle."

The easy smile I was wearing at the sound of my sister's voice dropped into a frown at the way she'd said this, like it was an accusation or something. "She was, and now she's coming back."

When Charlie spoke again, her words held a harsh tone. "Just a week ago you said you hadn't heard from her. Why is she coming back *with* you?"

"Seriously, Charlie? I thought you wanted her back."

"I did want her to go back to Thatch, I just didn't expect you to be bringing her back. What changed in the last week?"

"I went and got her. I don't understand the way you randomly react to Grey. You love her, you want to see her, you're upset she left . . . and then you're pissed off that I'm bringing her back and were weird as shit when you both hung out before you left for your trip. I thought you'd be happy . . . for me at the very least. Shit."

There was another long pause before she asked, "Happy *for* you? Why would I—what happened to make her come back?"

"Because I finally have the girl I've been waiting for my entire fucking life, Charlie! Now what is your deal?"

"Have her?" she asked quietly. "You're together?"

I blew out a slow, steadying breath and stared at the car in front of mine. "Yeah, in a way."

"When did you start dating?" she asked, her voice rising. "Seriously: What. Is. Your. Deal?"

"Just tell me, Jagger!"

"We didn't *start* dating, and I don't think either of us is going to consider this dating. It's not like we tried to make it official . . . there's not really a need to. She knows how I've always felt, and I know how she feels, that's all we need."

Charlie was silent for so long I started to say her name when she spoke again. There was an odd pain in the tone of her voice, and for the life of me I couldn't understand it. "I just—I don't understand . . ." She trailed off.

"What don't you understand? What *is* there to understand?"

"Nothing, it's not a big deal."

"Really. You sure about that?" I bit out. "Because I could've sworn you felt differently."

"Yes, really. And I am happy for you, Jagger . . . I am."

"Then wh—"

"You know, I should probably get going," she said, cutting me off. "We need to check out of this place and I haven't packed yet, so I'll talk to you later."

"Charlie," I groaned.

"Tell Grey I said hi, okay?"

I shook my head as my confusion grew. "Yeah, all right. You guys be safe, okay?"

She laughed softly and sighed. "Of course. See you in a couple weeks."

Once the call ended, I blew out a harsh breath and dropped

my phone back onto the passenger seat as I pulled up behind Grey at her parents' house. Stepping out of my car, I rested my arms on top of the door, waiting for her as she walked toward me with a shy smile on her face.

"Charlie says hi," I told her once she reached my side.

"Yeah?" she asked, her eyes brightening. "Is she having fun?"

I nodded and brushed back some of the hair that had fallen out of her bun, keeping my hand there so I was cupping her cheek when I finished. "Do you need help taking your stuff in?"

"No, I'll be fine, it's only one bag. Are you not staying?"

"I'm gonna go home and shower, and you should probably spend some time with your parents."

She took a step closer to me, closing the distance between us, and her lips parted on a soft exhalation as her body pressed up against mine. "And what about you?"

I looked up to find her eyes locked on my mouth, and a crooked smile pulled at my lips. "What about me?"

"What about spending time with you . . . ?" She trailed off, leaving the end sounding like a question.

"I can wait for you." Leaning forward, I pressed my lips to her forehead and left them there when I said, "Spend time with them, I know they've missed you. When you're done, you know where to find me."

As much as I wanted to keep her next to me forever, I couldn't, and I couldn't rush this. Even though I knew this girl was finally mine, I still needed to give her time to come to me.

Stepping back, I bit back another smile when I saw the disappointment briefly cross her face before she nodded. "Okay. I'll see you soon, then."

Forcing myself to not pull her back into my arms, I stepped

into my car and shut the door. With one last look in her direction, I pulled out of her driveway and drove home.

Grey
July 13, 2014

I BARELY HAD the front door open before my mom was swinging it back so hard that it bounced back toward us as she pulled me into a hug.

"I missed you so much, sweetheart," she murmured as she squeezed me tighter.

Before I could respond, my dad had his arms around both of us. "So glad you're home."

I laughed awkwardly as I pulled away from them. "I was only gone for a month and a half. I'd gone almost a year without seeing you before this."

"It was how and why you left. None of us knew if you would come back, how you were feeling."

"Mom, we talked all the time."

"I know," she said with a shrug. "But whenever you've left before this and we knew you were upset or hurting, you had . . ." She paused and gave my dad a look. "Well, you had Jagger with you. We knew as long as he was there that you would be okay."

I shook my head in amazement. Even after a month and a half of thinking about nothing *but* the fact that my parents, brother, and friends had all been waiting for the day I would realize what Jagger meant to me, it still blew my mind to hear how much they'd relied on—and trusted—him.

"Is he coming soon?" Mom asked, and glanced outside before shutting the front door.

"No, he went back to his place so I could spend some time with you."

"Well, you thank him for us for bringing our girl home."

I wrapped my arms around my dad's waist when I heard the tremor in his voice. For all his acting like such a hard-ass, he was the biggest softy.

"So now tell us what happened," Mom said eagerly. "I want to hear the whole story. Are the two of you dating now?"

"You didn't stay in his hotel room while he was there, did you?" Gone was the shaky tone I'd just listened to, back was my overprotective dad.

"Honey," my mom chastised.

"What? She's not old enough to—"

"So here's an idea," Graham said loudly as he walked into the entryway from the living room. "Why don't we let her actually get past the front door and let her relax before we start demanding the details of her time gone?"

I sent him a grateful smile and he winked at me as Mom and Dad agreed and started bickering about my staying with Jagger while Dad pushed my bag toward the stairs. With the things I'd found out, the feelings I'd sorted through, and the personal conversation between Jagger and me that had changed everything, I wasn't sure what I wanted to tell them—if anything. It was one thing with my friends, it was another when my dad and brother would be scrutinizing every word I said, and my mom would be hoping that I'd finally moved on from Ben.

"I didn't think you would be here." I stepped into Graham's arms and laughed when he squeezed too tight.

"Really, kid? Mom said you were coming home, so of course I'm here."

"Well, I'm glad, it's good to see you. And thanks for talking to Jagger while I was gone."

"Of course," he said, his eyes showing the smile he tried to contain. "I needed to make sure we didn't lose you; someone had to say something so he would go after you."

"Like I said, I really appreciate it."

"Don't worry about it, kid." Hooking his arm around my neck, he walked us into the living room, and his voice dropped to a low whisper when he said, "But I will kill him if you slept with him."

"Graham!"

"Does that mean you did?"

"No." I groaned and stepped away from him to go sit on the couch; he just followed. "You and Dad are both ridiculous when it comes to all that. But you can call Janie if you don't believe me, I stayed with her last night just like I had the entire time I was gone. No reason to kill Jagger."

"I will." He said the words like he was trying to make sure I knew how serious he was.

I rolled my eyes and huffed softly. "I know."

"Okay, you're sitting down!" Mom said excitedly as she and Dad came into the room. She sat down on the couch opposite Graham and me, and her face lit up. I swear she started bouncing up and down. "*Now* tell us everything."

"Mom," Graham grumbled at the same time Dad complained, "Darcy."

"What?" she asked, an innocent expression masking the curiosity and excitement that had just been all over her face. "I want to know!"

I let my head fall onto the back of the couch so I was looking up at the ceiling. This was going to be a long and awkward day.

I STOOD THERE hours later with key in hand, just staring at the door in front of me. Before everything had happened, I would've unlocked the door and walked right in. But now, well, everything had changed now. I didn't know if I should knock, if I should knock as I unlocked and opened it, or if I should call Jagger to let him know I was standing outside the warehouse.

I'd told my family as little as possible about the thoughts and feelings I'd sorted through while I was gone and what had happened the night before in the gallery. All while trying to turn the conversation to any other subject whenever Graham and my dad started freaking out over a small detail that they were blowing out of proportion—which was practically the entire time. My mom had still been begging for more details after noticing my evasiveness, and I'd only escaped by saying I'd needed to shower and get to Jagger's.

Thankfully my brother and dad were still trying to decode certain things I'd said by the time I'd gotten ready and come back down. With my mom acting as the peacekeeper on Jagger's behalf and mine, I was able to slip out after a quick good-bye without giving my mom the chance to corner me.

And now I was there, staring at the stupid metal door like it had the power of changing everything. Like what I decided to do in the next five seconds would give the wrong message to Jagger. I laughed to myself when I realized minutes had gone by with me just standing there, before finally unlocking the door and letting myself in.

"Jag?" I called out when I didn't hear music or see any sign of him. "Jagger?"

Shit. I should've called. Or knocked. I totally picked the wrong option.

Turning around, I took three steps toward the door before a deep voice stopped me. "Where you going?"

As I looked over my shoulder and up to the loft, a soft smile crossed my face when I saw him leaning over the railing, his hands covered in lingering charcoal, his face and neck covered in smudges.

"You have a little something there . . . well, kind of everywhere."

He rolled his eyes, but his signature lopsided smile offset the action. "I'm working on it. Are you hungry?"

"A little."

"Can I take you out?"

My smile widened. "Covered in charcoal?" I teased. "And since when do you have to ask me if we can grab food?"

"Since when do you take off after not being able to find me for half a minute?" he challenged.

I searched for something to say other than the unspoken questions lingering in my mind. *How much has changed between us now? What has changed?* When nothing came to mind, I simply shrugged. "Apparently since now."

Jagger watched me for a few seconds, and I knew he was trying to figure out the questions I'd just avoided. With a small nod, he pushed off the railing and took a step back. "Give me a couple minutes and I'll be ready."

In all the years since Jagger and I had become friends, I'd never felt awkward while waiting for him at his place. When he'd lived with his mom and Charlie, I'd wait in his room with Ben, or by myself. During college it had been the same. Just like he and Ben had always done with me. There had never really been any privacy among the three of us, and that had continued on after Ben died. But now I was terrified. I didn't know what he would think if I went up to the loft to wait for him, or what he would think if I didn't. I didn't want him to think something might happen if he walked out of the bathroom and found me waiting on his bed, but quickly realized he'd had years to think this and had never acted on it.

It was then I realized I was the one who was making things awkward. Not Jagger. Not the change in our relationship. I, with my fear of the unknown, was making this harder than it needed to be. I knew I couldn't worry about what might happen between us, or doing or saying the wrong thing. This was Jagger, my best friend and the one guy who knew absolutely everything about me, and had seen me at my worst. He was the guy I'd fallen in love with at some point in my life.

Just because I'd finally acknowledged that truth didn't mean that we had to change.

With a deep breath, I dropped my purse and keys on the bar and walked across the room and up the stairs to the loft. The water from the shower was running, and I caught myself looking at the closed door to the bathroom. I'd seen Jagger naked before. From the times we'd all skinny-dipped in the lake, and from others when I'd come to his place and he hadn't been expecting me while he was changing or just getting out of the shower. But now I couldn't stop thinking about him in the shower, the way his body looked, the way it would feel.

It took a second to realize my body was trembling and my breaths were too quick and shallow. I was on the edge of hyperventilating and, at the same time, welcoming the way my body slowly heated at the thoughts I'd just been having of him. The dizzying waves, shaking, and cold sweat that had just covered my body, mixed with a heat that had everything to do with the guy currently in the shower, were too much. I took hard and deep breaths in and out as I tried to calm myself, but my conflicting thoughts were only making it worse.

Knowing I was allowed to think about him in the way I had been didn't stop me from going back to my old way of thinking. That I couldn't do that to Ben, that it was spitting on his memory. *I can't do this. I can't do this.*

Gripping the chain around my neck, I tried to push those thoughts out of my mind, but they were loud. Too loud. Suddenly Jagger was right in front of me, and my eyes flew open when I felt him there. I focused on his worried expression as he knelt between my legs, both hands cupping my cheeks as he mumbled over and over again for me to breathe. And it was there and then, in the calm that poured through my body and the way my chest warmed as I stared into his green eyes, that I knew I *could* do this. That I remembered why I hadn't been able to let him walk away from me the night before.

Because, despite everything from our past, I was undeniably in love with him.

"Grey," he said on a breath when I'd calmed down, his eyebrows pinching together like he was in pain.

"I'm sor—"

"Don't," he begged. "Don't say you're sorry. You're fine. I swear I'll take care of you, and I won't push you into anything."

"I know you won't. I'm not scared of you or this, Jagger, I

swear. It's just so hard to stop the way I've been thinking for the last two years."

"You don't have to stop thinking that way. You don't. We will go as slow or as fast as you want. The only thing that has changed between us is that everything is out there now. We're still best friends, and we can stay *just* that for however long you want. Even if it's forever."

I hated the sincerity in his tone. Because even though that wasn't what I wanted for us, I knew he would do exactly what he was saying without a second thought. It killed me that after he'd waited for me for so long, there was still something between us. There would always be something between us. "I don't want that. I want you, and I want a life with you—one that's different from how it has been. I just . . ."

One of his hands left my cheek to curl around my fist, gripping Ben's ring. "I know," he said softly. "You don't have to explain anything to me. I already know." Standing up, he kept his hand on my face so I would continue looking at him. "Do you want to go home?"

"No! No, I don't. I was counting down the hours until I could come see you tonight. I want to go eat; I just want to be with you. I'm sorry that I—"

"Grey, I told you, it's fine. Please don't apologize. Let me get dressed and we'll leave."

My eyes automatically dropped to the towel wrapped around his waist for the first time since he'd come out of the bathroom, before quickly darting back up to his face. He took a step away before turning toward his dresser, and I watched as he pulled clothes out before walking to the bathroom.

"Jagger," I said before he could reach the door. He looked over his shoulder at me, his face blank. "I love you." It was true, and I'd wanted to say it over and again since the first time I'd finally said it the night before. But even I wasn't deaf to the way those three words had just sounded. Like a mix of trying to convince him *and* me.

A sad smile crossed his face before he nodded. "I know you do."

As soon as the door to the bathroom closed, I fell onto my back on the bed and tried to hold back the tears that had been threatening to spill since before Jagger had found me quickly losing it.

All I'd wanted was to spend time alone with Jagger after having gone so long without him, but I'd already messed everything up within five minutes of being there. I knew from his words, and from the fact that he hadn't kissed me since the night before, that Jagger was letting me set the pace. I didn't want anything holding me back from a relationship with him, but knew I was allowing Ben's memory to do exactly that. I wished I could say I could stop, but at that moment, it would've been a lie.

After clinging to it for so long, I wondered if I would ever be able to let go of my past with Ben.

Chapter 7

Grey
July 15, 2014

THREE LIGHT TAPS on my door pulled me out of my daydream just as my mom came walking into my room. I stared at her blandly for a second as I finished pushing aside the lingering thoughts I'd been having, until I caught on to the coy smile she was trying to hide. She was failing. Horribly.

"Hey," I said, drawing out the word in my confusion. "Am I missing something?"

She blinked quickly and straightened her back as she put on her "mom" face. "Why does there have to be 'something,' what if I just wanted to come in here and see what my daughter was up to?"

I glanced down at my phone and raised an eyebrow when I looked back up at her. "At nine in the morning?"

"Well, you were awake, weren't you?"

"Yes . . ." I drew out the word again, making it sound more like a question.

My mom hated mornings and was always grumbling at people who were "too perky" before ten. Which meant she was usually grumbling at me when I was home. I distinctly remember her throwing a mini-celebration for herself when Ben got his license and car because she wouldn't have to wake up to take me to school anymore. So for her to be out of her pajamas and have her makeup and hair done at this hour was something to be concerned about. Add on the creepy smile, and I wasn't sure I was talking to my mom anymore.

"Have you had a lot of coffee this morning?"

"Not a cup! But I'm working on it." She lightly bounced as she walked into my room and sat on my bed, facing where I was sitting at my vanity.

"Is that why you're so awake? You want to go get coffee?" I glanced down to what I was wearing and shrugged. "I'm ready if you are."

"Grey, don't act like I'm never awake at this hour."

"I didn't say that. I'm just saying you're usually a zombie at this hour."

She huffed and rolled her eyes. "Nice."

Neither of us said anything as her smile started slowly creeping across her face again. This was getting awkward.

"So, are we getting coffee or not? You're staring at me like you belong with other Stepford wives."

"Now, why are you being so grumpy this morning?" She leaned forward to whisper, "Are you on your period?"

"Mom, no. Seriously?" I laughed awkwardly as I waved a

hand at her. "You're the one being weird, I'm not grumpy at all. You come in here smiling like you have a secret and I'm pretty sure my mom has been replaced by a robot. That, or my phone is a few hours behind on the time for some reason."

"Like I said, I just wanted to come see you . . ."

"I usually wake *you* up in the morning!" I argued.

" . . . and maybe tell you that there is a very handsome young man waiting downstairs for you."

My head jerked back and I looked toward my bedroom door. "Wait, what?"

She put her hands out to the side and shrugged, but that excited smile was back on her face. "It's just a possibility."

"Jagger's here? Why didn't he just come up?"

"Because I had to make sure you looked ready for him."

A short laugh burst from my chest. "Mom. He's seen me in three-day-old pajamas and greasy hair. Nothing will faze him."

"Well, that's gross. Wait, where are you going?" she asked as she quickly climbed off my bed and ran over to me as I walked to the door.

"I'm going to see Jagger . . . unless he's not actually here . . ."

"He is, but you need to change," she hissed before shutting my bedroom door.

I once again looked down at my clothes, my expression morphing into confusion when I did. "What's wrong with what I have on?"

"You look like you're going to do yoga."

"And? I just got home from running and taking a shower, I wanted to be comfortable."

"And you can't look like you're not excited to see him!"

I laughed in frustration and looked at the door longingly

before shooting my mom a look. "I *am* excited to see him, these clothes don't say that."

"Grey Alexandra LaRue, change your clothes."

My eyes widened and a smile pulled at my lips. "Okay, that sounds more like you in the morning. What do you suggest I wear?"

"Something perfect."

My expression fell. "Perfect."

"Yes, and put some makeup on. I'll go distract your guest."

"Mom," I called out when she opened the door and walked out of the room. "This is *Jagger*. Not some random guy coming to see me. Jagger stopped being a guest when we were twelve."

She pointed a finger at me as she walked backward toward the staircase. "Change," she demanded quietly.

Biting back a groan, I walked over to my closet and flung open the door. I didn't know what qualified as "perfect" at nine in the morning, and at that moment nothing seemed better than what I was already wearing. After staring at my clothes for what felt like hours, I grabbed my green lace racerback tank and threw it on over the black spaghetti strap I was already wearing. Stepping out of my yoga pants, I searched for a pair of shorts and pulled them on as I walked to the door. I stopped abruptly as soon as I hit the doorway, and didn't hold back my next groan as I turned right back around and walked over to my vanity to put on some makeup—the entire time grumbling about my mom.

Maybe I was in a bad mood.

My mind drifted back to the dreams I'd had last night, and that I'd let replay through my mind all this morning. Jagger still hadn't kissed me again, and even though we'd spent all day together yesterday, every touch had been started by me. I knew he was letting me set the pace, but it was making me think that I'd somehow pushed him back with my mini-meltdown the other night. My dreams of never being able to get close enough to him just made my worries increase.

Once I finished with my makeup, I looked at my reflection for a few seconds before grabbing my phone and taking off toward the stairs. I shook my head and tried not to laugh when I heard my mom talking. She wasn't just being weird with me; she was being weird with Jagger as well. Questioning him like she was just meeting him for the first time, asking all about his life that she already knew just as well as his own mother.

"Mom, Jagger can't tell you anything about himself that you don't already know," I said by way of announcing myself when I walked into the living room.

Jagger gave me a look that I was sure matched the expression on my own face when the robot posing as my mom had been in my room, and I just sent him a smile. When I glanced over at my mom, she gestured to her clothes before giving me a thumbs-up while mouthing, "Perfect."

"Did your mom have a caffeine IV this morning?" Jagger whispered in my ear as he pulled me into his arms.

"You'd think so."

"Well, what are the plans for today, kids?"

Jagger turned back to look at my mom, his arm wrapped securely around my waist. "Uh, not sure. Do you need Grey for anything today?"

"No, no. Of course not, keep her as long as you want." I made a face and she quickly added, "Except for the night, of course! Bring her home tonight, you know, so she's here. In her bed. Without you in it too."

A husky laugh sounded next to me, and Jagger's fingers flexed against me. "Of course, Mrs. LaRue."

Mom blushed and waved him off. "You can call me Darcy, sweetie, you know that."

Oh my God. My mom was flirting with my boyfriend. Man friend . . . person. "Mom!"

"I know, but why change thirteen years of tradition?" Jagger replied easily. "I'll have Grey home tonight."

"Okay! Bye, you two! Have so much fun today—I mean, not *too* much fun. You know, don't get yourselves in any position you'll regret."

"Mom!"

"Not *that* kind of position . . . but, yes, that too! Protect yourselves."

Jagger busted up laughing, and I felt my face heat. "Oh my God. We're leaving. Now. We're going." Grabbing the hand on my waist, I towed a still-laughing Jagger to the door and outside. "What the hell?" I whispered as we walked down the driveway.

"I have never seen your mom like that."

I shot him a look as I slid into the passenger seat of his car. "And you think I have? I called her a Stepford wife when she came to tell me you were here."

"Did she act like that yesterday when you came over?"

"No, she was shuffling around in her robe still." I glanced down at my phone when it buzzed twice, and my jaw dropped and eyes widened in horror when I read the texts from my mom.

U have condiments just in case, right?

CONDOMS. I meant condoms! Y did it change what I wrote?

"What?"

Dropping my head, I shook it back and forth as I started

laughing uncontrollably at the ridiculousness of this morning so far, and held my phone up for Jagger to see.

"Oh Christ," he mumbled, and nudged my leg into the car before shutting my door. Once he was in the driver's seat, he turned on the car and threw it in reverse, his face covered in shock until we hit the road. "Did she, uh . . . was she like this with you and Ben?"

"No, not at all." I looked ahead and tried to find an explanation for her behavior. "This is the first time she's seen you since that morning I found out how you felt about me, and she's been rooting for you all along, I think she's just overly excited by it right now."

Jagger glanced at me and tapped on my phone. "I think that's an understatement."

"So embarrassing," I groaned. "New subject, please. What are we doing today? Just hanging out like yesterday?"

"No, I have a few things in mind."

"Oh really?" I reached over to place my hand on his leg, my chest warming when he switched hands on the steering wheel so he could grip my hand. "And what exactly do you have in mind?"

"Making you pancakes."

"You can't even make pancakes, Jag."

"No, but the cooks at Mama's Café can."

I groaned in appreciation. "My favorite."

Looking over at me, he sent me a lopsided smile and squeezed my hand. "I know."

"And what after?"

With a subtle shrug, he looked back at the road. "I guess you'll just have to find out when the time comes."

"All right, then." Settling back in my seat, I smiled to myself and got ready for a day of nothing but Jagger.

AFTER EATING PANCAKES and driving into the town next to ours to watch a movie, we spent a couple hours at the dock and were now walking around the touristy part of our town.

"I need to start looking for a job," I mumbled as we exited a store where Jagger got more charcoals.

"Why?"

"Why?" I laughed softly and sank into his side when he pulled me close. "Um, it could have something to do with me needing money."

"I'll pay for something if you need it."

I rolled my eyes and elbowed him. "I meant bills. I have to pay my student loan, and I want to get out of my parents' house and get my own place."

"You're going to get your own place," he stated dully. "Why?"

"Did you not see my mom this morning?" I teased. "Besides, I want to, and we've already talked about this. It's weird living by yourself for two years, and being away from your parents for four, and then going back to living with them. If you didn't have the warehouse, would you have moved back in with your mom?"

He gave me a look like I'd lost my mind. "No."

"See? I'm just ready to get back out on my own."

Jagger stopped walking, but kept me close to him. "Do you want to be alone, or do you just want to get away from your parents?"

"It's not that I *want* to get away from my parents. I just want space. I don't want my mom acting like she did today if you come to see me, I want some privacy sometimes."

He looked at me for a few seconds before letting his eyes drift away. Just before I could ask what he was thinking, he said, "We have privacy at my place."

"I know, but I'm not going to move in with you four days after we figured out that we want to be together."

"No, um . . . I didn't mean move in now. Not that you can't, you're welcome there whenever. If you want your own space, I can make up the extra room—it already has the stuff from your apartment in there."

My eyebrows rose and I got even closer to him. "You really think if I moved in there that I would sleep in a different room?"

His green eyes flashed down to meet mine, the want in them clear. "What I'm saying is that I think you should save your money. Am I hoping that you'll one day move in with me? Yeah, of course I am, but that's up to you and can be tomorrow or years from now . . . *if* it does happen. But if you think that it's a possibility, I don't see a point in you getting a place where you'll just waste your money and be stuck in a lease for however long. At the same time, if you want your own place, then you should get it."

I stared at him for a few seconds before grumbling, "You're no help."

"I won't push you—"

I stood on my toes and pressed my mouth firmly against his, cutting off the rest of what he was going to say. "I know you won't," I whispered against his lips. "The fact that it's been four days since you've kissed me is proof."

As soon as the last word was out, he crushed me against his body and captured my lips with his, a deep moan sounding in his chest when my tongue met his.

"If you wanted me to kiss you, all you had to do was ask."

"Okay. Well then, this is me telling you that I want you to kiss me whenever it crosses your mind." I giggled against his lips at the force of his next kiss, and swayed a little when he released me.

"If I kiss you whenever it crosses my mind, someone's going to start complaining about us. Come on, let's grab an early dinner before we go back to the warehouse, that way I'll have a table between us for the next hour."

I smiled wryly and easily fell into his side as he turned us to walk back to his car. We got to Wake—the only restaurant that wasn't a grill or a mom-and-pop-type place in town— and for the first time since we left my house, I was glad Mom had made me change. Wake wasn't so nice you had to dress up—nowhere around here was since we were on the lake, and people would go into the restaurants right after stepping from the water—but I would've felt trashy if I'd stayed in my yoga pants.

Jagger's hand tightened around mine as we followed the hostess to our table, almost to the point that it was painful, and before I could ask him what he was doing, I saw what he'd seen only seconds before.

"Here we are," the hostess said, standing off to the side of a booth. "Here are your menus, and your server will be over here soon to tell you about the specials."

"Thank you," I mumbled, and looked up to see Jagger's face, the expression unreadable. "Do you want to leave?"

His expression softened when he looked into my eyes, and he shook his head. "No."

I barely glanced at the table out of the corner of my eye, only long enough to know the woman sitting there wasn't looking at us, and an uneasy feeling settled in my stomach.

"Um, I really don't know what to say to you right now. You look pissed, but you haven't mentioned her in years. Is there something I should—"

"Grey, stop. Do you really think I'm uncomfortable because of something that I wouldn't tell you?"

"Well, I don't know. She's your ex-girlfriend, Jag, and the first time you see her, you shut down."

He leaned across the table so his voice wouldn't carry. "It's not the first time I've seen her since we moved back."

"It's not?"

"She came up to me when you were in Seattle. I was at the gas station grabbing some energy drinks, and she was just there all of a sudden. Said she'd been trying to get ahold of me, which I already knew, and was trying to talk me into getting back with her. She knows now that there's no chance in hell of that, but she asked if there was someone else. I didn't say yes or no, because there'd always been you, but at that moment you weren't talking to me. I just told her I was sorry that she'd still thought there would be something between us, and she got pissed. Asked who the person was, told me I'd come back to her . . . typical LeAnn bullshit. So I'm not uncomfortable that I'm seeing her, or that she sees me with someone. I don't like that she's seeing *you*. I don't want her to get on you because she thinks you're a threat or something."

"She would've found out eventually, it's probably already going around town after today," I mused as I grabbed the menu.

"Of course she would have. If I wanted to prevent that, I'd never go into town with you. I'm just worried about how she'll react. You remember how she was in high school to any girl I talked to, including you. She'd put threats in your locker because I was always with you."

"And sent me letters 'from Ben' that he was breaking up with me. How could I ever forget those lovely moments," I mumbled drily.

Jagger sent me a droll look. "All of that added with how pissed off she was last month, I just—"

"I know, Jag, I get it. She was a little intense in high school."

"A little?" One dark brow rose, and I rolled my eyes.

"Fine . . . she was borderline psychotic in high school. Better?"

He smiled, and the look on his face easily showed his agreement, but he didn't say anything.

"But that was also four years ago. She has to have matured in that time. Even if she did initially get mad when you saw her last month, you have to know that it was bound to happen. One, because . . . well, it *is* her, and she's the type of person who could easily be institutionalized for her actions. I'm pretty sure it's in her DNA to be loud and dramatic about everything. Two, if she waited for you that long with the hope that you *would* get back together . . . then I don't know who would expect a different reaction from her. Especially since you told her the two of you would be together."

"She wouldn't let me break up with her," he whispered harshly, and I had to bite back a laugh at the scene that had gone down that entire week.

Jagger had broken up with LeAnn the week before graduation, and that next Monday she had walked right up to him and kissed him in front of everyone. Once Jagger had finally pushed her back and asked what she was doing since he'd broken up with her only days before, she gave him a look like he'd lost his mind and said, "But *I* never said we were done" with the air of someone who controlled the entire world. But Jagger had never been one to be controlled . . . and he'd more or less told her that he wasn't going to wait around for the day that she was done with him, and broke up with her *again*. That same thing happened every day—sometimes multiple times a day—for the rest of the week. It wasn't the first time any of us questioned her sanity, but we all just shrugged it off because it wasn't a secret that she'd been obsessed with Jagger for years before they'd ever gotten together. But it wasn't until after graduation that Jagger had finally figured out a way for LeAnn to leave him alone by telling her he didn't want to put her through the hardship of a long-distance relationship, and they would be together again as soon as he moved back from college.

Not that anyone had thought he was serious. Well, except for LeAnn apparently.

The uneasy feeling I'd had when we sat down had quickly disappeared as we'd talked through everything, and I glanced back over at LeAnn. Her eyes glided in my direction, and she shot me a soft smile and waved before continuing the conversation with her date.

"Well, she definitely looks like she's moving on from you, and away from the psych ward," I mumbled as I looked back down at my menu.

Jagger huffed. "I know, and thank God."

"And the look she just gave me was definitely not one that said she was pissed off at you or me."

"Good. Maybe she did grow up and is already over it. The guy at the gas station pretty much said she's been with most of the guys in Thatch. I'm glad they're enough to get her over whatever happened."

"Like I said, you really couldn't expect a different reaction from her."

My menu was suddenly pushed down, and Jagger set his hand over mine, his fingers gently squeezing my wrist. "As much as I love talking about LeAnn, can we change the subject?"

"But she's such a fun topic," I whispered sarcastically.

"About as fun as your mom telling us to use protection and asking if you had condoms."

A sharp laugh burst from my chest, and I dropped my face into my free hand. "Oh God. Okay, neither of those subjects."

Jagger's phone rang, and after a glance at the screen, he quickly answered. "Hey, you okay? . . . You just usually call me early in the morning or late at night . . . All right. Well, hey, I'm about to have dinner with Grey, so I gotta run, but have fun tonight . . . Yeah, Charlie." Jagger sighed and his eyes flashed up to mine before they focused on the table again. "Okay, just text me when you get back to the house."

"Is she having fun?" I asked once he put his phone back on the table.

"Yeah, I guess one of their friends lives wherever they're stopped today and tomorrow, and they're going to a concert or something tonight."

I waited for Jagger to look up at me, or at his menu, but he just sat there with his eyes still fixed on the table. "Is everything okay with her? You seem . . . I don't know, but your entire mood shifted when you were talking to her."

Jagger blew out a long breath before looking at me, and his head subtly shook back and forth. "She's just been kind of weird this summer. I don't know what's going on with her; she'll just say things that are so unlike her. But it's random, she's Charlie most of the time, and then she'll say something that—I don't know, whatever. She's fine."

"You sure? We can leave so you can talk to her."

"No, it's not that serious." Jagger's lopsided smile quickly replaced the frown that had deepened as he'd talked to Charlie, but the smile looked forced. "Another subject we can leave alone for tonight, sound good?"

"Yeah, of course."

He quickly changed the direction of the conversation by talking about the guy in Seattle who owned the gallery, and how long he'd been giving him his work to show and sell. And as that subject turned into Jagger's drawings, and what he was working on now, his smiles came a little bit easier, but it was impossible to miss the vacant look in his eyes that stayed there for the rest of the night. Even when he dropped me off at my parents' house hours later, I couldn't help but wonder where Jagger's mind was—because it was obvious it wasn't with me.

Chapter 8

Jagger
July 24, 2014

STEPPING UP BEHIND Grey as she was putting plates in the dishwasher, I wrapped my arms around her waist and brushed my lips across her neck. A soft sigh blew past her lips, and as she leaned back against my chest, she tilted her head away so I had more access to her neck.

"Thanks for making lunch," I mumbled against her skin before placing another kiss there.

"I really don't know how you survived for two years on your own, Jag. I know *I* wasn't feeding you since I wasn't even feeding myself." Her hand went up to the chain on her neck, and I tightened my arms around her.

"Microwavable food and takeout. My best friends."

Grey laughed and dropped the ring she'd been grasping, then

turned around in my arms to face me. "Obviously." Her face fell and the tips of her fingers traced under my eyes for a few seconds before she repeated the words she'd been saying all morning. "You look so tired."

"I know. I never went to sleep last night."

Her head jerked back and she pressed her hands flat on my chest to push me back. "What? Why?"

"I had an idea for a drawing right before I got in bed, and the next thing I knew it was after nine this morning and I was just getting in the shower."

"Jagger, why didn't you tell me? I've been saying something all morning and you've just been blowing it off."

"Because you would've left if I'd told you."

"Of course I would have! You need to—"

I cut off her words by pressing my mouth gently to hers, and smiled against the kiss when she tried to push me away. "I didn't want you to leave, I wanted to spend the morning with you and force you to make lunch."

Her anger quickly vanished and she kissed me again, this time deeper. "So that's what I'm good for? Making you lunch?"

"Yeah," I responded automatically, and exhaled roughly when she punched my stomach.

"You need to sleep."

"I know." Moving so only one of my arms was around her, I bent down and swiped her legs out from under her with my other arm at the same second as I started walking.

"Jagger!" she screamed, and quickly wrapped her arms around my neck. "Warning next time!"

"Where's the fun in that?"

She kicked her legs in the air as I approached the staircase.

"No. Put me down! You're tired, and you are not carrying me up the stairs. And you *need* to go to sleep!"

"Why do you think we're going up there?"

"Jagger," she whined, but stopped wiggling around.

"Grey . . ." I mocked her tone, and smiled when she glared at me. "When in the last thirteen years have you ever left because I was about to take a nap, and vice versa."

"I'm sure there was at least once. Now put me down and go to sleep."

I stopped walking halfway up the stairs and let my arms shake. "You're right, this looks like a good spot." Bending down, I made my arms shake harder and let my eyes close. " 'Night, Grey."

Her legs kicked at the air again, and a hard laugh left her chest when I laid her down on the stairs, and lowered myself onto her so I was pinning her down. "Okay! Okay! Not here!"

"Too late."

"This is so uncomfortable, Jag," she complained.

I cracked one eye open and looked into her gold eyes. "You told me—"

"I take it back. Go to sleep *in* your bed." She grunted as she tried to push me off. "You're so heavy!"

"I don't know if I should be offended by that or not." Dropping my head to kiss her quickly, I jumped off her and left her there as I continued to climb the stairs.

"Good night," she called after me from her spot on the stairs.

"Get your ass in the bed, Grey. You're not leaving."

I didn't turn around to see if she would follow me. I already knew she would. I knew there were parts of our friendship that meant more now that things had changed between us, but I didn't want that to change the way things had always been. I didn't want her to feel awkward around me, and I didn't want us to go through a phase of trying to figure out what we should or shouldn't do now that we were together.

I had only been on the bed for a few seconds when she dropped down next to me. A smile tugged at my lips, but I didn't say anything. This was right. This was us.

WHEN I WOKE up, Grey was in my arms with her head curled under my chin. One of her hands was pressed to my chest while her other arm was wrapped around my back, keeping us locked together. The arm underneath her was asleep, and I was afraid to stretch out since one of her knees was locked between both of mine. It had to be the most uncomfortable position I'd ever been in; but it was perfect, and I would've stayed like that for hours if she hadn't woken up and started moving.

I waited to see if she would start to freak out over our position, but long seconds passed before she moved her head from under mine so she could look at me—her eyes widening when she found me awake.

"How long have you been up?"

"A couple minutes," I mumbled, and tightened an arm around her. "When did this happen?"

Grey's cheeks filled with heat, and I couldn't help but smile from the sight of it. "Uh . . . well, it was cold, and you were on top of the comforter."

She and I both knew she could've gotten under the covers on the side where she'd been lying when I'd fallen asleep, but if she was going to use that as an excuse to reproach me, then I'd swear that she'd had no way of getting under. Anything if it meant she ended up in my arms voluntarily.

"Are you mad?" she asked hesitantly.

"Are you kidding?" Brushing my lips against hers, I left them there when I said, " 'Mad' is the complete opposite of what I am right now."

She smiled against my mouth before kissing me again, and soon the teasing kisses changed into something more. The hand that had been resting against my back started clinging, and the hand on my chest curled against the material of my shirt like she was trying to pull me closer when there was already nothing between us. When her hands released me only to start searching along the bottom of my shirt, I rolled us over so Grey was on her back and pulled my shirt over my head before tossing it away from the bed.

Her hands were everywhere—lightly traveling up my stomach and chest, across my shoulders, down my back. This was something I'd dreamed of for years, and never thought I would experience—and for a second, I wondered if I was still sleeping and would wake up and find her on the other side of the bed. Her fingers trailed over my abdomen, and a low groan sounded in my chest when she moved them just inside the top of my jeans.

Sitting back, I took in her flushed cheeks, swollen lips, and hooded eyes, and knew I would never forget the way she looked right then. Dipping my head down to her stomach, I pushed the bottom of her shirt up slowly, my mouth following the movement. Her breathing deepened and her hands moved up to gently grasp the back of my neck as I continued to move upward. I pushed the shirt just past her breasts, and let my lips linger on them for a moment, then Grey was pulling me up and crushing her mouth to mine. I settled myself between her legs, and had to clench my fists against the comforter when she moved her hips against me so I wouldn't tear off her shorts right then.

"Jag," she breathed against my mouth, her hands trailing down to the top of my jeans again. "I want . . ." She trailed off.

"Tell me—"

"Jagger?" a female voice called out from below the loft, and Grey and I both froze. "Your car is here, where are you?"

"Charlie," we whispered at the same time, and Grey's eyes were no longer hooded or dark with need; she looked terrified, and one hand was quick to grip at Ben's ring when she realized the position we were in.

I turned my head and pushed myself off her so she wouldn't see how much that action killed me after the last ten minutes.

"Jag?" Charlie yelled from the hallway.

"Yeah! Be down in a sec."

I caught sight of Grey just before I pulled my shirt on, and wished I hadn't. She'd already fixed her shirt and was sitting up on the bed, her eyes wide as she stared straight ahead, not seeing anything.

"Grey." I waited until she looked up at me, and held my hand out to her. "Come on, let's go downstairs."

She nodded and mumbled something too low for me to hear as I pulled her off the bed.

Just before we hit the top of the stairs, I looked back at her and whispered, "I'm sorry."

Not waiting for a response, I jogged down the stairs and wished I could go back to sleep when I saw my sister's face. She was staring at Grey with a look close to betrayal, and once again, I was left not understanding my sister at all.

"Hey," I finally said to break the tension coming from each girl. "I didn't know you were coming back so soon."

Charlie finally looked over at me, her voice soft and unsure. "I told you I'd be back tonight."

"We just woke up. I don't even know what time it is."

Charlie didn't say anything, and Grey finally shook off whatever she'd been wrapped up in to say, "Did you have fun?"

"Um. Yeah, it was—well, I'm glad to be home. But I should leave."

"Charlie," I grumbled at the same time Grey said on a laugh, "What? No!"

Charlie took a step back and pointed behind her. "No, really, I should. I should've called or something so I wouldn't interrupt anything."

"You didn't," Grey assured her, and my eyes darted over to her. "Jagger stayed up drawing all night, so we fell asleep after lunch. We just woke up, you weren't interrupting anything."

Part of me knew that Grey would've said that no matter what. It's not like I wanted my sister to know what I did with Grey when we were alone, but I couldn't help but think of the panicked look on Grey's face when we'd broken apart, and the way she'd been gripping Ben's ring.

"Um . . . okay," Charlie mumbled before looking back at me.

"Oh my God, I had no idea it was this late."

I looked over at the microwave to check the time, but right now the fact that we'd slept until seven wasn't enough to faze me. My sister still looked hurt and betrayed, and Grey was standing far enough away from me that I couldn't touch her if I tried.

"Are you hungry? We can order something, or I'll make dinner."

Charlie's head jerked back, her eyes stuck on me before they slowly drifted to Grey. "Do you live here now?"

Grey's face fell at my sister's tone, and she scrambled to find something to say. "No . . . I don't, I just . . ." She trailed off and looked helplessly around. "Jagger doesn't cook, and I thought you might be—I'm gonna go home."

I didn't say anything; I didn't know what to say in that moment. I was pissed off and so fucking confused. My sister and my girl were trying to leave, both looked uncomfortable, and I had no idea what to do to fix it.

"No, don't," Charlie said just as Grey started walking toward the bar to get her purse. "I'm sorry, it's been a long day and I'm just crabby. I was with those girls in a car for a month and a half, it all got to be too much. We can order something, and I want you to stay, I've only seen you once since you moved back."

Grey turned to look at me, but my eyes were still on Charlie. She sounded and looked like my sister again, but there was still that underlying hurt in her eyes. When I realized they were both looking at me, I cleared my throat and shrugged. "I don't want either of you to leave. Decide what you want, I'll call the restaurant."

By the time the food had been delivered, Charlie and Grey were completely back to normal. But Grey was still sitting far enough away that I couldn't touch her, and even when Charlie went outside to get something from her car, she was acting like nothing had ever happened between us. I couldn't help wondering how much she regretted what little we'd done, and if she was blaming me for it.

Grey
July 28, 2014

As soon as I walked into The Brew, I spotted Charlie sitting at one of the large couches and started toward her just as she waved at me. She already had two drinks on the table, and I knew without having to look at the cup farthest from her that it was an iced caramel macchiato for me. Charlie and I had always taken turns getting something from this shop in the morning before classes during high school, so it was impossible to not know what each other's favorite was.

"Hey, sorry I'm late," I said as I sat down beside her on the couch.

She waved me off and pushed my drink closer to me. "You're not. I came here early so I could grab a few books."

"Get anything good?"

"Of course," she scoffed. "Some more romances from a few of my favorite authors . . . you could always borrow them when I'm done."

A sharp laugh burst from my chest, and I rolled my eyes. "Oh yes, please, I would love nothing more than that," I said drily.

"You never know, Grey, you might just fall in love with them."

"Doubtful. But, really, enjoy them for me."

I wasn't a fan of reading much, as it was, but romance was definitely the opposite of what I would look for if I was. Charlie had been trying to get me into reading since she started high school, but I didn't see the point. Because of romance novels, she had expectations that were absurdly high when it came to guys, and even though I'd always joked with her that she'd only ever find those kinds of guys in books, she'd just smile dreamily and say, "He's out there."

"I will get you to read one, Grey LaRue. One of these days, I promise you."

"They're all fairy-tale-ish, and there's always the happy ending that never happens in real life."

Charlie looked like I'd just stuck a knife in her stomach. "It does happen in real life, but not all the stories have happy endings. And fairy tale? Come on, Grey, this isn't *Cinderella*."

I laughed softly and took a sip of my drink. "You know what I mean. Girl meets guy, they're perfect for each other. Something happens that will threaten to keep them apart, and then they live happily ever after."

Charlie's expression told me she was trying to figure out a way to disagree, but then her shoulders slumped and she mumbled, "Yeah, that's usually how it goes."

"See?"

"But there's so much more in them! Yeah, okay, fine . . . that's generally the outline to any romance novel, but it's what happens to fill up that outline that makes it amazing. It's the different circumstances, it's the lengths they'll go to in order to be together, it's their *struggles* that are real."

"Your inner nerd is showing," I teased.

"I'm serious, Grey. They're not all perfect." She looked away

for a second, and I actually worried that she was too involved
in these books when I saw the deep sadness embedded in her
features.

"Hey, I was kidding."

Charlie looked back at me and smiled, but there was still that
sadness her eyes weren't able to hide. "No, I know you were. I
wasn't offended by what you said. But I don't believe everything
is a fairy tale, Grey. Life hurts; there are parts of life that are so
major that they'll change you completely. We're all on this giant
roller coaster and you never know when you're going to go down,
or just how far down you'll actually have to go. But those drops
and those climbs are what make us, and make our life what it's
supposed to be—whether it hurts or not."

I couldn't move or say anything as I sat there listening to her.
This girl I'd grown up with and who had always been so quiet
and shy because she lived in her books sounded like her world
had been crushed. I couldn't think of anything in her life that
would rock her enough to make her sound like this.

"Like I said, I don't believe everything is a fairy tale. But I
do believe that everyone meets someone in their life who will
make it seem like their life is as close to a fairy tale as it can
get."

"Okay," I said on a breath.

"Anyway!" She straightened her back and shook herself as a
bright smile lit up her face. "I will get you to read a book one day,
just you wait."

"And I'll just leave it there because I love the smell of books."
I looked behind me at all the shelves of books, and smiled. "I
would work here just so I could have two of the best smells in the
world. Coffee and books."

"Why don't you?"

"Hmm?" I turned to look at Charlie, my forehead creased. "Why don't I what?"

"Work here. You told me the other night at Jagger's that you were looking for a job. Unless you start your own business, you're not going to find much in Thatch. Or you could always travel into another town to work in an office."

"I don't want to work in an office," I grumbled. "I can't see myself sitting behind a desk all day."

"Didn't think so, and unless you're about to turn into my mom and go through a bunch of phases where you try to make things, I'd say you don't have many options."

"Your mom and her phases . . ." I trailed off and laughed. "Yeah, definitely not going in that direction either."

"So then what's wrong with here?"

I looked around The Brew, pretending to look at it like I was seeing it for the first time. Until I was six or so, the coffee shop and bookstore had been two separate businesses. We didn't have a Starbucks in Thatch; if you wanted amazing coffee, you went to The Brew. The bookstore had been owned and run by an old woman who really only carried books that she liked to read. When she got to a point in her life where she knew she needed to stop working, she'd just been planning to shut down the bookstore. And considering we didn't have a library or actual bookstore anywhere within an hour from here, that meant bye bye books.

The owners of The Brew had bought out her store, knocked out the wall separating them, and updated the books and the look of the store so it was now inviting and there was something for everyone. On Thursday nights there was live music, and it

really was one of the best places in Thatch to just sit and relax—
especially during the winter. Jerry and Anne were the owners,
and you never found the store without both of them in it. They
loved their shop and all the people in it, and would easily be the
best bosses around.

"I guess nothing is wrong with working here. I love this place,
I'd just never thought of working here. I'll talk to Anne before I
leave."

"There you go. Job search over," Charlie said confidently, and
I snorted.

"Uh, one, I never actually started searching. Two, no one said
they would hire me."

"Well, considering I talked to Anne while I was looking for
books, and she told me she was going to have to put up a sign
soon since one of the employees quit because she was having
twins, and two of the others put in two-week notices since they
were leaving for college . . . I'd say she'd be happy if you told her
you wanted a job."

"I *would* be happy."

I turned around to see Anne standing at the end of the couch,
bent over so she could rest her elbows on the arm.

"Good morning, Anne," I said with a smile.

It didn't surprise me that she'd chimed in on our conversation.
That's how she was, always flitting around the shop, talking with
everyone. If it weren't for Jerry, she'd probably stay out talking
the entire day.

"Morning, girls. So, Grey, you gonna come work for me?"

"Would you like me to?"

"Let me think . . ." She clucked her tongue and gave me a look.
"Um, of course! Why don't you come in next Monday around

two-ish, I'll have you do all the paperwork, and then we'll start training you for the registers and the coffee."

I looked at Charlie and she gave me an I-told-you-so smile before I could look back at Anne. "That sounds perfect, I'll be here."

"Great! Now I better get back to looking like I actually do something around here before that husband of mine starts complaining. Have a good day, ladies!"

Charlie and I called out our good-byes, and I turned to glare at Charlie. "You told her I was looking for a job," I accused.

"Of course I did. She'd just finished telling me about all the employees who were leaving and being short staffed, and I told her you'd been looking into getting a job. She was going to call you to *ask* you to come in, but I told her I was meeting you here anyway. So . . . done! You now have a job."

"Well then, thank you?" I laughed awkwardly. "Good to know I have people who will set up jobs for me."

Charlie smirked. "Whatever. You know you would've applied as soon as you saw that sign. You're in here enough as it is, you might as well work here."

"Clearly." I gestured in the direction Anne had walked off. "Anyway, on to other things. Is there anyone you've been interested in or seeing while we were at school . . . ?" I let the question trail off.

"No."

"No? Come on, Charlie, there has to be someone. You are gorgeous—"

"And shy around anyone who isn't you or my family," she added, cutting me off. "There's just no one here who catches my eye."

"That doesn't mean you haven't caught their eye. Has anyone *tried* to talk to you?"

She looked like she was trying really hard to think, and finally she shrugged. "I don't know; I don't pay attention."

"Why not? See? Those books you read are ruining you for real men."

"They're not!" she said on a laugh. "I've never had a boyfriend . . . I don't want one."

"So you're just going to become an old cat lady . . . or a nun?" I asked, my voice and expression flat.

"No, I'm not. I just—I haven't found someone who has shown himself to be worth my time." That same sadness I'd seen earlier was back, and her eyes seemed somehow unfocused as if she were seeing things I couldn't even begin to imagine. "Trust me, I'll know when there's a guy who's worth it."

I waited for a few moments to see if she would expand on that, and it wasn't until I started talking again that she shook off her expression. "You've never dated anyone, and you seem to avoid guys, but you look like your heart has been shattered by someone. I don't get it. Did something happen to you, Charlie?" I finished on a whisper, fear and panic clawing at my stomach at the thought of someone hurting her or taking advantage of her.

"What?" Her eyes widened when she got what I was asking. "No! Oh my God, no, nothing has happened to me. You would've known; Jagger would've been the first person I called if something like that ever happened."

The panic and fear eased up, but I still didn't understand how she could look like someone had broken her. "Then why—"

"It's like you said," she said loud enough to cut me off again, "the books I read are ruining me for real men. I know I'll never find someone like the guys I read about, and it's kind of depressing." Charlie tried to laugh it off, but I knew that wasn't it.

I stifled a gasp when it hit me, and leaned closer to her. "Charlie, no one will think differently of you if you're gay."

"Whoa, what? Grey, I'm not . . . I'm not into that. No. Really, you're looking into this too hard. There's nothing. No guys, no girls, nothing. Just me and my books and a depressing world of guys who will never be enough."

I sat back and blew out a deep breath. "Sorry, I was just trying to understand where you're coming from."

She shook her head, a smile crossing her face. "Really, it's fine. And I'm fine."

I would've tried harder to believe her if her voice hadn't cracked at the end, and if she didn't look like she was seconds away from breaking down. I couldn't think of anything to explain her sadness and knew she probably wouldn't admit to it even if I had guessed correctly. But seeing her pain, I knew I would keep trying to figure out what had happened to her to make her so unhappy.

Chapter 9

Grey
July 31, 2014

MY FOOTSTEPS FALTERED as I walked out of The Brew a few days later, and my spine straightened as a chill ran through my entire body. Looking around to see if anyone was watching me, I glanced back at the piece of paper that was tucked in between the windshield and wiper and slowly closed the distance to my car, my eyes never leaving the seemingly harmless sheet. After unlocking the car and putting the coffee inside, I climbed back out and looked around one more time before reaching for the paper, ice sliding through my veins as I did so. There were people I knew all around, but none that looked like they were waiting for this . . . for me to find whatever had been left for me.

I could have easily walked around my car, inspecting it to see if someone had hit it and left their information, but I didn't. And

I didn't let my mind even think of Jagger leaving me a letter . . .
because not only was he at his place waiting for this coffee, but he
wouldn't do something like this to me. Because he knew. Everyone who knew us knew. Ben had left notes on my car every day.
No matter what. It could've been something as simple as a smiley
face or an *I love you,* or it could have been something long that
had my heart melting. But every day after I got my first car, there
had been a note. Notes that stopped abruptly with his death.

Taking a deep breath, I opened the paper with shaky hands.
A cry burst from my chest as my eyes ran over the page, and I
stumbled back. I looked around furiously for someone, *anyone.*
There were people giving me worried looks, but none who
looked like they knew exactly what I'd just seen. None who
looked like they'd put Ben's wedding vows on my windshield.
His handwriting, words and lines crossed out as he'd tried to
perfect the vows.

"Grey, darling?"

"What?" I cried as I whirled around, startling one of my old
teachers from high school.

"Are you okay? You don't look so well."

"I—I, I don't . . . I don't know. I have to go!"

She reached out for me, but I quickly backed up into my car.
"Really, darling, you don't look well. Should we call someone
for you?"

"N-n-n-no. I'm fine!"

"Are you sure? Maybe you should—"

I swung open the door to my car and slid in as I nearly shouted,
"I'm sorry, but I have to leave!"

I tossed the paper onto the passenger seat, and fumbled
through my purse with shaking hands, looking for my phone so

I could call Jagger. This was a dream, this was a joke, I was going—I was going . . .

My blood ran cold and the world seemed to tilt as a high-pitched ringing started in my head. Blocking out my old teacher knocking on the window, blocking out the sound of other cars and people outside, blocking out everything other than that fucking deafening ringing.

My jaw trembled as I tried to open my mouth to deny out loud what I was seeing.

There, on the lock screen of my phone, was a Facebook message notification.

Ben Craft: Forever, Grey.

The phone slipped from my trembling fingers, and I pressed my hands to my head as the sound grew louder. It wasn't until my door was wrenched open and I was being pulled out of the car that I realized the deafening noise was my screaming.

Someone was shaking me, someone was gripping my face and forcing me to look at them, someone was shouting—but I couldn't hear the words, I couldn't focus on the face, I couldn't feel the jarring effect the shaking should've been having on my body. All I knew in that moment was the paper filled with vows, and the message waiting for me to view.

Impossible. I was going insane. This is what it felt like to truly lose yourself, and for a second, I wondered why it had taken so long for it to happen, or if it had been happening all along. I wondered if I was going to come back to reality and find myself in a bland, white room where a nurse would come medicate me. Because this—this couldn't be real, and I wasn't dreaming, because if this had been a dream, I would've woken up by now.

"Grey! Grey! What's happening?" someone shouted, followed closely by someone else's yell, "Has anyone called an ambulance yet?"

My screams had ended, only to be replaced by a hyperventilation so extreme, I was waiting for the moment when it would become too much for me to handle. I hung, hunched over in someone's arms, clawing viciously at them as I tried to steady my breathing, but the panic only seemed to rise.

"B-Ben!" I shouted through rapid breaths, and I heard the person behind me sigh sadly.

"Poor girl still isn't over what happened."

"You need to try to breathe, Grey," another voice said soothingly. "Calm your breathing. Big, deep breath in. Hold it as long as you can, and then let it out."

No matter how many times she said it, my breathing never changed.

"Graham's already on his way, I called him a few minutes ago. He'll be here soon. Big, deep breath in, Grey."

I looked back up at the girl, and even though I knew I'd grown up with her, I couldn't focus on her face, I had no idea who she was. All I knew was Ben.

Ben. Ben. Ben. Ben. Ben.

Forever, Grey. Forever, Grey. Forever, Grey.

Another scream tore through my throat before my world went blurry with tears. I placed my hands on the sidewalk below me, allowing the person behind me to continue holding me up as I sobbed toward the ground until I heard my brother's voice above everything else.

"What's happening?" he asked loudly to everyone surrounding me before pulling me out of the man's arms, and curling me onto his lap. "God, Grey, it's okay. What's wrong? What happened, kid?" he crooned. "Talk to me."

I sobbed into his chest as the people around me spoke to him.

"Grey, you gotta tell me what's wrong. The ambulance is almost here, do you need to go to the hospital?"

It was then I heard the sirens, and I shook my head fiercely as I tried to back away from him. My breathing was ragged again, and I tried to look past the crowd circling us, toward my car.

"B-Ben. H-h-he . . . vows."

"Grey," Graham whispered. "No, it's okay. He's—kid, he's gone."

"He's not!" I screeched, and tried to scramble from his lap, but he didn't let me get far. When I looked back at his face, I saw a look conveying thoughts I'd just been having. He thought I'd lost it.

"What the hell is going on?"

I turned quickly at the sound of Jagger's frantic voice, and Graham helped me stand in time for Jagger to wrap his arms around me.

"I've been getting calls for the last ten minutes. What's happening?" he asked Graham, but then cupped my cheeks and lowered his head to ask me, "Are you hurt? Why is there an ambulance pulling up?"

Even if I could say anything in that moment, Graham would've beaten me to it. "From what everyone's saying, she isn't hurt, but I think the medics should check her over."

Jagger's green eyes bounced over my face before looking over at Graham. "Why? What's going on?"

The EMTs started parting the crowd, making their way toward us, but Jagger just tightened his grip on me until Graham said, "She thinks Ben is here."

I felt a jolt go through Jagger's body, and he slowly pushed me back so he could look down at me again. "Grey, you . . . you think that—what?"

"Is this who we were called for?" an EMT asked, and reached for me.

"Don't touch me! I'm fine!"

"Grey," Jagger and Graham said at the same time.

Tears were still falling down my cheeks, and my chest was still rising and falling too erratically, but the last thing I wanted was to be checked over by these men. Despite the body-numbing terror that had filled me when I'd seen the note and the message, I needed to see it again to know I wasn't insane. I needed Jagger and Graham to see it to confirm my sanity.

"Ma'am, are you—"

"Please! I'm fine. I don't . . . I don't need help."

The three medics looked at each other before shrugging and asking around if anyone else had been hurt in the "incident."

Graham was busy getting people to back away from us when Jagger tilted my head back again. "Talk to me, baby."

"There was—he left . . . I don't know how it happened, Jag," I cried, and pressed my forehead into his chest.

"Mrs. Reil said Grey kind of freaked after she pulled something off her car," Graham said when he came back. "She said she tried to get Grey to talk to her because she looked like she was panicking, but Grey got in her car, and when she did, she just started screaming and wouldn't stop. They had to pull her out of her car and she kept screaming."

"What'd you pull off your car?" Jagger asked quietly in my ear, but fresh tears filled my eyes, and I couldn't force anything from my mouth. "Where is it, Grey?"

I shook my head against his chest for long seconds before whimpering, "I can't be crazy. I know what I saw."

"Babe, look, you *need* to help me here. I want to help you, but I can't if you're not giving me anything to go on. What did you pull off your car, and where is it?"

I stepped back from him, and looked from him to Graham's worried expression before glancing at the remaining people on the sidewalk. I didn't want them there; I didn't want an audience. Because if I was wrong—if I hadn't really seen what I thought I'd seen—I didn't want a dozen people who had known me my entire life to witness my loss of sanity. And if the letter and message were still there, I wasn't okay with anyone else getting a glimpse of something so personal.

Taking a ragged breath, I gripped Jagger's hand and walked slowly toward my open car door. Each step felt weighted. With each one, the dread of what might not be in there, and the fear of what I somehow knew *was* in there, continued to grow.

I reached down to grab my phone from the floorboard before sliding into the seat of my car. My hands shook when I saw the piece of paper lying on the passenger seat, and when I grabbed it, I turned to look at Graham and Jagger standing by the door, blocking my view of everyone on the sidewalk. Both looked worried, confused, and like they weren't sure what to do with me.

Once I calmed my breathing enough to speak, I told them about finding the letter. Both listened closely, neither saying anything as they listened to my weak and shaky voice.

"I was only in the shop for maybe six minutes, seven tops. I hadn't been looking outside while I was in there, so I don't know who went past my car. But when I came out, this was tucked under my windshield wiper." I held up the folded piece of paper, and both Jagger and Graham sent me looks of pain. They knew where my thoughts had gone when I saw the paper, but they had no idea how bad it was yet.

"It could've been a coin—" Graham started, but I kept talking.

"I opened it, and I thought I must have been dreaming, or someone was playing a joke on me. There was no—" I cut off on a sob. "No way this could've been here. I got inside my car to call you," I said, looking at Jagger. "But when I found my phone, there was a push notification on my lock screen, and that's when . . . that's when . . ." I shrugged helplessly, not knowing how to continue.

I clicked the lock button on my phone and a strangled cry bubbled past my lips when I saw that the message was still there. I hadn't imagined it. It had been real. Just as the guys began asking what had been on my phone and the paper, I handed over both, and a weighted silence seemed to fill the space of my car for a few moments before Graham erupted in curses.

Jagger's face went completely pale, his head shaking back and forth. "Who did this?" he asked himself before turning around to yell the same thing. Holding up the vows as he glared at the people still standing on the sidewalk. "Huh? Who the fuck pulled this shit?"

Graham was asking everyone who had been near my car, but the way he was asking was scaring people to the point where all they were able to do was shake their heads and back away from him.

The phone vibrated in my lap where Graham had dropped it, and I looked down to see a text from Janie, the notification from Ben sitting untouched below hers. My fingers felt like ice as I slid my thumb across the screen, opening up the Facebook messages. I looked at the small picture of Ben and me before glancing down at the message that had been sent to me almost thirty minutes ago, the ones before that from well over two years ago.

In my head, I knew he was gone. I knew this wasn't him, and I couldn't let myself believe he was sending me messages. *He's gone, Grey. He's gone.* With a steady breath out, I typed back a message and hit send.

Who is this, and why are you doing this to me?

Just before I closed out the app, a bubble popped up indicating Ben was responding—no, not Ben. Someone. I stared at the screen, holding my breath until it all came out in a hard rush when I saw the response. There was a picture of Jagger kissing my forehead from just a couple weeks ago. Below, the words:

Ben Craft: How could you do this to us? We were supposed to be forever, Grey.

"No, no, no, no," I whimpered. "Ben, no."

"I don't know how—Grey, what is it?" Jagger asked in a rush, reaching for my phone. I tightened my grip, but he somehow swiftly and gently pulled it from my fingers. "It'll be okay, we'll find out who did . . . what the hell? You sick fuck!" he roared out toward the street, and people turned to look at him. "Stop hiding, you have something to say, come and say it!"

Graham walked quickly over to where Jagger was turning in circles, his eyes looking suspiciously at everyone. Wrapping his arms around Jagger's chest, he started pulling him back toward the car. "Calm down, man."

"I swear to God I will find out who you are!" Jagger yelled at everyone, and yet no one.

"Calm down, Jagger," Graham grunted as he released him. "Calm down and get Grey out of here."

"This piece of paper came from *my* place. It was in my fucking house!" Jagger hissed at Graham, shoving the vows in his face. "You know I wouldn't do this shit to her, now tell me how this got here. Tell me who took this!" he yelled back toward the street. Jagger bent into my open car door and took my chin between his fingers, his eyes were wild and his voice was harsh. "That is not Ben, Grey. Whoever it is, is sick and twisted, but it's not him. Okay?"

I exhaled roughly and nodded my head once.

Everything about him softened as he continued looking at me. "I need to hear you say it. I need to know you believe it," he whispered, pressing his lips softly to mine. "It's not him, baby."

"It's not Ben," I finally choked out, and Jagger released a ragged breath as he moved his hands to cradle my face, holding me close to him. "You had the vows?" I asked shakily. "W-why . . . why would you?"

He moved back far enough to look at me better and shook his head slowly. "He'd been working on them at my mom's place the week before the wedding. He kept them there because he knew you'd look for them at his parents' house."

A startled laugh escaped my lips, because I *had* looked so many times in the days leading up to the wedding.

"I didn't know if you'd want to see them . . . after . . . but I knew you would hate me if I got rid of them. So I've just been holding on to them until you were ready. I knew one day you would ask about them. But they—I mean, they were *hidden* in my loft so you wouldn't stumble upon them, Grey. I don't understand. No one else goes in there . . ."

My eyes widened. "I'm not doing this!" I said quickly. "I'm not doing this to myself, I swear to God, Jag, I'm not!"

"No, baby, no. That's not what I was saying, I know you wouldn't. Someone cruel is doing this, and I promise you I'm going to find out who. Okay?"

I nodded and he pressed a firm kiss to my lips.

"I need to get you out of here. Where do you want to go? Do you still want to come to my place, or do you want to go to your parents' house?"

My mouth opened to say my parents', but I quickly shut it. Part of me screamed that I'd just seen the vows Ben had been preparing for our wedding, and now I was betraying him by being with his best friend. But I realized that is what the person who stole the copy of the vows was trying to do; they were trying to separate me from Jagger. They were trying to make me take ten steps back in my healing from Ben's death.

"Yours," I whispered.

"All right. Let's get you into the passenger seat, I'll drive you over there."

"What about your—"

"We can pick up my car later, it's fine where it is. Just let me drive you."

I don't remember the drive to the warehouse, or going inside. Actually, I don't remember much of that day at all except the fear of getting another message and cringing every time my phone went off. And most of all, wondering what Ben *would* say about us if he were here.

Chapter 10

Jagger
August 6, 2014

"I DON'T KNOW what you're seeing, but that is not a dinosaur." Glancing down at Grey when she giggled, I squinted at her, then looked closely into her gold eyes. "Are you stoned?"

"Shut up, Jag." She pushed against my chest and kept one hand there to lightly trail her nails against my skin. "That is totally a T. rex! You're just looking at it upside down."

I looked back up at the clouds in the sky, and shook my head. "That's not an upside-down T. rex either."

Her free hand splashed water up at me, and I laughed. "Babe, seriously, if anything, that's a tree."

"You have no imagination."

Leaning over her body, I brushed my lips just below her breasts and spoke against her skin. "I beg to differ."

Grey's hands went up to play in my hair as I placed soft kisses all over her stomach. "I see a T. rex, a bunny, a mug, and a heart. You think they all look like cotton candy or trees."

"That just means I'm the sober one here."

She tugged gently on my hair, but only sighed as she relaxed her head against the handles of the Jet Ski.

We'd gone out on a boat with a few friends from high school this morning to wakeboard, and I'd been prepared for it to be a disaster. In spite of her uncaring reaction when she saw Grey and me together, it didn't stop me from waiting for LeAnn to say some bullshit to Grey. Even when LeAnn's guy—a different one from the restaurant—went out on the water, LeAnn was talking with all the girls like they were just catching up.

After wakeboarding for a few hours, Grey and I had left them and rented a Jet Ski to spend some time alone before Grey had to get to work. We hadn't even been on the water for thirty minutes when I'd had to cut off the engine because the way Grey's hands were curling against my stomach had made it too hard to concentrate on anything else. She'd wiggled her way around me until she was sitting on my lap so she could lie back against the Jet Ski, and I'd been struggling to keep my hands and mouth only on places they'd already been. Her being in a bikini wasn't helping my self-control . . . or lack thereof.

Given the way Grey had reacted a week and a half ago when Charlie showed up at my place, I'd been afraid she would regret what we'd been doing. But by the next day, she was back to normal. Staying pressed up against my side, giving me teasing kisses that would quickly build . . . it was how it had been, and I was glad we hadn't gone back a few steps. But since the day she'd received the copy of Ben's vows and the message from his

Facebook account, I'd slowly watched her drift back into being the Grey I'd come to know so well over the last two years.

There were moments, like right then on the lake, but the rest of the time I'd find her staring off at nothing or she'd just slowly shut down and curl into a ball while gripping the ring around her neck. It was almost as if she'd remember the present and what I meant to her now, but then go back to cling to the past. Never moving on from the point we'd been at a week and a half ago, and going back a few steps for the majority of our days.

I didn't *need* more from her physically. If she needed to go back and slowly build up to where we'd been, I would do that for her in a heartbeat. But with the amount of time each day she spent in the past, I knew we wouldn't be starting over . . . I knew I was slowly losing the girl I'd had for what felt like only a few seconds.

I was slowly losing Grey completely.

She didn't want to talk about Ben, she didn't want to talk about what had happened . . . she just didn't want to talk. She was the Grey she had been after Ben died, but this time she was shutting me out too. So for the few moments I still had her, I wasn't wasting a single second. I wanted to have memories of the girl I'd waited for once that girl was completely gone.

"I have to go back soon," she mumbled.

I sat up and looked over at the shore. "What time do you have to work today?"

"Four. So, probably an hour or so."

"All right." I grabbed her upper arms and pulled her toward me. "Get behind me and we'll head in."

"I said soon," she said softly when she was sitting again, and

I looked up at her heated stare as she gripped my waist and adjusted herself on my lap.

Releasing one of her arms, I slowly traced the line of her bikini top down to the swell of her breast, and raised one eyebrow when she sucked in a sharp breath. "And what do you want to do until *soon* is here?"

Before she could respond, the roar of an engine and the sounds of yelling filled the otherwise quiet spot on the lake, and I dropped my hand to look at the quickly approaching boat.

"Yeah! Get some!" one of the guys yelled as they passed us, and I kept my stare on them until they were too far away to see clearly, because I knew exactly what I would find in front of me. Anytime we were physically close and something interrupted us, she would look at the position we were in in a whole new light, and go back to being the Grey who was stuck in the past.

Finally, looking back at Grey, I gave her a tight-lipped smile and reached behind me for her life jacket as she sat there staring at my chest and gripping her necklace.

"Put this on, sweetheart, I'll take you in."

Grey barely said anything more than a mumble as we went in and I returned the Jet Ski, and I don't think she even realized I wasn't walking with her toward her car until she started to get in. She looked back to where we'd been, then looked over to where I was standing next to my car.

"I'll see you later." She said the words almost like a question, and I just nodded. Without another word, she got into her car and drove away.

I got into my car and dropped my head back against the headrest as I replayed the good parts of the day. But it was hard to remember anything when three words kept going through my mind like a broken record.

I'm losing her.

Grey
August 10, 2014

"PUT ME DOWN, put me down, put me down!" I screeched as Jagger ran into the warehouse with me thrown over his shoulder a few days later. Before I could slap my hand against his back again, his hands were on my waist and he was bending over to throw me onto the couch.

"There. You're down." He smiled wickedly at me and stole a kiss, then stood up, but I grabbed his hand and yanked him back toward me.

"That was terrifying," I murmured against his next kiss.

"I only almost dropped you once."

"Exactly! You almost dropped me! I saw my life flash before my eyes."

He smiled widely and pinched my side. "You're being dramatic. I'm gonna go jump in the shower and change. Do you want to do the same when I'm done, or are you gonna head home?"

"I'll jump in when you're done." I placed my hands on his bare stomach, and pushed him away. "Go shower, you smell like lake water."

"And what do you think you're making my couch smell like?" he countered as he walked backward toward the stairs.

"Cupcakes and rainbows?"

He stopped and gave me a look. "There is something in that water that makes you high, woman."

I laughed and pointed up to the loft. "Go shower so I can too!"

As soon as I heard the water turn on, I got off the couch and went to find my purse where I'd dropped it near thc door. Putting it on the bar top in the kitchen, I searched for my phone and texted my mom to let her know I was staying at Jagger's for a while. I'd barely gotten the TV on when she responded, asking if we had protection.

I groaned and flipped through the channels until I found a movie, and had only been watching it for a couple minutes when Jagger came back down the stairs.

His skin was tan from spending so much time at the lake this summer, and it made the contrast of his black hair and green eyes just that much greater. I was still whiter than white, and praying I hadn't burned anywhere. I blamed my dad's Irish heritage.

"I left some clothes on the bed for you to change into," Jagger said as he flopped down on the couch next to my feet.

"So now I'm going to smell like you?" I teased, and nudged his side with my toes.

He grabbed my foot and immediately started massaging it with his large hands. "Better than smelling like the lake."

"Don't lie," I moaned through the foot rub. "You love that I smell like . . . fish."

Jagger barked out a laugh and tossed my feet away from him. "That is not what you smell like, but now all I can think about is you smelling like fish. Go shower."

"No. Foot rub!" I whined, and tried to put my feet back on

his lap. He just continued laughing and pushing them away. "Please?"

Grabbing one of my hands, he pulled me up and pressed a soft kiss against my cheek before pushing me toward the edge of the couch. "When you come back."

I sent him a pathetic look as I slowly stood up, and he leaned forward to grab me and pull me back down.

"Don't pout, beautiful," he whispered before placing his lips on my neck.

I tilted my head away and sighed softly. "I thought I smelled gross," I said when he continued making a line of kisses down my neck.

I felt his smile against my skin, then he said, "I never said 'gross.' I said 'lake.' You took it to another level with 'fish.'" Jagger bit down gently on the base of my throat, and his hand gripped the back of my thigh when he moved lower.

My breathing was uneven by the time he made it back up to my lips, and the hand that had been gripping my thigh slowly moved up to grab the side tie of my bikini bottom. Pulling until it came undone, he reached under my shirt to undo one of the ties of my top, then the other. I was still wearing my shorts and tank top, but I knew I would be pulling them off soon if he didn't do it himself, and suddenly I wanted that shower. I didn't want to smell gross if things were heading in this direction.

"Um, I . . . shower—I should shower," I stuttered.

"Then go shower," he challenged.

It took another few moments before I was able to gather the will to move away from him, and the only thing that had given me the strength to do so was knowing that I wanted to smell clean.

"Five minutes," I shouted as I ran up the stairs, his low laugh following me.

I'd never showered that thoroughly *that* quickly in my life. Barely giving myself time to dry off and towel-dry my hair, I ran into the loft and put on the clothes that were sitting on the end of the bed. I glanced down at the boxers and long shirt I was wearing, and fought with myself for a minute about whether or not I should take off the boxers. But I had nothing underneath, and I knew if I went down like that, Jagger would think I wanted something.

Something I knew I did in fact want but wasn't sure I was ready for yet. I wanted him, I wanted his hands on me, but that still didn't stop the fear of finally giving myself to him. By the time I stopped arguing with myself and was on my way down the stairs, I still had the boxers on and was trying not to seem as eager to get back to him as I was.

"That was longer than five minutes," he said with his signature lopsided smile when I made it down the stairs.

"Hey, at least I'm clean."

"And looking amazing," he murmured as he reached for my hand and pulled me down so I was sitting on his lap.

"Amazing?" I asked against his lips. "Somehow I doubt that."

Jagger leaned back and gave me a look. "You have no idea how amazing you look in my clothes."

The gravel in his voice was enough to make a shiver go through my body, and I sat up to crush my mouth against his. His hand slowly ran up and down my legs, each time going a little higher, but nowhere near high enough. I wanted to ask him to touch me, but couldn't find my voice even though the words were repeating in my head. Pushing away from him without ever breaking the kiss, I slid one leg over his lap so I was straddling him, and slowly rocked my hips against him.

His hands went to my hips to press me harder against him, and a low growl rumbled up his chest as I continued rocking against him. Jagger dropped his head and slowly ran his nose between my breasts before moving over to suck on one of my nipples through the shirt.

My phone chimed from where I'd left it on the other side of the couch, but I ignored it until it chimed again, and again, and again.

Jagger lifted his head and looked over for a second before reaching for it.

"It's probably just my mom." I leaned forward to kiss his jaw, and couldn't stop the giggle that sounded in my throat when I said, "She asked me earlier if we had protection, and I never responded."

Jagger's body went rigid, and the hand that was still on my hip gripped tighter. "Grey," he breathed.

I sat back quickly at his tone to look at him. I'd been expecting him to laugh or look embarrassed because of my mom, but instead he looked like someone had just beaten the shit out of him. He looked weak, exhausted, and pale.

"What is it?" I asked, my voice rising in panic. I tried grabbing my phone, but he held it away. "Jagger, give me the phone!"

"Grey," he whispered. "I'm here, okay?"

"What happened? Is it my family?" I practically shouted, and this time when I reached for it, he handed me my phone.

I looked at the screen, and my blood ran cold when I saw the Facebook message pulled up.

Ben Craft: Grey, I love you.

Ben Craft: Please don't do this to us.

Ben Craft: How could you?

Ben Craft: You're mine. You've always been mine.

I stared at the phone for a few more seconds before my stomach roiled and I jumped off of Jagger and took off for the bathroom. I threw up what little I'd eaten before we'd gone out to the lake and sat on my knees, hunched over the toilet as sobs racked my body.

Jagger came in and pulled me back into his arms, sitting up against the wall with me pressed close to his chest.

"Why?" I choked out, and his arms tightened.

"I don't know, baby. I'm so sorry." He paused for a second, and hesitantly said, "I think you should block his account, Grey."

"Do it," I said shakily, then took a deep breath and said more decisively, "Do it so they can't do this anymore."

He sighed softly and stood up, pulling me with him. "Come on, let's go back out there."

I stopped long enough to rinse my mouth out at the sink, and then let him tow me toward the couch. He pulled me onto his lap again, and I curled my head under his chin as he grabbed my phone. After a minute, I heard the soft thud of my phone hitting the cushion and felt both of his arms wrap tightly around me.

"It's done."

I didn't respond. I just clutched his shirt to my face as the relentless tears continued to fall down my cheeks.

It's over, I told myself. *It's over.*

MY EYES SLOWLY blinked open and focused on the empty side of the bed beside me. Letting my hand run over the comforter until my mind caught up with me, I finally remembered I was at Jagger's, but didn't know when I'd gotten upstairs to his bed. I felt groggy, and my eyes were scratchy, and it was then that the events of this afternoon all came back to me. The messages, blocking Ben's Facebook account, Jagger holding me as tears steadily rolled down my cheeks.

Quiet footsteps sounded on the stairs seconds before Jagger appeared at the top, his steps faltering when he saw that I was awake.

"Hey," he said softly. "Did I wake you up?"

I shook my head and pushed myself up until I was sitting against the headboard. "What time is it?"

"Late. You'd been asleep for five hours the last time I looked at my phone."

"Five hours?"

"And that was probably an hour or so ago," he guessed.

"Why didn't you wake me up?" I looked down at his blackened hands and raised an eyebrow. "And how did I sleep through your music?"

A smile flashed across his face seconds before his lips softly fell onto mine. "I used earbuds so you wouldn't hear it, and I didn't wake you up because you've hardly slept in the last week and a half. Let me get all this off my hands. I'll be right back." He quickly walked into the bathroom, and I rubbed at my sore eyes.

Six hours was more than I had been getting in two nights combined, and somehow, it still didn't feel like enough.

"You doing okay?" Jagger asked when he sat in front of me on the bed.

"With what happened?" When he nodded, I continued. "Yeah, I am . . . I guess. I've been constantly worrying about what would pop up on my phone the *next* time and when that time would be. Knowing whoever is doing this doesn't have that way of communicating with me anymore feels nice."

"I'm sorry you had to go through that at all, but it's over now."

"I just . . ." I trailed off, struggling to voice the jumbled thoughts in my head. "What could anyone have against me that they'd feel the need to do something like this? I don't understand, and I *need* to understand, Jagger. I feel like I'm going insane still. Knowing that it's not actually Ben is a lot easier to say than to believe. I know he's gone, I do. But I—I just feel like I don't know anything anymore."

Jagger placed one of his hands on top of both of mine, and I quickly stopped twisting my hands together to grip his. "We'll find out who did this, I swear."

I nodded absentmindedly, and kept my eyes on where I was now playing with his fingers. I couldn't stop fidgeting; something was bothering me . . . something that had to do with the Facebook messages. I just couldn't figure out what it was. Jagger was talking—saying something that I wasn't hearing. All I could focus on was our hands and the messages and the vows.

"The vows!" I shouted suddenly, and looked up in time to see Jagger's head jerk back from my outburst.

"What about them?" Jagger asked hesitantly when I didn't say anything else.

"This can't just be over. Not that easily." Removing one of my hands from Jagger's, I pointed in the direction of the front door. "They obviously know my car since the vows were on them, and they know about you, where you live, and can *get* inside your place since the vows were here. Just because I blocked one of their ways of torturing me doesn't mean it'll just be over."

"You might be right, but we can't know that yet."

"Where did you have the vows?" I looked around the loft at the dresser and desk. "We could see if something else is missing, or—"

"Grey," he crooned, and cupped my cheek so I would look at him. "I already did all that. I had some cops come and fingerprint the vows and the box that the paper had been in. Nothing else was missing, nothing was out of place, and I don't even know *when* they were taken. There was nothing but my fingerprints up here, in the closet, and on the box. And nothing on the vows except for mine, yours, and some unknown ones that they're expecting to be Ben's since he had smudged the ink with his finger, and it matched the rest of the prints they found."

My mouth had slowly opened as he talked, and I knew I was looking at him like I didn't even know who he was anymore. "So the cops now have the vows? You would just give them something like that? Something that means so much to me? Jagger! They probably ruined the vows!"

"No, I have the paper back because they couldn't find anything on it, and the vows are fine, babe."

"Why didn't you just tell me? Why didn't you tell me that you'd called them? You didn't even say anything about giving the vows that were *meant for me* to the police. What if I didn't want them to have that?" I looked around the room, shaking my head. "Were you ever going to tell me?" I asked on a humorless laugh. "For all I know, they could've found something, but you're still not telling me."

He laughed edgily, and I knew he was getting mad, but I didn't care. I couldn't believe he'd done all that without asking me first, or telling me after. "Are you—are you fucking kidding me? Of course I would've told you if there was something! Jesus, Grey.

You've been miserable since the morning you found the vows. Most of your days are bad days, and babe, that's fine! It's fine to be hurting. But I didn't want you to get involved with the police when there was a chance they wouldn't find anything."

"You can't protect me from everything, Jagger!"

He dropped my other hand and sat back, shock and pain covering his face.

"There are things in this world that you can't control or keep me from!"

"You think I don't know that?" he yelled back. "I've watched you disappear because of something I *couldn't* protect you from! Why wouldn't I try to protect you from the small bullshit when you have gone through so much more?" Getting off the bed, he took large steps toward the stairs, then turned around to look at me. His arms were hanging by his sides, palms up, his expression lost. "That's what I want to do, Grey, that's all I've ever wanted to do, to be there for you when shit gets bad, to take as much of it as I can away from you so *you* won't have to deal with it. I have spent my life doing that because I love you, and I will spend the rest of it doing the exact same fucking thing. If you need to know something, I'll tell you. You of all people should know that by now!"

I opened my mouth to say something—start apologizing, anything to erase that look from his face—but he kept talking.

"I'm sorry you're mad, I'm sorry you feel like I kept something important from you. But you have no idea what I'm seeing when I look at you. You have no idea what I've watched happen to you since the vows ended up on your car!"

That startled me enough to make my mouth snap shut for a few moments. "I don't—what are you *seeing*? I'm fine, I've been fine except for when it's happened."

Jagger laughed harshly, but he sounded defeated. "Grey . . . are you serious?"

"I have no idea what you're talking about!"

"I'm fucking losing you," he whispered, the soft, anguished tone hitting me hard enough to make me lose my breath. "I'll do whatever it takes to help you through your grieving for Ben and what's happening now. But you are slowly pushing me away more and more each day."

"I've never pushed you away."

He smiled weakly and nodded his head. "No, you never did . . . until now. I've seen you five times in the last eleven days, including the day you found the vows and today. Today is the longest I've spent with you. There have been days when I come over and you won't leave your room or look at me; there have been times when you told me you were coming over after work and you didn't show and never called. I had to call your mom to make sure you were even safe."

I stared at him blankly, my head shaking quickly. "No, I—I don't think . . ." I trailed off, trying to remember other times we'd seen each other.

"This is a hard time for you, I know that. But it's been killing me to watch you shut down and keep me out."

When I couldn't respond, he turned and slowly went down the stairs, and I just sat there listening to the echoes of his steps as he walked across the open space below. I didn't move for long minutes as I thought about everything he'd said and tried to remember those days he'd been talking about. I couldn't, but I knew he was right. Because what I did remember from the last week and a half was all the time I'd spent thinking about Ben.

After crawling across the bed and standing up, I walked across the loft and down the stairs. Before I could get to the hall leading to the back rooms, I saw my phone on one of the couches and walked over to pick it up. After tapping out a quick message to my mom about not coming home tonight, I turned the phone on silent and dropped it back onto the couch.

Jagger was leaning against a wall in the main hallway when I turned the corner, his forearms were pressed to the wall as his head hung down to his chest. His head snapped up when he heard me walking toward him, and he slowly straightened to face me. His face and eyes were guarded.

Without saying a word, I reached out to grab one of his hands and turned to walk back the way I'd come. I didn't let go of his hand until we were next to the bed and didn't say anything until we were both lying on it, facing each other.

"I don't want to shut you out," I whispered. "I'm sorry I've been hurting you, but you have to know I would never purposely hurt you. It would kill me to lose you, Jagger, and I swear to you that you aren't losing me," I choked out, my voice breaking.

Jagger ground his jaw and wrapped one arm around my waist to pull me closer. "Okay, Grey," he murmured as he pressed his lips to my forehead.

"I've always loved how protective you are, and I'm not just saying that because of what you or I said earlier. I love it; it's comforting. I know you'd do anything to keep me safe, and I'm so thankful for that. I'm sorry that I used that against you, and I'm so *so* sorry that you've thought for one minute that I was taking myself away from you." I curled my hands against his chest, and tried to fight back the tears stinging my eyes. "Everything has been harder since I first got the messages from Ben's

Chapter 11

Grey
August 13, 2014

I RAN INTO the safety of my parents' house from the summer storm, and tripped over myself as I worked at kicking off my shoes while simultaneously heading toward the stairs. Before I'd even hit the fourth step, my mom's voice stopped me.

"Honey! You got something in the mail today."

I stopped and let my head hang back so I was staring at the ceiling. "If it's a bill, I don't want it," I grumbled even as I turned around and headed into the kitchen, where my mom was sitting at the table sorting through the mail.

"Not a bill." She smirked as she handed me the large manila envelope, and I blew her an obnoxious kiss as I turned around to head toward the stairs again.

"I'm getting ready and going for a run!"

account. So many things have gone through my mind, and it makes everything so confusing. But that doesn't mean I'm confused about you, or us. I love you and I want to be with you, and I need you to know that and not have any doubts. Because when you look at me, I know exactly how much you love me, and—"

Jagger pressed his mouth firmly to mine, cutting off my emotional rant, and I threw everything I had into that kiss. I needed him to know how much he meant to me, to see it when he looked at me and feel it in every kiss and touch we shared. I had spent so long blinding myself to him and keeping myself from feeling anything for anyone. After having this—having Jagger—I couldn't ever lose him or go back to who I had been.

When the kiss slowed, I pushed myself away from him to slide under the comforter. He watched every movement like he was afraid to miss any of it, and when I was settled into his bed, he got up and kissed my forehead before jogging down the stairs. The lights went off and seconds later he was back and flipping off the lights in the loft. Pulling off his shirt, he let it fall to the floor before crawling back into the bed with me. With a murmured good night, he wrapped his arm around me again and pulled me close as we slowly drifted off to sleep.

"Okay. How was work?" she called out after me.

"Fine," I mumbled as my steps slowed to a stop, my eyes stayed glued to the envelope in my hands.

My brow furrowed when I didn't find a return address, and even though my name and parents' address was completely filled out, there weren't any stamps or postage markings. A sense of dread slowly unfurled in my stomach and spread throughout my body as I carefully pried up the metal holding the envelope flap down.

I pulled out a stack of papers and tucked the envelope under my arm before flipping the stack over, and the feeling of dread intensified as the open space of the entryway seemed to close in on me.

The top sheet of paper had the typed-out words: *Don't let him make you forget what we have.* My head shook back and forth as I fanned through the remaining pages, each one a printed-out picture of Ben and me, with a blank page at the end. Like some fucked-up type of manuscript—complete with blank page at the end and a dedication at the beginning. All it was missing was the title page.

"What'd you get?"

My head snapped up at the sound of my mom's voice, and I had to swallow past the tightness in my throat twice before I could ask, "This was in the mail?"

"Yeah, honey, why? Are you okay?"

I shook my head quickly as I handed over the stack to her. "It's another . . . it's another message."

She didn't even make it past the first two pages before gasping and dropping it all to the floor.

"I n-need to call Jagger. I need to tell him."

Mom didn't respond, she just stood there with her hands over her mouth, staring at the mess of papers on the floor, and I couldn't make my arms move fast enough to call Jagger. What should've taken seconds felt like hours, and I didn't even recognize my own voice as I explained the pictures to him, and when I looked down at the fanned-out papers, my sharp inhalation had Jagger's voice rising in panic.

"It wasn't blank. The last page—it wasn't blank." On shaking knees, I bent down to the floor and moved aside a picture to reveal the rest of the small picture on what had been the last page. "Oh God," I mumbled.

"What, Grey, what does it say?" Jagger asked over the roar of his car.

"It says: 'Three more days, and Grey LaRue will finally be mine.' It was his last status on Facebook, Jag, they printed it out."

"Son of a bitch," he growled. "Okay, I'm on my way. I'll be there soon, and we're calling the cops immediately this time, Grey. This bullshit has gone on too long."

"Yeah, okay," I said shakily.

"Breathe, baby. I'm coming for you."

AFTER THE POLICE had come and talked to us for who knew how long, had taken fingerprints off the mailbox and the envelope and printed off pictures with them, I was exhausted. Emotionally and mentally drained. It took everything in me just to lie down on the couch and close my eyes as my parents and Jagger talked quietly around me. At some point I remember briefly waking up when Graham came over, but when I woke again, it was completely dark outside, and no one was in the living room with me.

"Jag?" I called out, and slid off the couch when I didn't get a response. Stretching the tension out of my muscles, I walked through the house until I found my parents. "Where's Jagger?"

My mom looked at my dad, as if she needed his help, and he sighed heavily. "He'll be back. He said he had to go take care of something, he left about ten minutes ago."

"Then why do you both look so . . . I don't know, but why do I have a feeling there's something going on that you're not telling me?"

"We got the call about an hour ago. They were able to look at the fingerprints immediately today. The only fingerprints on everything from the envelope and mailbox were matches to the prints you, Jagger, and your mother gave today, Grey. Nothing else, just like with the vows."

I took a step back. "What are you saying?" My voice rose as denial and anger tore through my body. "Jagger didn't do this! Is that why he left? Because you all think—"

"No! No, Grey, no one thinks that," Mom said. "He left because he thinks he knows who's doing it."

"What?" I asked, my voice now barely a whisper. "W-who? Did he say?"

"No, we were sitting here trying to figure out *something* . . . *anything* that would make someone want to do this, and suddenly he just froze. His head snapped up and he froze. It was like he wasn't even here anymore. Then he just started whispering, 'No, no, she wouldn't.' We asked what was happening, and he just took off saying he would be back." Mom shrugged sadly, like she didn't know what else to say.

"She?" I stumbled over to the table and sat down roughly as I tried to think of any girl who would do something like this. My first thought was LeAnn, but I pushed it aside when I remembered how she'd been acting the last couple weeks. I stared down at the wood of the table as I tried to think of anyone else.

Grabbing the house phone sitting in the middle of the table, I dialed Jagger's number, but his voice mail eventually picked up. I ended the call without leaving a message, and set the phone down before placing my head on the table. I didn't know who this person might be, but hopefully Jagger was right. Hopefully this would all be over soon.

Jagger
August 13, 2014

"CHARLIE!" I ROARED, slamming the door to my mom's house behind me. "Charlie, where are you?"

Mom rounded the corner that led from the kitchen to the living room just as I hit the living room; she looked carefree even with Keith screaming in her arms—her expression confirming that Charlie *was* here. "What is wrong with my oldest son?" she asked above the cries.

"Stay out of this, I don't have time for your bullshit tonight," I hissed as I walked past her.

"Jagger, honey. Calm yourself. We just need to be calm. This house is a love-only zone."

I turned on her just as a man I'd never seen before stepped in behind her and took Keith from her. "Shut up, Mom! Just shut up! Stop pretending to be some free-spirited hippy who doesn't have a care in the world, when you and I both know who you really are!"

Her eyes narrowed and her face looked pinched for a second, showing the woman I knew was there deep down, then she relaxed back into the mask I'd grown up knowing, and the man spoke.

"If you want me to call the cops on you, keep it up." His tone was deep and full of authority. "You can't just come in here and threaten your mother and scare the baby."

I snorted. "Threaten? Hardly. And he was already crying before I got here. And who are you anyway, number eight?" Without waiting for him to respond, I turned around, heading for Charlie's room. "Charlie!"

I yanked open her door and watched her jump as she scrambled to pull off her headphones. "You scared the crap out of me!"

"Are you the one who's doing this?"

Her eyes widened as the tone in my voice registered. "Doing what?"

"Don't play with me, Charlie!" I yelled, hitting my hand against the door frame. "Are you the one doing all this to Grey?"

"Doing what?" she yelled back. "I don't know what you're talking about!"

"Ben's wedding vows on her windshield. Messages to her from Ben's fucking *Facebook account*! The envelope full of pictures of her and Ben in her mailbox today. *Are you doing it?*"

"What?" she breathed out, her hand covering her chest. "Wait—what? How is that poss—his Facebook?"

"I don't have time for you to act like you don't know what's going on, Charlie! Tell me if it's you!"

"Of course it's not me! Why would I do that to Grey? *How* could I do that to her?"

"I think it's time you should head on out," Mom's latest man said over Keith's screaming, and I turned to glare at him. Stepping inside Charlie's room, I slammed the door and locked it behind me.

"I can't believe you would think I could do something like—"

"You can't? Are you sure about that? Because *you* are the one who wasn't okay about Grey getting better. And even though *you* told me you had always wanted Grey and me together, the minute you found out we were together, *you* were the one to got upset about it! A week after *you* got back from your trip, this shit started. *That* is how I can think it is you! I love you, Charlie, but I swear to God, if you're doing this . . ." I trailed off and raked my hands through my hair.

"But it's not me! I swear it's not!"

I flung my arms out to my sides and yelled, "I don't even know if I can believe you right now! Those vows were in my goddamn place, Charlie! You, Grey, and me are the only ones who have keys to the warehouse unless Mom made a spare that I don't know about. But even Mom isn't smart enough to figure out how to hack into Ben's fucking Facebook!"

"I don't have my key!" she said quickly, and jumped off her bed, heading for her purse. "I lost all of my keys." She handed me a set of two keys, and I looked at them.

"Why isn't my key on here, and when did you lose it? And what are these?"

"I don't know. I must've misplaced them when I was packing for my trip; I've been looking for them ever since I came back. But I took them out of my purse since we weren't taking my car and I was afraid of losing them on the trip, all I took with me was the key to the house just in case Mom was gone when I came back, and I kept it in my wallet. The only way I'm driving my car is because of the spare key."

"You got into my place the night you came back!"

"It was unlocked, and I opened it because you hadn't answered and your car was there."

I sighed heavily and handed her keys back as I began pacing.

"Jagger, I swear it's not me."

"Then tell me who it is, Charlie. No one else is upset about us being together. No one else has, or *had,* a key to my place. And I know Grey isn't doing this shit to herself. This is like torture for her." When I turned to look at her, tears were streaming down her face.

"I don't know, but I wouldn't do this to Grey, I love her."

I gritted my teeth, trying to hold back what was rushing through my mind, but it came out anyway. "I love you, Charlie, but you're the only person who makes sense right now. If you actually loved Grey, you would be happy for us, you would be happy for *her.* I don't understand you," I snapped, and she flinched back. "I don't understand you, and as much as it is *killing* me, that is why I think it's you! Because if you loved her, you wouldn't be mad that she was trying to move on! That she was trying to be happy for the first time since Ben di—"

"I loved Ben too!" she yelled before covering her mouth, her eyes wide as she backed up to her wall. And I knew . . . I knew in the way she said it and in the horrified look on her face that her words went much deeper than the love she had for Grey. She'd loved Ben the way I loved Grey.

"What?" I finally asked, the word barely audible.

A sob tore from her throat, and she shakily slid down the wall until she was sitting on the floor. "I loved him too," she repeated, the ache in her words forming an ache in my own chest. "I was selfish, I wanted Grey to be with you because I wanted Ben. But that's not the only reason I wanted you together—I swear!" she said quickly, her eyes wide as she tried to convey the truth in her words. "You and Grey belonged together. Anyone could've seen that."

When she didn't say more, I walked over to her bed and sat down. Leaning over, I rested my elbows on my knees and put my head in my hands. "Why didn't—how did I not know?" I asked, looking back up at my sister.

"Because you're my big brother. I couldn't tell you! And he was with Grey, what was I supposed to do? What was I supposed to say?"

A heavy silence filled her bedroom as we sat there, and I tried to process that my little sister had been in love with my best friend—and while I had been busy taking care of Grey after his death, Charlie had dealt with it on her own. "Charlie," I groaned. "God, Charlie, I'm sorry. If you had told me, I would've—I would've been there for you."

She shrugged and sent me a shaky smile before it was disturbed by another sob. "It was hard enough for you, and for her . . . I knew you had to be there for her. And you were in Pullman most of the time anyway."

"I'm so sorry. I've always taken care of you, I still should've been there," I whispered. After another few minutes, I shook my head and sat up straighter. "I don't understand. You have to know how hard this has been on Grey. I've told you how much she's struggled over the last two years, and now suddenly you're so mad at her? Now you're pissed off that we're together? I don't—I just don't understand how you could change the way you felt about Grey and me so drastically, and so fast."

Charlie laughed sadly and looked down at her hands, which

she was nervously twisting. "The way you were talking about her when you were still in college, you told me the bad things. I knew she was still struggling. When I saw her at the graduation, she looked horrible. But when you both came back to Thatch? She looked happy, and you guys looked closer than I'd ever seen you, and I didn't know when that had happened. I didn't know when she'd started getting better. And I . . ."

"You what?" I asked when she didn't continue.

For a while she didn't respond. When she finally looked up at me, tears were streaming down her face. "I've never even had a boyfriend because of Ben. I always only wanted him. When he died—I felt . . . God, I felt like a part of me died, and I had to keep how I felt to myself. And now I'm going on with my life, just like you and Grey are . . . just like everyone is. But that first day I hung out with her after you both moved back, I could see the way Grey looked when we talked about you. I knew she was falling in love with you even if she hadn't realized it yet, and I hated her for it. Because even though that's what I've always wanted for *you*, and what I've always wanted for *her*, I hated that she could move on from loving him when I can't."

The rest of the air in my lungs left me in one hard rush. "Charlie," I whispered. "I'm—I'm sorry. I don't know what else to say." I shook my head and looked at her helplessly. "I'm sorry that you went through all that grief alone, but don't take your hurt out on Grey. After everything she went through, she doesn't deserve it."

Charlie let out a sad laugh and nodded, then we just sat there in silence for a while.

Charlie loved Ben and was upset that Grey could move on, but whoever was trying to drive Grey insane wanted to keep Grey and me apart . . . reminding her of what she was supposed to have with Ben. While my mind kept saying the only person who made sense was Charlie, I knew it couldn't be her. It would've been too hard for Charlie to go through everything this person had been.

"You swear it's not you?" I asked softly.

"I swear, Jagger, I could never do that to her."

I nodded and fell back onto the bed, staring up at the ceiling fan. "I need to find the person doing this, they need to stop. This is killing Grey."

"I would help you if I could, but I don't know who it is. I honestly thought my keys were just lost in here somewhere."

I blew out a ragged breath, got off the bed, and walked over to Charlie. Holding a hand out, I helped her up and pulled her into my arms. "I'm sorry for yelling at you. I'm sorry for blaming you—this is making me crazy and I just freaked when I remembered how mad you've been."

"I understand," she mumbled against my chest.

"I'm sorry," I repeated. She would never know how sorry I was. For not being there for her, for blaming her . . . for so much.

My phone vibrated in my pocket, and I reached for it, thinking it would be Grey and knowing I needed to get back to her. My body froze and I stopped breathing as I looked at the message on my screen. With shaking fingers, I opened up the Facebook message and ground my jaw when I saw a picture of Ben and Grey kissing. Looking closer at the picture, I knew it was from the day they'd officially gotten engaged. Underneath were the words: *Don't forget, she's always belonged to me.*

"Jagger?"

Kissing the top of Charlie's head quickly, I backed away from her. "I have to get back to Grey. We need to figure out who this is. I'm sorry, Charlie."

Her eyes widened. "Wait, what's wrong? What just happened?"

"Whoever this is isn't done. And they need to be stopped. I have to go." Turning around, I left her room and walked quickly down the hall and into Keith's room. After checking his closet and the kitchen pantry, I walked toward the front door and didn't even look at my mom or her boyfriend as I let them know I would bring diapers and food the next day. As soon as I was out of the house and in my car, I pulled up Grey's name to call her as I flipped my car around and tore off down the street.

"Hey!" she answered on the first ring. "Where are you?"

"I'm coming back to you, are you okay?"

"I'm fine, I just—did you find out who it is?"

I blew out a slow breath and shook my head as guilt filled me. "No, I didn't."

"Well, who did you think it was? My parents said you'd said 'she.'"

As much sense as it had made earlier, I felt like a dick. No matter that everything pointed to Charlie, I couldn't believe I'd accused my sister of everything that had happened. "Let's talk about it when I get to you, okay? But tell me, has anything else happened since I left?"

"No," she said slowly, drawing out the word when she noticed my eager tone. "Why did you ask like that? Should I be expecting something?"

"No," I assured her. "No, I just needed to know. I'm only a couple minutes away, I'll see you soon."

There was a pause before she reluctantly said, "Okay. Be safe."

I ended the call and sank deeper into the seat as I ran one hand over my head. I knew I'd have to tell her where I'd gone, and I knew in telling her this, I'd have to tell her about Charlie, and it was killing me. Grey hadn't known that Charlie had been getting upset about us, or that she'd been mad at her . . . and right now seemed like the worst possible time to tell her. But I couldn't lie to her. When I pulled up to a red light, I quickly tapped out a text to Charlie.

I have to tell her. I'm so sorry . . . for everything.

By the time I'd pulled into Grey's neighborhood, Charlie had responded.

I know. Tell her I love her.

I replied with an *I will* as I walked up the driveway to Grey's parents' house and took a deep breath before knocking on the door and letting myself in.

Grey launched herself at me before I even had the door shut behind me, and I stumbled back a step. "Hey, you wanna go to the dock?" I asked into her ear; her only response was to nod her head against my chest. "Okay, hold on a second and we'll go." Unwrapping myself from her, I kept a hand on her waist as I looked up at her parents, both of whom were looking at me expectantly. "I was wrong, and I'm sorry I ran out of here. But do you mind if I take Grey for the night?"

"She is not staying with you overnight again. You'll bring her back tonight," Mr. LaRue said firmly, and I smiled.

"Of course, sir. It'll only be for a couple hours."

"Mark," Mrs. LaRue hissed, and slapped at his chest. "Just bring her home whenever, Jagger."

As I backed up with Grey in my arms and walked us out the door, I could hear Mrs. LaRue whispering harshly to her husband about how we were grown and he needed to lighten up.

"Are you going to tell me what happened?" Grey asked when we got in my car.

"When we get to the dock, but until then . . . I got this while I was gone." Opening up the Facebook messages, I tapped on the one from Ben's account and handed it to her.

A choked cry left her, and my face tightened from the pain I knew she was going through. "Why?" she asked softly. "Why are they doing this?"

"I don't know. You still have that account blocked, right?"

"Yes."

"Okay, well, they've already pretty much done everything they can. We'll just hope they're done."

Grey looked at the picture of her and Ben for a little while longer before putting my phone down, and a broken sigh filled my car. Reaching out, I grabbed her hand and was relieved when she squeezed mine tightly.

"We'll figure it out," I promised.

"I know. It's just hard, and it makes it worse because I still can't figure out who would want to do this to both of us." She said the last part to herself and stayed silent for the rest of the drive to the lake; the entire time I was dreading telling her about Charlie.

I tried thinking of a dozen different ways of telling her so it wouldn't reflect badly on my sister. But by the time Grey again asked me where I'd gone, when we were lying on the dock, I still hadn't figured out a better way to tell her, and I ended up saying it exactly as it had gone. From that first night in my place to how Charlie had reacted when she found out we were together, and then finally tonight.

It was safe to say Charlie had been the last person Gray had expected me to start talking about, and I hated how unsure of herself she looked, and confused about everything she'd thought she'd known. Like me, Grey hadn't had any clue that Charlie had been in love with Ben, and everything my sister had confessed to me tonight seemed to hit Grey twice as hard as it had hit me.

"It makes sense, I guess. Ben always had a soft spot for Charlie . . . he was just as protective of her as you were. Why wouldn't she fall in love with a guy who treated her the way Ben did?" she mumbled a couple minutes after I'd finished telling her everything. "God, I feel so stupid. Every time I've seen her I've thought—I don't know, but I feel like—I just don't understand," she rambled. "And what does that say about me if I'm moving on, and she's not—and she wasn't even with him?"

"Grey," I crooned. "Nothing. It says nothing about you. It just says that Charlie hasn't tried to get past it. No one knew about her feelings for Ben, so she probably didn't grieve the way she should have. But this . . ." I rolled over so I was looking down at her and cupped her cheek. "Us? It doesn't say anything about either of us, I promise."

She nodded, but I knew by her expression that she wasn't sure whether or not she should believe me, and that terrified me. I wanted to kiss her, I wanted to tell her what she meant to me, but only because I needed to reassure myself that we were okay, that she wasn't pulling away from me again because of what had happened. And I knew I couldn't do that when it was only days ago that we'd gotten past her shutting me out . . . and now it was happening all over again. The one thing that had stopped her from acknowledging her feelings about me in the first place— her relationship with Ben—was now constantly being thrown in her face.

What she and Ben had before he died was something I knew I'd never be able to have with her. They'd promised each other forever—and now she was moving on with me . . . his best friend. I knew she felt like she was cheating on Ben again; it was all over her face.

Trying to hide my own pain and fear, I rolled back over and stared up at the night sky as we fell into a silence—only this one felt weighted. It was scaring the shit out of me.

By the time I'd gotten her back to her parents' house, she'd said only a handful of words, and she hugged me good-bye as if it were an afterthought. I stood there for long minutes after she shut the door before I was able to force myself to my car and drive back home. I'd known I was slowly losing her over the last two weeks, but everything about tonight screamed that I wasn't losing her anymore. I'd lost her.

Chapter 12

Grey
August 13, 2014

I GOT READY to go to bed in a daze, everything Jagger had told me tonight playing through my mind over and over. I was embarrassed that I'd been going on with my friendship with Charlie when she'd been so upset and angry with me. I didn't know what to feel anymore about everything from "Ben," and I was back to feeling like I was betraying him.

It wasn't until I was in my bed that I realized I couldn't remember even driving back to the house with Jagger, and I didn't remember saying good night to him. I didn't know what he was thinking about all of this, and at the moment, I didn't know where we stood in our relationship.

I lay there for what felt like hours, going over everything that had happened with Jagger, and everything from my time with

Ben. I'd told Jagger that I couldn't lose him, and promised him that he wasn't losing me, but it felt like that was exactly what was happening. And I was causing it to happen. I was the reason there was this sudden distance between us, and I knew it would only grow if I let it—and I knew I would. I could easily get so lost in my grief to the point where I'd make sure my future with Jagger never happened.

Gripping Ben's ring in my hand, I blinked away the tears that were forming in my eyes and scrambled out of bed. I didn't bother with a bra, I just slipped into my sandals and threw my hair up in a messy bun as I ran down the stairs and out to my car.

I raced down the roads of our small town, and was thankful none of the sheriffs were around since I'd left my purse and driver's license at the house in my rush to leave. Pulling into the lot, I stared ahead as I gripped the steering wheel and, after a few calming breaths, finally got out of my car. I walked slowly until I was in front of the shiny stone, and sank down to the ground.

"Hey," I whispered as I traced the letters and dates. "I miss you so much," I choked out, and had to swallow down the tightness in my throat a few times before I could speak again. "I miss you, and I still love you. I know whoever is doing this isn't you. I know that even though there are times when it's easy to let myself think you're the one trying to force Jagger and me apart. But you wouldn't do that, would you? Just like I would want for you to be happy, I know that's what you want for both of us. And somehow I know that Jagger is the only man you would trust to keep me safe. Maybe it's because you knew he loved me and tried not to flaunt our relationship in front of him. Maybe it's because you knew him better than anyone. Whatever the reason, I know when I'm with him that this is right. I love you, Ben, but I love him too."

A sob broke free from my chest, and I leaned my head against the stone as I gripped his ring.

"I'm not letting this person take me from Jagger," I said a few minutes later. "Your death was the hardest thing I've ever gone through, and I will never forget you or what we had, but I can't lose him too. There is a man who loves me and who loved you, a man who knows exactly what I need in my healing from losing you—and now it's time I gave him my heart." Pressing my fingers to my lips, I shakily pressed them to the stone and whispered, "I'll always love you, Benjamin Craft, but it's time for me to love him now. Please understand."

On weak legs, I stood up and slowly walked back to my car. The drive was smoother and not nearly as rushed as the drive to the cemetery, but I needed the time to cry as I let a part of my life go.

When I was sure I was done crying, I wiped my face and took some deep breaths as I sat outside the place where I knew I needed to be. And just before I got out of my car, I unclasped the necklace I'd worn every day for the past two years and set Ben's ring down in one of my cup holders. Slowly climbing out of my car, I walked up to the door of the warehouse and unlocked it. I could have called him to let him know I was coming—I should have. But I would've started explaining why I was coming, and this wasn't something that could be said over the phone, and I knew he was awake by the loud music that met me before I even had the door open. Slipping out of my flip-flops and setting my keys and phone down on the counter, I steadied my breathing as I made my way through the large room and to the halls.

My breath caught as I saw Jagger working furiously on a piece in front of him, and just like the last time I'd caught him working—the picture was of me. I looked lost. A part of me wondered if he was replicating what he'd seen on my face tonight, and I hated that I'd zoned out and fallen back into a place where I wasn't sure of anything.

Jagger hung his head, one hand moving to grip the back of his neck as he stood there in front of the drawing. Dropping the charcoal in his other hand, he looked up and started using his fingers to continue creating what was in his mind, and a small smile crossed my face when I saw the streak of black on the back of his neck.

When I was halfway down the hall, his body suddenly straightened and he slowly looked over his shoulder to where I was standing. Shock crossed his face, but not soon enough that I didn't see the pain and fear that had been there seconds before. He turned to face me, and just stood there for a few moments before hitting the stereo until the music abruptly cut off.

"What are you—what time is it?"

I shrugged and shook my head. "Um . . . late? I don't know."

"Are you okay?" he asked as he closed the distance between us, and my smile came back as I got a better look at his charcoal-streaked face.

Lifting my hands to wipe them across the streaks, I looked up into his green eyes. "You have a little something."

Jagger gripped my wrists, loose enough so it didn't hurt, but tight enough that I could feel the way his body was vibrating. "Why are you here, Grey?"

My smile fell as my stomach turned. I'd hurt him tonight, it was clear. Brushing my fingers across his cheeks again, I locked my eyes with his and knew I was ready. Knew that I was making the right decision. Jagger already knew I loved him, but this—it was different, and he would know. "I love you, Jagger Easton."

His worried face softened. "I love you too."

"I needed to tell you that I'm in love with you, and I'm ready."

A lopsided smile pulled at his lips as he bent his head lower. "Yeah?" he asked when his forehead rested against mine. "What are you ready for?"

"Everything," I whispered. Looking directly into his green eyes, I hooked my fingers inside the top of his jeans before slowly unbuttoning them. "Everything with you."

"Don't do this for me."

"I'm not," I promised. "I'm doing it for us." Pulling away from him, I started walking backward down the hall, my gaze locked with his the entire time.

With shaky hands, I moved the thin straps of my top off my shoulders and down my arms, and the desire was clear in Jagger's eyes as I turned the corner to the hall leading out to the main room. I made it to the stairs leading up to his loft before he grabbed me from behind and slammed my body to his. One hand pressed against my stomach as the other trailed up my arm to my bare shoulder. His lips pressed to the base of my neck as his trailing hand moved over my breasts and slowly pulled the shirt down to free them.

"If you need to stop—"

"I won't," I assured him.

Pulling my shirt down the rest of the way, I pushed it past my hips and down my legs as his large hands explored my torso and chest. I leaned back against his bare chest and wondered briefly when he'd taken his shirt off; then my thoughts were only on his lips and hands. One of his hands slid down to cup me through my thin shorts, and I moaned as I arched my back off him.

"Jagger," I whimpered.

His lips brushed against the sensitive skin of my neck as he mumbled, "I'm getting charcoal all over you."

"I don't care."

A soft laugh rumbled through his chest as he pushed me up the stairs and simultaneously finished undressing me. Never once did his hands and lips leave some part of my body, and the ascent that should have taken seconds ended up taking a few minutes.

Jagger lowered me onto his bed, and I watched him through hooded eyes as he slowly reached for the zipper on his jeans—his eyes raking over me as he let his pants fall to the floor and stepped out of them. As he crawled onto the bed to hover over me, his head dipped and he pressed his mouth to mine, then continued in a line down my neck toward my chest. I ran my hands over his short hair before intertwining my fingers at the back of his head to keep him against me and feel his lips curve up into a smile.

A breathy sigh fell past my lips when he settled himself between my legs and gently rocked against me. Releasing the hold I had on him, I slid my hands over the muscles of his back until I hit the band of his boxer briefs. I pushed down with one hand while the other gripped his back, and a rough needy noise sounded in his throat as I slowly rid him of the only material separating us.

Moving back up my body when the briefs were on the floor, Jagger gently grazed my ear with his teeth before mumbling, "You're mine, Grey."

Raising himself a little higher above me, he captured and

held my eyes as he positioned himself against me before pressing into me. My mouth fell open in a wordless plea at the most perfect torture I'd ever known as he slowly filled me inch by inch. I wrapped my legs around his narrow hips to bring him closer to me, and his next kiss quieted my moans as he finally began moving inside me.

My eyes fluttered shut and my head fell back against the bed when his pace quickened. My hands clung to Jagger's body as he quickly became my everything. He was everywhere physically and emotionally, and yet I still wanted more. I wanted more of him, I wanted all of this, and I wanted it forever.

I wanted *him* to be my forever.

Something deep inside my soul broke open as I let go and gave everything that was left of me to Jagger.

Burying my head in the crook of his neck, I breathed him in and focused on his shuddering muscles and harsh breathing as he brought us both over the edge. I continued to cling to him as I slowly came down off the high he'd just given me, refusing to give this moment up just yet. After what we'd just shared, I didn't know if I would ever be able to get enough of him. I didn't know if I would ever be able to get used to this feeling he gave me. This calm, this safety, this appreciation, and this sense of finally being whole and having everything I would ever need.

He was my best friend. He was my protector and healer. And I was so in love with him.

Moving to press his lips to my cheek, he stilled against me and I felt his body tighten. Before I could question the sudden terror in his eyes, a broken exhalation left him and he wiped his thumbs against my cheeks as he sat back.

"Grey," he breathed. "God, Grey, I'm sorry."

My eyebrows pinched together as confusion engulfed me. "What?" He was sorry about what we'd just done? "I don't—why?"

I watched as his features softened and he leaned closer to me. "Babe, you're crying," he explained, and his fingers brushed against my cheeks again.

Releasing the grip I had on him, I wiped at my own cheeks—my head shaking back and forth when I saw the wetness on my fingers. "I didn't know." Understanding covered his face, and I quickly cradled his face in my hands. "No! No, it's not what you think, I swear."

"It's okay," his deep voice crooned.

"No. Jagger, just no, please listen to me." Pushing him to the side, I rolled us over until I was on top of him, my legs straddling his waist. "I didn't know I was crying, but it has nothing to do with Ben. I finally let go. I let go, and giving myself to you was . . ." I trailed off and looked around the room as I tried to find the words for something that was beyond describing. "It shook my soul, Jagger. What just happened was perfect, and indescribable, and more than I ever imagined it could be."

Brushing away loose strands of hair, he cupped my cheek with his large hand, and his lips slowly tilted up in a soft smile. A smile that quickly disappeared when his eyes fell to my chest. Releasing my cheek, his fingers lightly traced along the bottom of my neck to my chest, the question clear on his face. "Where's his—"

"It was time. I was clinging to a memory, and it was time to let that memory go. I couldn't let the past get between us anymore."

"Grey . . ."

"I'm yours." Bending down to rest my forehead on his, I whispered, "I'm yours, and you're mine. Finally giving myself to you was what broke me in the most beautiful way. Those tears weren't sad. They were freeing."

Reaching up to kiss me, he mumbled against my lips, "I love you."

"I love *you*," I choked out, my voice breaking on the last word.

Lifting my hips off him, I moved back and slowly lowered myself onto him—chills coursing through my body at being filled by him again. When I looked up, his green eyes were locked on mine, and the intensity in them had my stomach heating. And I loved the feeling.

"I'll never get enough of you," I assured him.

I WOKE UP the next morning with my body half draped across Jagger's, one of his arms tightly wrapped around my waist, the comforter somewhere on the floor, and the sheet tangled around our legs. A smile broke across my face as my body slowly rose and fell in time with his steady breathing. I ached in a way I hadn't ached in years, but it just made this morning that much more real and perfect. Last night had changed our relationship, and it had changed me. I was ready for whatever this brought for us.

Kissing Jagger's bare chest, I smiled when a low rumble let me know he was waking up.

"The sun is up, Jag, it's time for you to get up too."

His free hand lightly fell to my messy hair and trailed down to my bare back. "Tell me I'm not dreaming," he pleaded, his voice rough and raspy from sleep.

Wiggling out of his grasp, I hovered over him and smiled. "Not dreaming. And as much as I want to spend all morning in this bed with you, I'm covered in black smudges, and so are your sheets."

A lopsided grin covered his face as his eyes roamed over my naked body. "And they look perfect on you."

I gave him a droll look then rolled my eyes. "I'm sure. I'm gonna jump in your shower."

"Don't be gone long."

Kissing him quickly, I climbed off him and the bed before he could get me to stay there, and laughed at the way he pouted before lying back down.

As soon as the water was hot enough, I pulled my hair back up into a bun and stepped into the large, open shower. My eyes shut as I enjoyed the hot water spraying all over me, and before I'd even begun trying to de-charcoal myself, Jagger was stepping in behind me.

"Took too long," he grumbled as he wrapped his arms around me, pulling me back against his chest.

"Three minutes is too long?"

"After last night?" His lips went to my neck, causing me to shiver. "Yeah, it's too long."

Jagger
August 14, 2014

I IMPATIENTLY DRUMMED my fingers on my knees as I waited for the food I'd ordered. I'd only been away from Grey for fifteen minutes, and I was anxious to get back. I was still struggling with the thought that all this was a dream, and that I would wake up and Grey and I would be exactly where we'd been when I'd dropped her off at her parents' house the night before. If it was a dream, I wanted to enjoy it as long as possible. If it wasn't, I wanted to enjoy her every second for the rest of my life.

An order came up, but it wasn't mine, and I shook my head when I realized how ridiculous I was being. She would be there. We would eat our late breakfast and hang out until she had to go to work—like we usually did. Nothing would be different, and yet everything would. The knowledge that Grey LaRue was finally mine after nine years of waiting was making it impossible to stop smiling.

I felt like such a girl.

Grabbing my wallet, I pulled out the worn and torn piece of paper from behind my license and unfolded it. As I looked over the four words I'd written down almost a decade ago, a strange sense of peace coursed through my body knowing that I was finally going to get the chance to give her this note—that I was finally going to get to ask her what I'd wanted to for far too long.

"Jagger."

My head shot up as I quickly refolded the note and started putting it back into my wallet, but my fingers froze when I saw LeAnn standing in front of me.

"How are you?" she asked as she sat down next to me.

I looked up to where the orders were coming out and bit back a curse as I slowly finished putting the note in my wallet and my wallet in my back pocket. "I'm good. How are you?"

"I'm really great," she said excitedly. Her voice softened and she placed her hand on my forearm, causing me to look over at her when she said, "I wanted to talk to you."

"LeAnn, I already told you—"

"No, I know. I wanted to tell you how sorry I am for how I

reacted a couple months ago. I felt so stupid that night after I'd thought about it, but I've been too nervous to say anything to you. And then the only times I've seen you, you've been with Grey, and I didn't want to make it awkward by apologizing about something like that in front of her."

"She already knows," I said with a shrug, and looked around the restaurant again. "I told her awhile ago."

Her eyebrows shot up. "Oh, you did? Well, that's embarrassing for me, but it's good that you two are so open with each other."

My fingers started drumming faster. I wanted to get away from LeAnn . . . I wanted to get back to Grey.

"So, she's the lucky girl, huh?"

My hands stilled, and I slowly looked back at LeAnn.

She started talking again as soon as I was looking at her. "I think it's great, Jagger, really I do. I always knew how you felt about her, that's why I never liked her in high school—but you two really deserve each other. She deserves someone like you after what happened with Ben, and you deserve the girl who's always held your heart." LeAnn smiled shakily and looked away for a second. "I'd always hoped you'd feel that way about me one day, and I think that's why I was so mad when I saw you in the convenience store the other month, because I finally realized that you never would."

I didn't say anything as I continued to stare at her. I didn't know how to respond to her words, or what she expected me to say. I couldn't apologize, because I wasn't sorry for getting away from LeAnn, or for loving Grey. And, honestly, I didn't know how to deal with the sane LeAnn I'd seen three times now. This was completely unlike the girl I'd known.

"Anyway!" She pointed toward the seating area of the restaurant for a second before shooting me a bright smile. "I should get back to breakfast, I just saw you over here and thought this would be my only chance to apologize."

I nodded and looked up when my name was called for the order. "Well, I appreciate it, but I'm fine with keeping everything that's happened in the past," I said when I stood up and grabbed the bags of food.

"Right. In the past." LeAnn looked behind her, and I noticed the same guy from the restaurant a few weeks ago watching us. "Anyway, have a good rest of your week. I'll see you around."

"Bye, LeAnn." I turned and walked out of the restaurant with her still watching me, but I refused to look back.

No matter how she was acting now, I would never forget the person she had been. I could keep it in the past, but that didn't mean I trusted her now, or ever would.

I'd just gotten into my car when my phone started ringing. My brow scrunched together when I saw it was from the LaRues' house.

"Hello?"

"Mr. Easton, I distinctly remember telling you my daughter was not to stay at your house last night."

My chest tightened and my head fell back onto the headrest as I prepared for Grey's dad to yell at me, tell me he wanted me to stay away from his daughter, something bad that would match his pissed-off tone.

"Sir, I'm—"

"And seeing how my daughter took off in the middle of the night, and she's still not home, I can only guess that she's with you."

I waited for a few seconds to see if he would continue, then admitted, "She's not with me at this exact moment, but she is waiting for me to come back with breakfast."

"Jagger . . . tell me something. Do my wishes for my daughter mean nothing to you? Do you not care about my demands?"

"No, that—I mean, yes, they all mean something to me. But that's not what this is. I'm not trying to go against your word. I'm sorry you're upset with me, I did drop Grey off at home last night, and I had no idea she was coming over until she showed up."

"So, then why didn't you do the smart thing and send her back home?"

I sat there staring at the roof of my car as I tried to think of an answer that would make him happy—but there was none. "To be completely honest with you, Mr. LaRue, I would never ask Grey to leave if she came to me. No matter what it was for."

He sighed heavily and mumbled, "I know you wouldn't. I'm glad she has you, but you have to understand something. That's still my—" He cut off abruptly, and all I heard was his broken breathing. "That's still my little girl, and she's been through hell. It is my job as her father to protect her until she belongs to someone else."

"I know she has, I want to protect her too."

There was a long silence before he cleared his throat and said, "Grey is an adult, and I can't stop her from doing what she wants to, just the same as I can't stop my son. But that will never stop me from trying to keep her heart from breaking again. Grey's heart and well-being are my priority."

"I'd do anything to make sure I never hurt her. Her heart means everything to me," I assured him.

"Well then, keep her fed and make sure she comes home safely."

I smiled for the first time since LeAnn appeared in front of me. "Yes, sir. Mr. LaRue?"

"Hmm?"

"I plan on marrying your daughter one day."

Another beat of silence, then, "I know that too. And you should know now that I don't think there's a better match for her than you. Darcy and I would be happy for our daughter to marry you."

"Thank you. Thank you—that means a lot to me."

"Now go on and get my daughter something to eat. If she comes back to us starving, I may have to rethink what I just told you."

I barked out a laugh and turned on my car. "You don't have to worry about that. Have a good day, Mr. LaRue."

As soon as the conversation was over, I pulled out of my spot and started back to the warehouse. The smile that wouldn't leave me seemed to widen as I replayed the conversation over in my head.

Grey was waiting on one of the couches in nothing but one of my shirts when I returned, and her face lit up as soon as she saw me. "You were gone forever!"

"Felt like it," I agreed, and set the food down on the counter before walking up to her. Pulling her off the couch, I lifted her in my arms and started walking toward the stairs.

"What about the food?" she asked on a laugh, her arms going around my neck as I climbed the stairs.

"I saw LeAnn, and she apologized for how she reacted back when you were in Seattle, and she said she was happy for us."

Grey's eyes widened. "Really, now?"

I rolled my eyes and nodded. "And then your dad called me when I got in my car . . ." I trailed off and laughed when Grey's face completely fell. "He's not mad at you, he was unhappy with me. That is, until I reminded him how much you mean to me."

"Are you serious? What did you say?"

I lowered Grey onto the bed, shrugged slowly, and crawled in after her, taking her shirt off once I was kneeling over her body. "All you need to know is that your dad is fine, and that he threatened me if you came back starving, and that I'm going to love you forever."

She smiled just before I could press my mouth to hers, and she pushed against my chest so she could slowly inch my shirt up over my head. "Well then, you better let me eat."

"I will, as soon as I get done showing you how much I love you."

Chapter 13

Grey
August 16, 2014

I CALLED OUT a good-bye to everyone at work and headed out to my car. I was pulling my phone out of my purse to call Jagger to see what he wanted for dinner when I stopped short at the sight of the woman who was standing next to my car. My eyebrows pulled together as I looked closer at the sobbing woman and took another few steps toward her.

"Mrs. Easton?"

She whirled around and wiped quickly at her cheeks when she saw me. "Oh, Grey, I'm so sorry—"

"Did something happen to Jagger?" I asked in a rush, my heart pounding at the thought of losing him.

"No! No, God no. He's fine, it's me."

I took calming breaths as I closed the distance between us and wrapped my arms around her. "I'm sorry, I just—sorry. How are you, and what's going on that has you crying?"

She wiped at her wet cheeks again when I released her and tried to laugh, but it sounded forced. "I feel so stupid coming to you for this. I need to ask you a *huge* favor."

"Of course, anything."

"But you can't tell Jagger."

I paused for a second, and she noticed my hesitation.

"Please, Grey, it would kill him if he knew. He would try to do everything to make it better, and I just can't do that to my son."

"Okay," I said warily. "What is it?"

Taking a large breath, she held it for a few seconds and blinked rapidly, like she was trying to stop more tears from coming on. "I need money. I got laid off, and Mike took everything and bailed on me."

My head jerked back. "What? Oh my God. I'm so sorry. I didn't even know you had a—wait, who's Mike?"

She waved her hand dismissively. "He's gone, it doesn't matter. But Jagger told me not to date him, he *begged* me not to. He said Mike would do something like this to me, but I didn't listen to him. I didn't believe Mike would leave me, and now I have nothing. No money, no car, nothing. I'm going to lose my house . . . I can't even afford to buy Keith's food," she sobbed.

"Mrs. Easton, I'm sorry. I don't even know what else to say."

"And I know Jagger. He'll go after Mike. Mike threatened him every time Jagger stopped by the house, and the last time Jagger was there, he told Mike he'd kill him if he did anything to me. I can't let my son go to jail because I was too stupid, and I know he'll go to extremes to make sure I'm okay. He'll give me everything he has, that's just how he is. I *can't* do this to him."

I stood there in shock. I wanted to know why Jagger hadn't told me about Mike, but knew that he would do anything to keep me from anything painful. "That's why Jagger was mad at you," I mumbled.

Mrs. Easton's eyes widened. "What?"

"That day we were moving Jagger into the warehouse and you came by, that's why he was mad. Because of Mike . . . right?"

"Oh, sweet girl. I'm so sorry you had to see that. He was just trying to protect me."

Of course he was. Because that's what Jagger did. Protect people. "How much do you need?"

"Two thousand. That will cover the bills until I can find another job."

"Two thousand?" My jaw dropped, and I scrambled for something to say. "I don't—I don't have that kind of money. I just started working and I'm trying to pay off student loans as fast as possible."

A hard sob burst from Mrs. Easton's chest, and she covered her mouth to quiet her cries. "Oh God. Oh God." She turned her body away from me, but I still heard her whisper, "What am I gonna do?"

"I can . . ." I trailed off, and felt sick at the thought. But this was Jagger's *mom*. I couldn't let her lose her house. "I can give you a thousand." The offer came across as a question more than anything. "I'm sorry it's not enough, but it's all I have. If I could just tell Jag—"

"No!" she nearly shouted, and turned to face me again. "That's fine, anything you can afford is fine, but you can't tell him. If he knew about this, he would give me everything . . . I told you that. He'd give me money even if it meant he wouldn't be able to pay his own bills."

I looked around helplessly for a few seconds before nodding. "Okay. I have to write a check, though. I can't pull all that out at the ATM."

"Oh, Grey, you're a lifesaver. I swear, as soon as I get another job I'll pay you back."

"I know you will." I gave her a weak smile as I searched for a pen in my purse and walked over to my car.

Setting the checkbook on the hood, I wrote out a check to her for one thousand dollars. I tried not to think of the fact that I would now only have enough left in my account to pay my cell-phone bill and buy gas. I just swallowed back the sick feeling and continued chanting to myself that this was Jagger's mom and little brother, and I needed to help them.

"Here you go, Mrs. Easton. I'm so sorry that all this happened to you."

Pulling me in for a tight hug, she held me for a few seconds as fresh tears began welling up in her eyes. "Thank you, honey. Thank you so much." Cupping my cheek for a moment, she smiled shakily at me. "You're such a sweet girl, I'm so glad my Jagger has you."

I watched as she turned and began walking away. "Do you need a ride home?"

She glanced back and rested her hand over her chest. "No, honey, the walk will give me time to think. Thank you."

Once she had turned the corner, I got into my car and gave myself a few minutes to gather myself before calling Jagger.

"Hey, I was just getting ready to call you."

"Sorry."

There was a long pause, and just when I realized that I hadn't said anything else, he asked, "You okay?"

"Of course!" I shook off the sick feeling and straightened in my seat. "I'm sorry, it was a long day, and then I got caught up at the end . . . I'm just a little out of it. But what do you want for dinner?"

"I already ordered Chinese so you wouldn't have to cook or anything since you had to go in on your day off."

A smile pulled at my lips. "Sounds perfect, I'll be there in a few minutes."

After ending the call, I knew I was right in helping his mom and in not telling Jagger. She was right. Even though Mrs. Easton had always been a little flighty, Jagger would do anything to take care of his mom. Just as he had always done for Charlie and me.

I KNOCKED ON Graham's door a few hours later after spending time with Jagger, and jumped back a little when it immediately opened and a big mass of a guy bear-hugged me.

"Where've you been all my life, girl?"

"Can't breathe," I choked out, and hit him as hard as I could. "God, Deacon!" I hissed when he released me, and hunched over to pull in quick and uneven breaths as I tried to fill my lungs.

"Don't be so dramatic, Grey. You're fine."

I glared up at him like he'd lost his mind. "Fine? Do you know that it feels like being slammed into a brick wall when you do that?" I tried to hold my anger, but the face he was making made it impossible, and by the time I finished talking, I was smiling.

"See? You're not even mad at me."

Pushing at his chest to walk into the house, I shook my head. "I *am* mad at you, you just make it hard to stay mad."

"When are you going to stop breaking my heart and realize

you're in love with me?" he asked as he slung an arm around my neck, pulling me in close to his side.

I barked out a laugh, then pulled away and skipped ahead of him. "Hmm . . . let me think."

"Never," Graham answered for me, and I turned around just in time to be engulfed in his hug.

"Come on, dude," Deacon complained. "She's breaking my fucking heart."

"She's my fucking sister!"

"And I'm also taken," I chimed in, and Deacon did a dramatic move like I'd just wounded him. "Don't act like you're hurt, how many *different* girls have you been with this week alone, Deacon?"

"Three," he responded immediately, and a wry smile crossed his face when the doorbell rang. "And that would be number two coming back again."

"You're gross, and obviously not brokenhearted."

Grabbing the back of my head, he landed a loud kiss on my forehead before dodging Graham's fist and backing up toward the entryway. "I'll always be brokenhearted when it comes to you, Grey LaRue," he teased.

"I fucking hate my roommates," Graham growled once Deacon had disappeared.

Turning to look at him, I raised one eyebrow and walked over to plop down on one of the couches. "No you don't, and I don't know why you had me come *here* when you know they're going to act the way they do." I looked around for a second before asking, "Speaking of, where's Knox?"

"Gone. Thank God. I don't think I'd be able to stop from punching one of them if they were both here."

"Once again: I don't know why you had me come here when you know how they always act."

Knox and Deacon had been Graham's best friends since middle school, and after years of partying together in a fraternity, they all decided they weren't ready to settle down or give up the party. They bought a large house in Thatch, and continued to live like frat boys.

Both were handsome in a way that had women of all ages turning to look at them, and they knew it. Their egos as well as Graham's added up to a recipe for destruction for any girl who entered their lives, and many did. I'd grown up with Knox and Deacon and viewed them as two more obnoxious brothers to deal with, but Graham never seemed to get the memo that we all viewed each other as siblings. Knowing his annoyance at my involvement with Ben and Jagger, both Knox and Deacon had been declaring their "love" for me since I was sixteen just to piss him off, and six years later, it still worked.

Deacon walked back into the living room with a busty, black-haired girl against his side, and shot me a wink as they continued on to the hallway leading to his room.

I gestured toward the hallway they'd disappeared in and whispered to Graham, "At least he's starting to go for girls outside of Thatch. The three of you have half the female population simultaneously hating you and waiting for another chance to be with you." Graham laughed, and I slapped at his arm. "It's not funny. Do you know how often I get asked about one of you, or receive phone numbers from women wanting you to call them again 'just in case you lost it'? It's annoying."

"Come on, you haven't even been back in Thatch for a total

of a month and a half when you take out your trip to Seattle. It can't be that bad yet."

I didn't respond to that, I just gave him a look telling him he was so wrong.

"And I wanted you here because I'm hiding from Mom," he continued.

"Wait, what? Why?"

"Haven't you heard her lately? Or have you been too wrapped up in your new relationship."

I opened my mouth to deny that, and smiled when I realized I couldn't.

"Exactly."

"Oh, whatever. Tell me why you're hiding."

Graham groaned and got comfortable on the couch. "She wants me to move out of here and get my own place, without a roommate, and she's trying to get me to settle down. She has a new list of *eligible girls* every time I come over or talk to her."

"Eligible?" I asked on a laugh. "Oh my God, are you serious?"

He sat up and tried to imitate Mom's voice. " 'They're single and absolutely *darling* girls. You'd be lucky to be with any one of them; besides, they're not like the floozies you normally date.' "

I laughed harder and had to wait until I could breathe normally before asking, "Floozies? She really says that?"

"Now you see why I'm hiding?"

"A little," I admitted.

"She acts like I'm in my midthirties or something. She just keeps saying all the good ones will be gone by the time I realize I'm ready to settle down, so she's trying to help me see what I'm missing. I'm only twenty-four."

"Or maybe she's saying that because she's secretly hoping you'll stop whoring yourself around."

Graham's foot shot out and connected with my knee. "Don't be a brat, you know I'm not getting paid." He grinned wickedly and shrugged. "Whatever, I think she just wants me to be like you."

My eyebrows rose. "Like me?" I asked dully.

"Yeah. Twenty-two and already with the guy of your dreams, or some bullshit like that. You've always known exactly what you want when it comes to who you want to be with, there's never been a question with Ben or—" Graham cut off quickly, his eyes widening when he realized what he was saying.

I waited for a second to see if he would continue or backtrack, but he just sat there staring directly past me, looking like he was kicking himself for saying anything. "With Ben or Jagger?" I offered, and Graham's eyes flashed back over to mine.

"I'm sorry, I didn't mean to—"

"Graham, it's fine. You're allowed to talk about Ben. Jagger and I talk about him."

"But it—I don't know, and then after what's been happening . . ."

I smiled and squeezed his arm for a second. "But it's fine. Even with everything that's happened, I can still talk about him. When all that shit went down, I was struggling, yeah, but only because I was confused and upset. I had a hard time dealing with the stolen vows and the Facebook messages, but none of that made a difference for me with what happened to Ben."

Graham watched me for a minute before speaking, and when he did his voice was soft—the worry in his tone clear. "But you look so depressed sometimes, Grey. You look like you're *not* dealing or something."

"I *am* dealing. I've dealt with it. Are there days when it's hard? Yeah, there are, but it was a sad thing that happened. And you have to remember that a lot of the days that you've seen me were really bad or hard days. Like at graduation and the two-year anniversary of Ben's death. Or coming back to Thatch for the first time in a year. Or when I found out how Jagger felt about me, and felt like everyone was spitting on Ben's memory. Or the times when I got the messages from his account, or pictures of us together. It would be hard for anyone to go through what I did."

"I just worry about you."

"I know. So do Mom and Dad, and so does Jagger, but I really am doing fine." I grabbed the collar of my shirt and pulled it to the side. "Did you notice I'm not wearing my necklace?" Graham shook his head and I released my shirt. "It was time to take it off."

"When did you do that?"

"A few days ago. It's now in the box with my engagement ring and some other things."

"I don't know what to say to something like that," he admitted softly. "I want to say I'm happy for you, because I know what taking off the necklace had to mean to you. I want to say I'm glad you're moving, and moving on with Jagger. But I hate that you've had to go through any of this. It kills me knowing how much you've hurt over the last couple years."

I looked up and blinked quickly to stop the tears that were welling up in my eyes, and gave Graham a soft smile. "Now you're going to make me cry because you're being all sweet and stuff."

Graham sat up and clapped his hands. "Okay, no crying. Because I'll find someone to hit for making you cry, even if it is my fault. New subject? Something not so depressing?"

"Sure."

"The love of my life is here!" someone shouted from behind me, and I turned to see Knox standing there with his arms open wide, a bag of greasy food hanging from one hand, a case of beer in the other. "Have you finally realized we're meant to be together?"

I laughed and Graham grumbled, "Not that subject."

"What, no girl tonight, Knox?"

He winked, the action so much like Deacon's, and one I'd come to expect from both of them during the times they were pissing off Graham. "Already left her for the night; somehow I knew I needed to be home, and look what I find."

"That's it. I'm killing both you and Deacon," Graham said simply, as if he'd just decided on what shirt to wear for the day rather than murder.

Knox huffed. "You can't kill me, your sister loves me. She'd hate you if you killed me." Graham stood up, and Knox raised his arms higher. "Food! I brought food and beer! You can't kill me, dude."

Snatching the bag of food, Graham punched him in the stomach and walked calmly back to the couch while Knox stayed bent over, holding himself up against the wall.

With an unapologetic look at his roommate, Graham turned to me and shrugged. "That'll hold me over until next time."

Jagger
August 23, 2014

I watched Grey shrug into one of my shirts as she got off the bed, and followed her every move as she walked to the bathroom.

She barely glanced over at me before she realized I was awake and watching her, and did a double take. "Hey," she said softly, and turned around to walk over to me, her voice still raspy from sleep. "When did you wake up?"

"When you moved away from me."

Grey smiled and leaned over to kiss me. "I'm sorry, I didn't mean to wake you—" She cut off on a laugh when I grabbed the backs of her thighs and pulled her toward me.

"I'm not. I'm just sorry you put clothes back on." Running my hands up her legs and over the curves of her bare ass, I pressed her down against me and swallowed her moan when she rocked against my erection.

"Then maybe you should change that?" she offered, and sat up so she could look down at me while she slowly eased herself onto me, a soft moan sounding in her chest when she was fully seated.

I'd barely inched the shirt up to her waist when we heard the front door open and shut, and Grey scrambled off me and the bed to look for more clothes to put on.

"Jag?"

"Son of a bitch," I growled. "Yeah, hold on a sec!" Grabbing the pair of jeans on the floor, I pulled them on and looked back at Grey.

"Charlie has the worst timing!" she hissed as she finished putting on her shorts and ran into the bathroom.

I bit back a smile and leaned over the railing to look at my little sister. "What's up?"

"Were you seriously still sleeping? It's almost eleven!"

And Grey and I didn't go to bed until sometime around four this morning. "Uh, yeah. We were tired."

"We—oh. Why do you always leave your door unlocked?"

I raised an eyebrow at her exasperated question. "I didn't."

"Actually, you did. It was definitely unlocked, and the key you just gave me doesn't work." She held up her key ring. "It wouldn't even fit in the lock, so I just tried the handle."

"Yes it does. I checked it before I gave it to you."

"Obviously not, I tried it this way *and* that way." She showed me as if she was actually trying to unlock an imaginary door in front of her. Holding her key out before turning it upside down and trying again.

"Really, now? Is that exactly how you did it?" I smiled when her answer was to glare at me. "Fine, I'll make you another key. Give me a second to find a shirt." Pushing away from the railing, I walked over to the closet and put on the first shirt I touched, then opened the bathroom door. "You coming with me?" I asked Grey.

"This is so embarrassing!" she whispered harshly. "This is the second time she's walked in when we were starting to do something."

I took a step forward and wrapped my arm around her waist then hauled her against my chest. Nipping at the sensitive spot on her neck, I whispered, "Just think of how much worse it would've been if she came in a few minutes later and heard you screaming."

Grey scoffed and pushed against my stomach, but I just laughed and kept her close against me.

"She thinks we were sleeping." Grey shot me a look and I sucked in air through my teeth as we walked out of the bathroom. "Or at least that's what she wants to pretend we were doing."

"Yeah. That sounds more believable," she whispered, and then called out brightly, "Hey, Charlie!"

Charlie's eyes widened, and she looked over at me for a second before smiling awkwardly at Grey. "Hi. Good morning . . ." She trailed off, her greeting sounding more like a question, and that's when it hit me. This was the first time Charlie and Grey were seeing each other since we'd found out about Charlie's feelings for Ben.

If it hadn't been for the unwelcome surprise of Charlie showing up at the same moment Grey had settled herself on me, I would've remembered this sooner, and I would've worried about how Grey would react to seeing Charlie. Whether Grey remembered everything given her embarrassment, she wasn't showing that anything had ever happened; and it was obvious that Charlie had expected her to be colder toward her.

"How are you?" Grey asked as she walked out of my arms and pulled Charlie in for a hug.

"I'm fine, I just—uh—sorry for waking you up."

"It's fine. Do you want anything to drink?"

Charlie watched Grey walk toward the kitchen and looked back at me. "Did you decide not to tell her?" she asked softly so her voice wouldn't carry.

I shrugged and shook my head. "No, she knows."

"Babe?"

I looked up at Grey, who was waiting expectantly. "I'm good."

"Water is fine," Charlie said without looking at her, then lowered her voice again. "Was she okay with it?"

"I don't know, she was upset that you'd been acting like you were fine, but she wasn't mad that you liked him. She just thought it looked bad on her that she was moving on with her life. But she got past that, she's a lot better now."

Charlie nodded absentmindedly and turned to look at Grey just as she came back with water for her and Charlie.

"If you want to hang out with your brother today, I can go

home or go hang out with Graham," she offered, but Charlie waved her off.

"No, I'm glad you're here, and I can't stay long, I just wanted to come say hi before running back home. Mom's leaving for somewhere, so I'm gonna watch Keith."

My eyes narrowed. "Again?"

"Don't start, Jag," Charlie pleaded softly.

I bit back the response I wanted to make and asked instead, "Where's Mom going this time?"

"I'm not sure, but she said she'd be gone for a couple days, so I'm guessing she'll be home in a week or so."

My face went blank. "Charlie, we've talked about this—"

"And I've asked you to stop bothering me about it!" she shot back, cutting me off. "I have nothing else going on right now except for a couple online classes. I'd be watching Keith anyway."

"He's not your responsibility."

"And I wasn't yours! But you took care of me anyway!"

"Hey, Charlie," Grey said suddenly, her soft voice enough to stop what was sure to be another argument. "How *is* your mom doing?"

"She's fine, I guess. I mean she's the same as she always is, the sky is made of love and all that, so she's good."

Grey kept a smile plastered on her face, but I could see the eagerness as she waited for something else—like Charlie's answer hadn't been what she'd been looking for. After a few seconds of awkward silence between the three of us, Grey asked, "Was she able to find a job?"

I forced out a quick laugh, and Charlie's face lit up with a weary smile. "Find a job? Mom? Uh . . . no. Definitely not."

Grey's smile faltered, and my eyebrows pinched together. "Wait, why are you asking if she found a job?"

"She said she was trying to get one."

"Said? When did you talk to her?"

Both girls looked at me in surprise at my harsh tone, and Grey's head shook back and forth quickly. "I don't—a week or so ago? Maybe?"

I tried to calm down and sound bored, but I was too afraid that instead of going to my sister—like I'd always feared—my mom had gone to Grey. "Where did you see her?"

"In town. I ran into her and we talked for a few minutes. She told me she was trying to find a job—that's it!"

"What is wrong with you?" Charlie asked, and by her expression, I knew I still needed to calm down.

"Nothing."

Her eyebrows rose as she continued to stare at me. "I don't believe you, but whatever. You're in a bad mood today anyway." Finishing the rest of her water, she turned toward the kitchen. "I need to leave, I told Mom I'd be back before eleven."

"Charlie," I groaned. "Come on, stay for a little while. I'll make lunch."

Grey laughed and Charlie looked terrified. "You'll . . . make . . . sweet Lord, someone save me."

"I'll pick up food. Sound better?"

Charlie's expression turned teasing, and she nodded once as we walked to the door. "It does, but for Grey's benefit. Because I really do have to go."

After hugging Grey, Charlie skipped over to me and threw her arms around my neck.

"If Mom's leaving, you could always bring Keith over here if you didn't want to stay there alone."

"Or you could always just come see us?" she countered, and kissed my cheek.

"All right, I'll think about it."

With a little wave, Charlie ran through the rain to her car and got in as quickly as possible. As soon as she drove away, and Grey and I were back in the warehouse with the door shut, Grey turned on me.

"Why did you react that way about me talking to your mom?"

I wanted to tell her, but at the same time I didn't. We'd just gone over my keeping things from her, but I'd told her then that I would continue to do whatever I had to in order to protect her. And letting her know about Mom would only worry her and make her ask too many questions. If Charlie could stay in the dark on this, then Grey could too. They needed to. "I don't know what you mean."

Grey made a face. "Yes you do. You went from fine to freaking out in half a second. Talk to me."

"I'm sorry if that's how I came across, but I'm fine."

She continued to watch me closely with those honey-gold eyes until I ran my hands over her arms and then pulled her into my chest.

"How about we get ready and go out on the lake?"

Grey laughed until she realized I was serious, and then pointed to the door behind her. "It's pouring outside."

"Then how about we order in some food, and spend the rest of the day in bed?"

She smiled against my kiss and pushed me back enough to

look at me. "You really want to do that after your sister just walked in on us? Kinda killed the mood for me."

My face fell and I dropped my arms as I took a step away from her. "Thanks for killing it *again*." Turning away, I walked quickly toward the stairs and up to the loft.

"Where are you going?"

"To get ready," I called back. "We're leaving and spending time in public until I can stop thinking about my sister walking in on us."

I heard her soft laugh from below, and the sound made me feel worse than I already did. I'd wanted to get her mind off my mom, knowing that this wasn't something she needed to worry about, and knowing she'd continue bringing up the subject until I told her what she wanted to hear. And while I was glad she had dropped it for now, I hated that I'd forced the change in conversation for my benefit.

Instead of protecting her like I'd promised I always would, I felt like I'd tricked her.

Chapter 14

Jagger

August 29, 2014

PLACING A HAND on either side of Grey, I leaned down and pressed my lips to first her throat, then her jaw and cheek, and finally her mouth. She smiled against the kiss, and the tips of her fingers traced along my jaw before I moved back.

"Morning," she mumbled sleepily.

"Good morning, sweetheart."

Her eyes finally opened, and her brow furrowed when she got a good look at me. "Why are you dressed?"

"I'm gonna go pick up something for breakfast. Unless you want me to cook . . ." I trailed off, and laughed at her horrified expression.

"No! Go get something."

"That's what I thought." Kissing her softly once more, I stood up and started walking backward toward the stairs. "I'll be back soon, I just didn't want you to wake up while I was gone."

Her face softened into a dreamy smile, and I had to fight with myself when all I wanted was to crawl back in bed beside her. "Thank you. Be safe and come back to me soon."

"Always."

Turning around, I jogged down the steps before I could talk myself into staying and walked outside—my steps immediately halting when I looked up.

"What . . . the . . . fuck."

I looked quickly around the alley where our cars were parked before jogging to the corner to look down that side of the building. When I didn't find anything, I walked back to Grey's car. A low growl built up in my chest when I saw what was on the paper, and my arm automatically reached out to rip off the one closest to me before I stopped myself. Pulling out my phone, I called the police and told them what was going on before looking at my own car.

Covering my car were thousands of pieces of paper, all with pictures of Grey and me together. Across the pictures were the words "whore" or "backstabber." It was the same on Grey's car, except the papers had pictures of her and Ben, with the words "What about forever?" The other papers were copies of Ben's vows. Over. And over.

I wanted to keep Grey out of this, but I knew I couldn't. Taking pictures of every angle of both cars, I finally walked back inside, standing just at the doorway.

"Grey?"

"What'd you get?" I heard the bed shift a few seconds before she appeared at the railing. "Are you coming inside?" she asked on a laugh that died as soon as she saw my expression. "Jagger?"

"I need you to put some clothes on and come outside, babe. The police are on their way."

"What?" Her soft voice barely reached me, and I hated the way her face fell.

I swallowed thickly and looked behind me toward the cars before looking back at her. "I'm here for you, Grey, and we'll find whoever is doing this. I swear to God."

A pained exhale came from the loft as she shook her head back and forth and took slow steps away. She hadn't even seen the cars, but she knew what was happening. I hated this for her, and silently vowed to do everything to find this person and make them pay.

The cops showed up before Grey made it outside, and I was in the middle of talking with the officer who'd helped us last time when I noticed his eyes trail to something behind me. Turning around, I saw Grey standing in front of her car with a mix of pain and fear covering her face. I walked over to her and pulled her into my arms as I backed us away from the cars and toward the officer.

"It'll be okay," I whispered in her ear. "I'm sorry."

She just nodded slowly, her eyes never leaving the cars. Not even a minute later, she gasped and gripped at my arm. "Jagger."

"What?" I looked around quickly, first to her and then around the alley to see if she'd seen someone who shouldn't be here. My eyes barely glanced at where another two officers were taking the pieces of paper off the cars, then darted quickly back. "You've got to be kidding me," I groaned.

The officers started removing the paper faster when they saw what Grey and I had seen, and soon both cars were paper free. Now you could see that someone had painted in white letters on all the windows of both cars. Mine had the words that had been typed over every picture covering my windows. Grey's were covered with Ben's vows. I pulled out my phone and took more pictures while the officers took pictures with their cameras, and stared at the writing. It was nondescript. It didn't look masculine or feminine. Every letter was capitalized, but that was it. Nothing else could be said about it.

We stood out there until the officers were gone, and when I got Grey back inside, she surprised me by looking pissed.

"You need security cameras, or something."

"What?"

She pointed at the front door. "You need cameras out there so we know if the person comes back, and can maybe figure out who it is. You changed the lock, but they obviously know I'm here with you most of the time. So changing the locks isn't going to stop them from doing something to the outside or, obviously, our cars."

"Okay, you're right. I'll call someone today and we'll get some cameras set up as soon as they can come out. I'll get an alarm too, just in case. It'll make me feel better if you're here without me."

Grey nodded and looked around at the large space. "This needs to stop, Jag," she mumbled.

"I know." Pulling her into my arms, I pressed my lips to her forehead, and left them there for a few seconds. "I need to go get the cars washed to get all that shit off them. Do you—"

"I'm coming with you," she said in a rush, and her body began shaking. "I'm not staying here alone after that."

"All right, then let's go. We'll take one car at a time. If you're coming with me, I'm keeping you next to me."

She sighed slowly and tightened her arms around me for a moment. "Thank you."

Grey
August 29, 2014

JAGGER WALKED ME out to my car later that afternoon, and just before I opened the door, I turned and wrapped my arms around him—pressing my face against his chest. It had been a long day with the cars and police, calling a security company to set up an appointment for someone to come out, and sitting around on the floor of the kitchen as we snacked on food and went over everyone we could think of in Thatch who would and could do what this person had been doing to us.

The list hadn't been long.

And even though I knew I needed to go back to my parents' house to get ready to go to work, the last thing I wanted to do was leave Jagger at that moment. Part of it was because I was worried about what someone could do, and being away from Jagger would have my mind constantly going in that direction. But it was also because I knew when I went to sleep tonight, it wouldn't be in his arms.

"You're going to be fine," he mumbled against the top of my head. "If anything happens, I'll be there in a second, okay?"

"I know you will." I reluctantly unwrapped my arms from his waist and turned to open the driver's door. Jagger's voice stopped me from closing it once I'd gotten in.

"Grey?"

"Hmm?"

Jagger stood there looking unsure for a few moments, then he gripped the top of my car and leaned in so his face was inches from mine. "What if you didn't go to your parents' tonight?"

"Whoever's doing this to us already knows where my parents live. They know where I am, they know my car. No matter where I sleep, if they want to do something, they'll find a way to do it wherever I am."

"No, uh . . ." He trailed off, and looked away from me again. "I meant what if you come here, and stay here." Just as I started to tell him that I had been staying there, he cut me off. "You've been sleeping here most nights anyway, why don't you just stay? Grab whatever you need from your parents' house and come stay here with me."

I tried unsuccessfully to bite back a smile, and acted like I was considering what he'd asked me. "You know, it only takes a few minutes to get to my parents', if something happens I'll be able to hang on for the amount of time it'll take you to get to me," I teased, and his green eyes narrowed at my nonchalant tone.

"I don't want you here just so I can be with you as soon as something happens. I want you here because I don't like watching you leave. Even if I know I'll see you again tomorrow, tomorrow's never soon enough when it comes to you."

"You really want me here? In your space . . . girly-ing up your warehouse?"

He laughed and rolled his eyes. "If it means you'll be here, you can do whatever you want with the place. And if you want, I'll talk to your parents or I'll be there with you when you tell them."

Cupping the back of his neck, I pulled him down so I could

kiss him. "I think I better talk to my parents alone. I'll never forget how this conversation went last time, so it's probably best if you're not within seeing range of my dad."

"If that's what you want, but I need to know that you want to be here. I don't want you staying here just because it's what I want or asked—"

"Jagger, stop. I want to be here, trust me. I'll talk to my parents tomorrow, and regardless of what happens, I'll see you after that, okay?"

"Okay." He stepped back, and his lopsided smile quickly took over his face. "Have fun at work tonight, and call me if anything happens."

"I will."

"And call me if you change your mind about wanting me there when you talk to them."

"I will!" I said on a laugh, and pushed on his stomach so he would take another step back. "Now go back inside or I'll think of a reason to call in to work and tell them I'm not coming in, and it'll be all your fault."

He raised one dark brow in an obvious challenge, but stepped away and put his hand on the door. "Come back to me, Grey LaRue. Tomorrow is already too far away."

"I'm calling in," I breathed, my heart warming with his words.

Before I could say anything more or try to get out of my car, he shut the door and gave me a wicked smile as he backed up toward the warehouse and walked inside.

THE NEXT DAY I walked into the kitchen and sat down at the table opposite my dad.

"Can I talk to you guys?"

Mom and Dad both looked up at me—Dad's eyes immediately narrowed, and Mom looked like she was ready to talk about the weather.

"Are you pregnant?" Dad asked suddenly, and I jerked back in my chair.

"What? No!"

"Now, I've been telling you to use protection," Mom chimed in as she walked closer to us from the stove, and Dad's mouth snapped shut as he turned to look at her.

"What? You've been what?" Dad looked back at me, and I watched as his face quickly turned red. "You've been—you and—that's it! I don't want you going over there anymore; if Jagger wants to see you, he can come here under my supervision."

"Dad," I groaned, and Mom clucked her tongue.

"Honey, don't be absurd. This isn't the 1800s." After rolling her eyes at my dad, Mom turned back to me. "Now, Grey, I've told you countless times, and I've asked if you had protection. You could've talked to me and we could have prevented this."

"Mom, I'm not—"

"Young lady, you are grounded."

"Dad, I'm not—"

"How could you go and get pregnant?" he demanded.

"You're pregnant!" Graham roared seconds before the front door slammed shut and he stormed into the kitchen. "Hell no. Where is he?"

"I'm not pregnant!" I yelled over everyone as Mom started trying to calm down Graham, and Dad started lecturing me. "And why are you even here?" I asked, looking up at Graham.

"I'm hungry and have no food in the house," he said with a shrug as he walked toward the pantry.

"Graham, I was thinking about Melissa Davis. She's such a lovely—"

"Mom, I'm not here to talk to you about which girls you think I should settle down with. Besides, we have bigger shit to talk about if Grey's knocked up."

"Oh my God, for the last time—" I started, but Dad turned his anger on Graham.

"We do not use that language in this house!"

"Since when?" Graham countered.

"Since right now! Too much sin happening here."

"Please." Graham snorted and sidestepped Mom when she walked up to him from the opposite side of the kitchen with a piece of paper in her hands. "Mom, I don't want to know which girls you want me to date."

"But they're all so—"

"I'm moving in with Jagger!"

Everyone stopped and looked at me with wide eyes before they erupted again.

"Like hell you are!" Graham shouted, and waved off my mom as she tried to hand him the paper again.

"You are grounded! You are grounded twice over. You aren't leaving your room until you're forty."

"Dad! I almost got married two years ago, you can't act like this now!"

"But we weren't going to let you move in with Ben before you got married," Mom said calmly as she stuffed the piece of paper in Graham's hand and moved away from him.

"You are not moving in with him, because you're not married," Dad continued, and I watched as Graham tore up the paper and threw it in the trash.

"Fine. Then we'll elope."

As if having two of them yelling their displeasure with the conversation wasn't bad enough, having my mom join in on it had a headache from hell forming.

"I'm not going to elope with Jagger!" I said above their voices and waited for them to stop screaming at me and each other. "I was just trying to show you that I don't really care what kinds of demands you make. I'm going to move in with Jagger one way or another. Dad, if you try to ground me, I'll just leave anyway. Mom, stop bringing up the subject of using protection, and don't worry, I wouldn't get married without you there. And, Graham, just calm down. I love you all but I'm going to do this; this is what I want to do. I'm not wasting time anymore waiting for the right time for things. The right time isn't set by any rules society makes; the right time is when you're ready for it—whatever *it* may be. And right now is the right time for me to make up for all the lost time with Jag, and start my life with him. Okay?"

Everyone was silent for a minute as they continued to stare at me. Graham looked annoyed, Mom looked ridiculously happy, and Dad's expression was unreadable until he opened his mouth again.

"Are you sure you're not pregnant?"

"Mark," Mom chastised.

"Oh my God," I groaned, and got up from the table. "I'm not pregnant. End of that discussion. I really wanted this all to go differently—smoother. I wanted to just talk to you about my decision, but you all started freaking out and I had to stop you. Like I said, I love you. I just have to do this, okay?"

When no one answered, I walked out of the kitchen and took off for my room, where I'd already packed most of my things.

Minutes after I got in there, Graham was walking in and plopping down on my bed.

"That was intense," I mumbled as I packed.

"Yeah, well . . ." He trailed off and looked around my room. "Promise you're not already married or pregnant and just don't want to say anything?"

"Graham. I promise. I just want to be with him, that's all. This wouldn't be a huge to-do if you were moving in with some girl, but because I'm the youngest *and* the girl, it's like all hell breaks loose."

"Exactly."

I stopped on my way back to one of my drawers and turned to look at him. "What do you mean 'exactly'? That's not fair to me. Why do the rules have to be different because I'm younger and female?"

"Because you're still their baby or whatever." Graham snorted as he lay back on my bed. "They want to keep you as long as they can. And girls are expected to be the ones who don't do the stupid shit."

"And moving out is considered stupid shit?" I asked in a monotone voice with one eyebrow raised.

"With a guy you've only been dating for a couple months? Yeah."

"I've known him since I was six! We've been best friends since we were nine. Mom, Dad, and you all know him as well as you knew Ben—hell, you know him as well as you know me."

Graham turned his head so he could give me a dry look. "Yeah, that's not the point, though. Think about it this way: I move in with some girl I started seeing a month or two ago. Sound stupid?"

"Of course it does, because you're with different girls all the time, and no one would expect you to actually want to stay with *just* her for any amount of time! And like I *just* said . . . I've known Jagger for sixteen years! You can't compare that with you meeting some chick and deciding you wanted to see her for more than a week."

"But what if I didn't just meet her? What if I grew up with her too?"

I laughed and dropped my head back to stare at the ceiling for a moment. "Still can't compare it. You haven't touched Thatch girls in who knows how long because you, Deacon, and Knox went through all of them long ago. So to go through your whore-ish ways for all these years, and then decide you want to do what Mom's been suggesting and actually settle down, and even more, if you decided to do it with a girl you hardly knew . . . well, it would seem stupid on both your parts. Even though I was with Ben all that time, I was never apart from Jagger. He's been a constant most of my life."

Graham's eyes narrowed for a few seconds, but his mouth never opened.

"Come on," I challenged. "Give me something else so I can shut you down again."

With a heavy sigh, Graham lay back down. "That was all I had."

"It was weak."

"Hey, I had to try and I didn't have a whole hell of a lot I could go off of. It's not like any of us have anything bad to say about Jagger that I could've used. But I still say you shouldn't move in with him."

"Fine, I'll move in with you. I'm sure Deacon and Knox will

be happy," I offered, and Graham gave me a look like I'd just suggested the most disturbing thing imaginable.

"Fuck. No. Move in with Jagger!"

"If you insist," I said in a singsong voice, and went back to packing.

"That was evil."

"If you say so."

Graham and I were silent for the next twenty minutes as I continued to pack, and he lay there still as stone. When I was done, I sat down on the bed next to him with an exhausted sigh and eyed all my packed things warily. I wasn't exactly looking forward to moving all of it by myself, and I didn't think it would be a good idea to ask Jagger to come help me when everyone was still in a mood over the fact that I was leaving.

"There has to be something wrong with him," Graham mumbled, and I looked over my shoulder to give him a questioning look. "Jagger. There has to be *something* that isn't perfect about him."

I laughed awkwardly. "Uh . . ."

"He took care of you after Ben with no questions asked. He never said anything to you about the way he felt until you accidentally found out. He brought you back here. He's there in a second when anything bad happens. He just seems too perfect. There has to be something."

"You left out that he pretty much raised his sister." Graham shot me a glare and I smiled back. "Jagger's still Jagger," I began, and turned so I could see Graham while I talked to him. "He's not perfect; granted, he's changed a lot in the last few years because of what happened to Ben, but he's still the guy who always got us in trouble when we were growing up. He's the reckless one, and the one who wants to have fun; but Ben changed all of us. And what happened made Jagger push the crazy side of himself back, and the protective side to the forefront. You can't really use that against him, though."

"No, I can't," Graham agreed. "I still say there has to be something."

I groaned in annoyance and hit his arm. "If you want something on him, then you already know what it is. The best thing about him is also his biggest flaw. His need to protect everyone from everything is one of the things I love most, but also something that can drive me crazy because there are some things that are out of everyone's control, and he'll still try to take it all on himself."

"Wonderful. Way to confirm his sainthood."

"Don't be a dick," I said in a huff.

My mind instantly went to Jagger's mom, and the guilt I'd been struggling with ever since I'd seen her came back to twist at my stomach. I'd told Jagger he couldn't protect me from everything, and I was doing the exact same thing. Well, I was protecting him from one thing . . . one thing that—as the days passed—felt like it was consuming my world and mind.

"Hey, Graham, I have a question."

His eyes drifted back to me, both eyebrows rising to show he was waiting.

"So, hypothetically—"

"Don't start anything with that," he said quickly, cutting me off.

"What?"

"When people start off a question with a hypothetical scenario, that just means it's actually happening and they're trying to act like it isn't."

"Well, maybe I'm trying to act like it isn't," I shot back, and he waved his hand out in front of him.

"Then continue."

"*Hypothetically,* if you know that someone close to someone you're close with is having trouble with some things in life—"

"I'm already confused," Graham cut in, and I sighed heavily.

"I'm confusing myself too. Okay, let's try this again. Let's say that Knox's older sister came to you because she was struggling. Like she lost her job, and her boyfriend stole absolutely everything from—"

"She's gay."

"Really? I didn't know that. Well, fine, her girlfriend. And stop cutting me off! So her girlfriend stole everything from her and then took off. But you know that Knox hates her girlfriend and is always fighting with her. So his sister comes to you because she needs money, and she's afraid if Knox finds out he'll give up everything he has to help her or get himself thrown in prison by going after the ex-girlfriend."

"Knox would never do anything to a girl, and he doesn't have much to give up."

"Graham!"

He sent me a teasing smile. "I'm kidding! I was just trying to piss you off. But he really wouldn't do anything like that to a girl."

"Anyway! So if all this happened, would you help her and keep it from Knox because you'd think he'd do exactly what she's afraid of?"

Graham sat up and looked at me for a while like he was trying to figure out whether he should answer honestly, or go back to trying to find out what was really going on with the "hypothetical" situation. Then he exhaled heavily and shrugged. "I have no idea. If that shit actually happened to his sister, I'd tell him because he deserves to know."

"What if this was kind of a repetitive thing for her? Like she always finds girlfriends that end up stealing from her and leaving her with nothing."

"Then she'd deserve it because she's too stupid to realize she deserves better than those type of girls. I wouldn't give her money. You can feel sorry for a woman if she happens to get involved with an asshole. If she repeatedly gets involved with them, then it's her fault."

All the air slowly left my lungs and I sat there feeling even more confused, guilty, and somewhat defeated.

"Hypothetically . . ." Graham trailed off, the word sounding like a question.

I looked up and nodded, but didn't say anything.

"Knox loves his sister. We all do. Any one of us would probably go after someone who hurt her, but Knox would be uncontrollable. He was always beating up people who used the fact that she was gay against her—whether they wanted something out of it, or they were just being assholes and making fun of her. So hypothetically, if all that shit happened, I would help her out once . . . and, yeah, I'd probably even keep it from Knox. Only because I know how he is when it comes to her. But if she came to me a second time, I would tell Knox in a heartbeat. Not only because she would be practically welcoming the destruction her partners always brought on her, but also because at that point, he would definitely deserve to know what was going on with his sister."

"Okay," I said on a breath. "Thank you."

He leaned closer and lowered his voice. "Grey, who asked you for money?"

"It was a hypothetical situation."

"Grey."

"No one asked me, they asked a friend of mine."

Graham gave me a disbelieving look and ground his teeth. "That's just as much bullshit as saying it's hypothetical."

"Graham, I don't even have money to give someone. I barely make a dollar over minimum wage at The Brew, and most of it goes toward paying off school loans. It was a friend of mine."

He sat there for a minute without saying anything, the look on his face showing he was waiting for me to come clean. But I couldn't do that. With an annoyed grunt, he leaned forward and kissed the top of my head. "I don't believe you. Just don't give them money again."

"Graham . . ."

"Come on, I'll help you move everything over to Jagger's. Most of this can fit in my truck."

My body stilled as my mind raced. It wasn't exactly a town secret that Jagger's mom couldn't keep husbands or boyfriends, but she'd stopped being talked about in the town back when we first went to high school. I wondered if Graham was putting everything together and that's why he wanted to help me . . . so he could talk to Jagger . . . but my mind and body eased when he turned and saw the look on my face.

"I'm not going to say anything to him about you moving in, I swear! I told you what I think, and you're the only one I need to tell. It's up to you if you tell him about the war you started in the kitchen."

With a relieved smile, I accepted Graham's hand to help me

off the bed, and filled my arms with things to take downstairs. "I appreciate it."

Graham snorted as he walked out to the hall. "This would take you three trips in your car. We already got on you once about you moving out, I'm not going to force you to go through it another two times each time you come back here to get the rest of your shit."

"Ah, well, if that's the only reason you're helping me . . ." I trailed off, and laughed at his confirming glance.

"Besides, I need to get out of here before Mom can—"

"Oh, Graham, there you are!" Mom called out from the entryway. "I thought you'd left. Okay, so if you don't want to talk about Melissa Davis, what about—"

"Mom! No. No more trying to set me up."

"But you need to settle down," she argued as we walked outside.

I grinned at Graham. "Why do I feel like Mom's never-ending list of girls is the real reason you're helping me?"

Graham grumbled something incoherent and walked faster. "Shut up and let's get this done before Mom calls one of the girls and invites her over."

"That might be—"

"If you want my help, you won't finish that sentence."

I shut my lips tightly to silence my laugh, and nodded. "Whatever you say."

Chapter 15

Jagger
September 10, 2014

I LOOKED TO the side when I felt Grey's breathing deepen, and smiled when I saw her eyes were shut and her mouth was slightly open. Reaching over with the arm she wasn't lying on, I brushed her hair away from her face and trailed my fingertips across her cheek, nose, and lips.

We'd been going all day. After sorting through everything of hers in the extra room yesterday, we figured out what we could put in the warehouse and what was going to go. We drove a few towns over to donate the things we didn't need, and then went shopping for stuff for the warehouse. Stuff that I couldn't care less about, but Grey was having fun decorating, and I loved that she was taking her move-in seriously and making it obvious the warehouse was ours instead of mine.

Once we'd gotten home and put up everything she'd chosen, we went to work on painting the spare room, then decided to go out to eat. We'd gone to Ben's favorite restaurant in the next town over to celebrate his birthday—that had been the day before. After visiting the cemetery, we'd gone back to the warehouse to set up the extra room and had just finished when Grey was called in to cover a shift at The Brew. I'd finished a piece I'd been working on while she was gone, and went to pick her up for dinner, which led to us driving over to our dock to just relax.

We'd been lying there talking for hours when her words began to get slower and then stopped altogether. And now I couldn't stop looking at my beautiful girl as she clung to me while sleeping on my shoulder.

"Grey," I whispered, and my smile widened when she grumbled in her sleep. "Babe, it's time to go home."

One eye cracked open then shut again, and she cuddled closer against my body. "Not yet," she mumbled.

"It's been a long day. Let me take you home and put you in bed."

Her eyebrows lifted, but she didn't open her eyes as she muttered something I couldn't understand.

"What was that?" I asked on a laugh.

"I said: 'You're getting there.'"

"Getting there, huh?"

She made some sort of affirmative noise in her throat, and her eyes slowly opened when I slid out from underneath her to hover over her.

Placing my mouth against her throat, I moved up until my lips were barely brushing her ear. "I'll slowly undress you from the front door to the loft," I breathed into her ear, and glanced down when her body shook slightly to see her arms covered in goose bumps. Settling down between her legs, I dropped my voice even lower. "Then I'll lay you down on the bed and memorize every part of your body with my lips and hands . . ."

Grey's fingers dug into my back, and her lips parted on a soft exhale, but she didn't say anything.

"I'm going to bring you to the edge again and again until you're screaming in frustration." Moving away from her ear, I looked directly into her dark gold eyes that were now locked on me. The heat and want were clear in the way she was staring at me. "Then I'm going to spend the rest of the night wrapped up in you . . . inside you."

A soft moan blew past her lips and she whimpered my name.

"Is that okay with you?" When she just nodded, I placed a soft kiss on the corner of her mouth and pushed away from her to stand up. After I'd helped her up, I nodded toward the car in the lot as I handed her my keys. "I'll get the blanket, wait for me in the car."

My phone started ringing as I was gathering up the blanket, and I answered without looking at the screen. My mind was on nothing but Grey, and what was coming for the rest of the night.

"Hello?"

"Is this Mr. Easton?"

"This is, may I—"

"Mr. Easton, this is Janelle, I'm with ADT Security. I'm showing that your intruder alarm is going off, did someone accidentally trigger—"

"What? No! We're not home." I took off running for the car, and Grey stepped out when she saw me.

"Do you want me to notify the police, Mr. Easton?"

What kind of question was that? Our alarm was going off and

we weren't home. Why wouldn't I want the police contacted? "Yes!"

"What's—"

"Get in the car, Grey," I barked, and opened the back door to shove the blanket in there, then got into the driver's seat as the ADT employee spoke.

"I've alerted the police for you, and they're on their way. Are you out of town? If so, can someone you trust go to your residence to speak with the police?"

"No, we're not out of town. We're driving back to my place right now." I took off from the lake, not caring about how fast I was going or that Grey was staring at me in shock.

"It's safest for you if you don't go inside until the police are there. I'll let them know you're on your way."

"Thank you, I appreciate it."

"Of course. Is there anything else I can do for you, Mr. Easton?"

"No, that's all."

As soon as we ended the call, I dropped my phone into one of the cup holders and started talking before Grey could ask what was happening.

"The alarm was triggered at the warehouse."

"Are you serious?" I'd expected her to freak out, or to be yelling at me because of the way I'd snapped at her. But her voice was soft and shaky. "Why does this keep happening?"

"I don't know, but hopefully the cameras got a picture of the person."

"Are you going to call the police?"

I glanced at her and offered her a reassuring smile. "Security company did that for us, they'll be there right before us or after."

"Okay." She blew out a harsh breath before repeating, "Okay."

"If there's anything there . . ."

"I want to see. I need to."

Grabbing her hand, I brought it up to my mouth and placed a kiss on the inside of her wrist. "All right, I'm here for you."

"I know, Jagger." She laughed softly and squeezed my hand. "If there's anything I've learned in my life, it's that you're always there for me."

I looked over to see her smiling at me, even though the smile was strained from the fear of what we might find at the warehouse. I'd vowed I would figure out who was harassing us like this, and I hoped we would identify the person tonight. I couldn't let Grey continue to be tormented even if it wasn't affecting our relationship the way I'm sure this person had planned. I knew even though she was doing better than she had in the last two years, it was still hard for her. There was no way it wasn't; it was still hard for me. No matter how much time passed, I would always think I'd taken my best friend's girl from him; and having it thrown in our faces every couple weeks didn't help push away those thoughts.

We pulled up behind three police cars from the city next to us, and I had Grey wait in the car while I went to talk to one of the officers.

"Are you Mr. Easton?" he asked as I walked up to him.

"Yes, you can call me Jagger." I offered him my hand, and looked over to the wide-open door. Someone had turned off the alarm, and other than the officers, the warehouse looked normal from the outside. "So what happened that you can see?"

"No signs of forced entry. Is it possible you left the door unlocked?"

"No, not at all. We've been paranoid about the alarm and locks since the last time this person came and messed with our cars."

His eyebrows rose. "You know who's doing this?"

"No, we don't. But someone has been harassing my girlfriend and me for about two months now. I've been dealing with Officer Rand about all this."

He nodded and wrote something down on a small notepad, then gestured toward the door with his pen. "If you didn't leave the door unlocked, then the person had a key. I don't know how long they were in there, but we cleared the entire space, the person isn't in there anymore. You'll have to look to see if anything is missing, but it looks like the alarm startled the intruder and they bolted. Come look inside, I need to ask you about something we found."

Turning around, I gestured for Grey and waited until she was by my side before taking her hand and following the officer. A dozen feet inside the doorway near the kitchen counter was a plastic container on its side with torn papers spilling out of it.

"Is this yours?"

"No," I answered, and tightened my grip on Grey's hand. When the officers began taking pictures, I turned to speak in her ear. "They said there was no sign of forced entry, the intruder had to have had a key."

Her face was covered in shock when I pulled back. "That's impossible. No one else has a key and Charlie's didn't work."

"I know, but I locked that door."

"I watched you do it. It just doesn't make sense."

We glanced around the large room to see if anything looked out of place, and then followed an officer throughout the rest of the building and up to the loft to see if anything was missing. By the time we came back down, the first officer I'd spoken with was waiting for us by the plastic container.

"We need to take all of this for evidence, but I wanted to let you look at it to see if anything in it might help you to give us a name. Because these seem pretty personal."

He flipped through the only pieces of paper that weren't shredded; each had a picture on it that Grey and I had seen too often over the last month and a half. The only new picture was one of Ben's headstone.

I sighed and shook my head. "No, that's pretty much what we've been getting this whole time."

He nodded and placed the photos back in the container. "The rest looks like it's going to be the same pictures, just torn up."

"Figures, that's not surprising. We have the cameras outside if you want to come look at the recording."

"That'd be perfect."

He followed us to the TV, and I knelt down on the ground to open the cupboard that held the hard drive, and started slowly rewinding after we had all the cameras up on the screen.

"There it is," the officer said quickly, and I continued to rewind until we had an image of the outside of the building looking like it was any other night.

We watched a car pull up, and right away the sight of that car triggered something for me—I just couldn't figure out where I knew it from. The person stepped out with their back facing the camera, a hood pulled up over their head, opened the back door, and took out the plastic container filled with paper.

Grey exhaled roughly, and my blood started to boil when the hooded figure turned around. The hood only covered her hair, her face on perfect display for the camera.

"But she . . ." Grey began, but didn't continue.

"This is a fucking joke," I growled.

"Do you know her?" one of the officers asked as the figure went right up to the door and pushed a key into the lock.

"Yeah. Her name is LeAnn Carson, we grew up with her. I dated her over four years ago."

The main officer started writing on his notepad again. "Do you have any idea how she got a key to your house?"

"No. No clue." My conversation with Charlie a month ago came back to me, and I bit back another curse. "She got in here before the first time she ever did anything, and I think I know how. She knows my sister, does her hair, and my sister lost all of her keys—my key was on the key ring. I don't know how she originally got her keys, but that has to be what happened. We've changed the lock since then, though, and I don't know how she'd have a key to this new lock unless she somehow switched the old one out with the new key I gave my sister." Looking back at the officer, I gestured toward the door. "My sister's new key didn't work when she came over, and I know I checked it before I ever gave it to her."

"Do you have an address for Miss Carson?"

"No, but I'd bet she's still living with her parents, and if she's not, they know where she is. I can show you were they live, but I don't know the address."

"That's fine, there's a clear shot of the car and plates; we'll look it up." He cleared his throat and nodded in the direction of the doorway. "Mr. Easton?"

As soon as he walked to the door, I gave Grey a confused look and stood up to follow him.

"I have to ask because of the personal nature of this situation.

Could Miss Carson's behavior be explained by her trying to make trouble because of your relationship with the woman here?"

"Of course it is," I responded immediately, and he eyed me curiously.

"Is there anything still lingering between you and Miss Carson that we need to know before we talk with her?"

I laughed loudly and shook my head at the ridiculousness of this night's events. "Hell no. She approached me at the beginning of summer to see if there was anything between us still, and I told her no. My girlfriend and I run into her every now and then because it's impossible not to in a town of this size, but she's with a different guy every time we see her. I figured she was over me. Like I said, my relationship with her ended *years* ago."

He wrote in his notepad and asked his next question without looking at me. "Could she have someone helping her? I noticed the pictures were of your girlfriend and another man, could he have something against you two?"

"No, uh . . . that *was* Grey's fiancé. But he's, um . . . he died more than two years ago. That's just what she's been using to try to get Grey and me apart. We knew that was the purpose this whole time, just didn't know who was doing it."

"Okay. Well, we'll take this evidence and I'll have someone come by tomorrow to get a copy of the video if that's okay with you . . . ?"

"Of course it is."

"Once we have that, we'll proceed with the investigation. Officer Rand or myself will contact you once there's news."

"I appreciate it." I shook his hand, and automatically looked around until I saw Grey watching us.

"There's a chance Miss Carson knows we'll be coming for her.

What with the alarm going off, and also, I don't know if you noticed, but it looked like she caught a glimpse of the camera before she took off. Do you need an officer to keep an eye on the two of you?"

"No, it's fine. We'll just set the alarm again."

"Okay. Well, call us if anything happens, otherwise you'll hear from us tomorrow about the video recordings."

He motioned for the other officer who was still there, and once they were gone, Grey and I locked the door, pushed a couch in front of it, and turned on the alarm.

"You okay?" I asked her after we got in bed.

She rolled around in my arms until she was facing me, and got comfortable before answering. "Yeah. I'm glad we know who it is now. I want to say I'm surprised, but at the same time . . . I'm not. I thought it was her not long ago, but stopped thinking that as soon as I remembered seeing her out with different guys."

"Yeah, same here. I still don't know how she hacked into Ben's account. She wasn't smart enough to pass most of her classes, she definitely isn't smart enough for that."

Grey laughed softly, then sighed. "Maybe one of the guys she dates is a computer nerd or something."

Her eyes slowly closed, and I watched her for a second before asking, "Do you want to move?"

"What's the point?" she asked without opening her eyes. "It's Thatch, no matter where we move, everyone will know where we end up."

"Yeah, that's true."

"But I would like to get out of here at least until the police arrest her."

I looked down to find her staring at me again. "Like where?"

"Anywhere, as long as we can hide. I'll call in to work for tomorrow and Friday, I'll just tell my boss what happened. Then we can find a hotel in a city close to here, we can just drive until we feel like stopping and stay there. We can even go back to Seattle. You can give some of your work to that guy who sells it for you, I can see Janie, and then we can spend the rest of the time alone."

I smiled down at her and then kissed her softly. "Okay, then that's what we'll do. As soon as the police come for the video, we'll leave for wherever you want to go."

"Good. What did the officer say when he pulled you to the side?"

"Basically wanted to know why LeAnn might do this, if I still had a relationship with her, and if Ben was working with her since there were pictures of you two in there."

"Even if he was alive, Ben wouldn't do this," she mumbled.

"What?"

Grey was silent for a few minutes, and I'd thought she'd fallen asleep until she said, "It's something I've been thinking about since our cars had all that stuff pasted and painted on them. Did I ever tell you what Janie told me about Ben when I ran to hide out at her apartment?"

"What she told you about Ben? No."

"Ben knew how you felt about me." Grey scooted up on the bed so she could look over at me, and one shoulder moved up in a shrug. "At first I wondered if you'd known that he knew, or if the two of you ever talked about it. But I knew that night in the gallery that there was no way you would've ever talked to Ben about me."

"He knew?" I asked softly. "What do you mean, and how did Janie even know this?"

"One of the nights when we went cosmic bowling, Janie asked him why he never really touched me or kissed me when we were at parties or whatever. And Ben said something about having the rest of his life to hold me, but not being able to do that to you."

I didn't say anything as I thought about Grey's words. Ben had never given any indication that he'd known about my feelings, and I didn't know how to feel about finding out that he did, or that he tried to tame down their PDA in front of me *for* me.

"Anyway," Grey began through a yawn as she slid back down to get comfortable, "I was just telling you that Ben wouldn't try to keep us apart."

"And how do you feel knowing that?"

There was another long pause, but I waited, knowing she was still awake. "Comforted," she finally said. "As should you. I think Ben would want this for us." Kissing my chest, Grey sighed softly. "Good night, Jagger."

"Sleep well," I murmured, but I knew sleep wouldn't be coming for me anytime soon. Not after what I now knew. Not after my girl had just told me how she felt about the situation. There were too many thoughts and emotions coursing through me to sleep now.

Grey
September 14, 2014

"Wake up, beautiful."

I mumbled something even I couldn't understand, and tilted my head when his lips touched my ear. As I slowly opened my eyes, I felt the pillow dip down in front of me. A pair of green eyes met mine, and I smiled when he wrapped an arm around me to pull me closer.

"Time is it?" I asked groggily.

"Early."

"Hmm? Why?"

Jagger's low laugh rumbled through his chest, and he started trailing a path of kisses across my jaw and down my neck. "Because we have to leave today, and I wanted a few hours with you before we had to start packing."

"Just a few?" My body broke out in goose bumps when he lightly bit down on the sensitive part of my neck; and when he kissed me in the same spot, I felt his lips pull into a smile.

"Yeah, just a few." He sat back so he could look at me again, his face serious. "You gonna be okay when we go back?"

"I think so. If LeAnn starts acting up again, we'll call the police. I doubt she will now, though. Not with the possibility of going to jail for an extended period of time."

Jagger nodded, his eyes drifting away as he thought over either my answer, or the possibility of LeAnn's revenge. They'd arrested her Thursday night on charges of burglary, stalking, criminal mischief, and harassment. But with bail set at only five thousand, it wasn't hard to figure that someone would pay the five hundred to get her out, and on Saturday, someone had done exactly that. Now she was out of jail, and the officer was telling us to get a protective order against her as soon as we were back in town.

"What about you? Are you going to be okay?"

Jagger's lips slowly curved into a smile. "I'm fine, Grey. She can only hurt me if she hurts you, it's you I'm worried about."

"Well, I'm okay. I really do think she'll do anything to avoid jail."

"You're probably right." Releasing his arm from where he had it wrapped around my body, he slowly brushed my hair away from my face, and my eyes fluttered shut when his fingers traced across my cheekbones, down my nose, and across my lips.

The last three days in Seattle with Jagger had been perfect, and exactly what we needed. Friday afternoon he met with the guy who owned the gallery, and I'd gone out to a late lunch with Janie and Heather for a few hours until Jagger practically dragged me back to the hotel and bed.

I hadn't complained.

Other than that afternoon, answering the door for room service, quick trips to the bathroom, and a shower together, we hadn't left the bed. We'd ordered a few movies, talked about everything from here on out and what was happening with LeAnn, and spent the rest of the time wrapped up in each other. I couldn't remember a time in my life when I was happier than I had been in this suite with him, even when Ben had been alive.

I refused to compare my relationship with him to the relationship I had with Ben . . . but I knew that if I did compare the two, I would quickly realize they weren't comparable. Everything was different with each of them. And now Jagger was my life while Ben was my past.

There was something about Jagger that felt perfect despite everything we'd gone through to get here. There was something about the timing that felt like it couldn't have been more perfectly planned. And there was something about the way he loved me and I loved him that left me speechless whenever I'd focus on it.

It was easy between us. Ever since I'd let go of the past, nothing with Jagger ever felt rushed or too slow. I knew that at no matter what speed we took the rest of our lives, everything would end up feeling the way it had so far. Perfect.

"What are you thinking about so hard?"

I looked up at his curious green eyes, my eyebrows rising in question when I realized I hadn't actually heard what he'd said. "What?"

"It was like you weren't here with me for a few minutes. What were you thinking about?"

"Us," I said without hesitation.

"Yeah? And what about us were you thinking about?"

"Everything."

"Really?" he said on a laugh. "Anything I should know?"

Looking directly into his eyes, I embraced the tingling feeling that had started in my stomach and quickly expanded throughout my body. I knew that the words that were on the tip of my tongue were exactly what I wanted to say, and I felt light-headed as I realized how true the words were.

"Babe?"

Jagger's eyes looked panicked for a few seconds then widened with surprise at my next words.

"I want to marry you."

He blinked a few times, his lips twitching like he didn't know if he should smile or not. "What did you just say?"

"I want to marry you."

Before I could register the way his entire face lit up, his mouth was on mine and he was pushing me back onto the bed so he could hover over me. "When?" he asked through our kisses.

"Whenever. I just know that I want to be with you for the rest of my life."

He pushed himself up so he was on his hands and knees, and I looked at the way his chest rose and fell with each labored breath. "What brought this up?"

I grasped his shaking forearms, and knew they were shaking for the same reason he was breathing so hard. He was trying to control his excitement, but his bright eyes gave him away. "I've loved you my entire life. I've been *in* love with you for . . . I don't know. Years. Whether I knew it or not. But now that I've let go of everything that was keeping me stuck in the past, I've realized how much time I wasted with you, and I don't want to waste any more."

"I would spend forever with you just as long as you were mine, Grey. Don't say this because you think it's what we need to do."

"I'm not," I promised. "This is what I want as long as you want it too."

His signature lopsided smile crossed his face and he kissed me again. "Are you kidding?" he growled against my mouth. "Why wouldn't I want that? I just want to make sure you've thought about what you're saying."

Pressing a hand to his chest, I pushed him far enough away that I could look at him fully. "I *have* thought about it. Jagger, I love you, and I want this. I want you. With our past together, and with how unpredictable life is, I want to start *this* future with you."

Moving my hand away, he spread my legs with one of his knees to lie down on top of my body. A deep groan sounded in his chest when I wrapped my legs around him and he slowly pressed into me. His mouth cut off my gasp when he began moving inside me, and I gripped him tighter to me when he backed away to look down at me. "Then let's start that future, Grey."

Chapter 16

Jagger
September 19, 2014

I WALKED SLOWLY across the grass until I got to the right stone, then squatted down in front of it. For long minutes no words came as I stared at the engraved letters and numbers and tried to figure out the words to explain the hardest thing I'd ever had to say. Grey was working, and I'd just finished having lunch with her dad and asking him the very thing I was trying to say now, but saying it to Mr. LaRue hadn't seemed nearly as hard as this.

And that didn't make sense.

I was trying to talk to a slab of marble. It couldn't respond and it couldn't give me a judging look. It couldn't even give me the permission I was looking for and had already been given by Mr. LaRue. But somehow, asking this stone meant more to me than asking anyone else.

"I can't imagine what you would say to me or think of me if you were here. There are so many times when something happens, or Grey says something, and I can hear what your response would be. Typical Ben bullshit that we all miss. Always trying to reel me in, to stop getting your girl in trouble, to bash my drawings just so I wouldn't feel like I was the only one who doubted them . . . so much. So much that I know both Grey and I hear clear as day. But this? I can't begin to guess what you would say. Probably because if you were still here, none of this would be happening.

"Because if you *were* still here, I know that you'd be furious. I know that you'd do everything in your power to stop me from being with her, and I know that you wouldn't give her up for anything in the world—because that's exactly how I feel now that I have her. But when I try to think about it, all I see is you standing there staring at me. Saying nothing, with no emotion on your face whatsoever."

I sat back and rested my elbows on my knees as I continued staring at the stone, memorizing everything about it as I waited for a response that would never come.

"I love her, man. You knew that, but knowing that you knew doesn't make any of this any easier. I love her and I'm going to take care of her for the rest of my life. I'm going to marry Grey, Ben. I have a ring and I'm going to ask her to take my last name. And you wanna know the fucked-up thing about all of this? It's that I hate that you won't be there when I marry her." I let out a strangled laugh and shook my head. "I hate that my best friend can't be there on what I know will be the best day of my life so far, and yet you were days away from that exact same day with the exact same girl. Like I said, it's fucked up. And sitting here telling a piece of stone all this somehow makes it that much worse. If you were here you'd laugh and tell me I'm insane, and God I feel like it . . ." I mumbled the last sentence to myself.

"I wish you could see her. See how much better she's doing. There were so many times I thought she'd never get past what happened, there were so many times I was terrified that she was destroying herself—just waiting until she could be with you again. Even now, regardless of how much better she is, there are days when it looks like she's on the edge of going to a place worse than where she ever was. But she's strong, and I have no doubt she'll continue to pull herself out of those places, and keep moving. And I'll always be there with her to help her.

"I feel like I need to ask your permission to marry Grey, that's why I came here; but I can't ask a stone. I can't ask something that has nothing of you other than your name and dates on it. So this is me letting you know what we're about to do. This is me saying I'm sorry that you can't have this chance with Grey, and I'm sorry for taking her. This is me telling you that she still loves you, and we all miss you. And this is me promising you I will take care of her and cherish her forever." Standing up, I took two steps away from the headstone and shoved my hands into my pockets. "You always have been and always will be my best man, Ben. See you."

Grey
September 20, 2014

THE BED SHIFTED, I felt something heavy settle down on my hips, and my eyes cracked open to find Jagger sitting on me with an unreadable expression on his face. My lips pulled into a lazy smile, and my eyes blinked slowly a few times before I could finally focus on him.

"Interesting way to wake me up considering we're both fully clothed."

One side of his mouth curved up, but he didn't say anything. Leaning forward, he placed a soft kiss on my cheek before doing the same to my lips. I reached up to run my hand over his head, hoping to prolong the kiss, but he pulled back, and my hand slipped to his face.

"You have a little something there," I teased, and started to brush at the black smudge on his cheek. Then I noticed my left arm.

In my groggy state, it took me a few seconds to realize that, one, it wasn't a bug; two, it was charcoal; and three, it was the words "WILL YOU . . ."

I mouthed the words a couple times and my heart began racing. My eyes flickered over to Jagger. His face was still unreadable, but his green eyes were full of a mostly hidden excitement. With his eyes locked on mine, he lifted my right arm, and I slowly slid my gaze to it.

And my heart sank.

MAKE BREAKFAST? was there in charcoal on my right forearm.

"Seriously?" I whined, and pushed at his stomach. "You drew on me so you could ask me to make breakfast? You could've just woken me up and asked, or waited for me to wake up on my own."

"So, is that a yes?" he asked earnestly, and I glared at him.

"Fine."

"That's not a yes."

"Yes, Jagger, I will make us breakfast because you are incapable of even pouring a bowl of cereal for yourself." I tried to stay mad, but that was impossible with Jagger. "You're such a nerd. I'm getting you cooking lessons for your birthday."

"It won't help."

"One can dream." Grabbing the back of his neck, I pulled him down to kiss him then pushed him away. "Now get off me so I can make something."

As soon as he was off the bed, I grumbled something about only making him toast as I climbed off and started walking toward the stairs.

"Seriously, who messes up cerea—" My words and feet immediately stopped when I was two steps down and looking at the ground floor.

My next breath was audible as I took in the sight. Made up of dozens of the thick papers that Jagger used for his drawings was the outline of a large heart, the bottom of which looped around to make the heart also look like an infinity symbol—my name making up the right side of the heart. Inside of the open space was WILL YOU MARRY ME?

Jagger's arm went around my waist, and his lips went to my ear. "So, is that a yes?" he asked softly as he lifted a ring in front of me.

"Jagger," I said on a breath, and took the ring from his fingers.

I felt his lips pull into a smile as he placed soft kisses on my neck. "That's not a yes."

I turned in his arms and crushed my mouth to his. "Yes, that's a yes!"

His arm tightened around me as he pressed his lips to mine again and deepened the kiss, and we both grunted when we fell back onto the stairs before laughing—never once stopping the kiss.

Pushing against his chest to lift myself up, I looked into his bright eyes and shook my head to gather myself. "I thought—I thought I'd kind of asked you in Seattle. We'd already talked about it, and—"

"And did you really think I was going to let you take this from me?" His wide smile matched my own, and I tried to figure out how to respond to that before giving up and holding the ring between our faces.

"Are you going to put it on for me?"

"That is part of my job," he teased, and took it from me. Grabbing my left hand, he slowly slid the ring onto my finger, his green eyes holding mine as he did. "Grey LaRue, will you let me take care of you and love you for the rest of our lives?"

My eyes started watering, and I nodded my head quickly.

"Will you marry me?"

"Yes," I choked out, and leaned in to kiss him again, but sat back when I felt him reaching into his pocket.

"Grey, there's something I've wanted to ask you since we were thirteen years old. I will admit I was fucking terrified to ask you; for weeks I tried to say something and it just wouldn't come out. We'd been best friends for so long by then that I kept thinking I'd lose my friend if I actually asked, so I stopped trying. Then one morning I decided I'd rather ask and risk losing you than never tell you." His lips tilted up in a quick smile and his eyes shifted down to the folded-up paper in his hand, then up to look at me again. "I knew I'd chicken out again, so I wrote it down to give to you at the dock. But when I got there, I saw Ben kiss you, and when you finally saw me, you ran up to me to tell me that he'd asked you out. You were so excited that I put the paper back in my pocket and never showed it to you . . . but I kept it."

I wiped at my wet cheeks, and stared at him in amazement. "What is it, Jag?"

With a deep, steady breath, he gave me another tight-lipped smile and handed the paper over. It looked and felt old, and for long seconds I couldn't open it—I could only stare at it, in disbelief that Jagger had written this more than nine years ago and had kept it all this time. I slowly unfolded the note that had obviously been opened and refolded countless times, and my heart stopped when I read the words.

Can I keep you?

"You were going to give me this the day Ben asked me out?" Jagger nodded and my chin started trembling even harder. "You'd been trying to tell me this, and I'd had no idea. And you kept it all these years? Why didn't you say something then?"

"It wasn't our time then," he said simply.

I hung my head and kept my eyes on the paper. I couldn't believe what I was holding, and I couldn't believe that he'd chosen *those* words for me. But it shouldn't have surprised me, this *was* Jagger we were talking about; and when he started explaining the note, I couldn't stop smiling even through my tears as the memories came back to me.

"Do you remember when we were nine and you kept watching *Casper* over and over again . . . and making *me* watch it with you?" Jagger laughed hesitantly. "I hated that movie because it was like five or six years old, and about a little boy ghost who turned into a teenager, and I thought that was creepy, but you couldn't seem to get enough of it. But I still watched it with you every time because I loved the way you smiled like Casper was talking directly to you when he asked the girl while she was sleeping if he could keep her. Four years later I still thought about that smile of yours, and even today I can remember how you seemed to melt at that line every time."

I read the words on the small paper over and over until my tears made it too hard to see. Jagger took the note out of my hands and placed it on the stairs before cupping my cheeks so he could wipe at my tears.

"So, Grey, can I keep you?" he whispered, and a soft sob left me as I threw my arms around him, crushing my body to his.

"Yes. Yes, you can. I love you," I choked out, and his arms tightened around me.

"I love you too, Grey LaRue."

He held me there on the stairs as I finished crying and we talked about the movie that I was now dying to watch again—to Jagger's horror—and started talking about when to get married.

"Oh my God! I need to tell my parents! I need to tell Graham and Janie, and you need to tell Charlie."

Jagger grinned sheepishly and his eyes squinted like he was somewhat worried about my reaction to something he was about to say. "You mean the people who are going to be at Wake in about half an hour to celebrate with us for breakfast?"

My mouth popped open, and I waited to see if he was going to tell me that he was joking. "Are you serious?"

"Yeah, but if you don't—"

"They're going to be at Wake? All of them? They knew about this?" I asked rapidly and excitedly.

"Yes to all of that. Do you want to go?"

"Of course I want to go!" I kissed him roughly and pushed off him so I could run back up the two steps we'd made it down. Just before I hit the bathroom, I whirled around to find him behind me, and launched myself into his arms. "You're amazing. I love my ring. I love the way you asked. I love the note. I love you. This morning has been incredible and more than I could've ever asked for. Thank you for asking me, and thank you for knowing I would want to share this with all of them."

"Thank you for saying yes." He kissed the side of my head and released me. "Now go get ready."

I squealed and ran into the bathroom to freshen up and get ready. Calling Jagger in there, I made him take a picture of my arms before I jumped in the shower to clean off the charcoal. When Jagger stepped into the shower behind me minutes later, I quickly forgot about Wake, our family and friends, and every-thing else except for Jagger, how in love with him I was, and how he felt against me and inside of me. My legs were wrapped around his waist and my back was pressed to the cool tile of the shower wall while hot water pelted down on us and Jagger moved slowly and easily inside me. The differences in tempera-ture and the feel of his body were an exhilarating combination, and I gripped at his shoulders like only the touch of him under my fingertips could keep me tied to this earth and this moment.

Jagger unwrapped my legs from his body and we stumbled out of the shower and bathroom, and over to the bed. We'd barely landed on the bed before Jagger was pressing his thick length inside me again, and I fused our mouths together to quiet my moans as our slick bodies moved against each other and he quickly brought me to the edge. He hooked one of his arms under my leg, and my mouth left his as my thigh slid up near his shoul-der when he steadied himself on the bed with the same arm, and began moving faster and deeper.

My stomach heated and tightened in eager anticipation for what was coming, and my eyes locked with Jagger's when he reached down with his other hand and ran his fingers over my aching clit. My mouth opened on a soundless moan as my body shattered around him, and minutes later he came with a deep groan, his arms shaking as he tried to keep himself above me before finally lying down on top of me.

Our chests moved roughly against each other as we lay there, and I lightly ran the tips of my fingers over his back to keep him there when he started moving away. I wasn't ready to let go of him yet. Once we both calmed our breathing, he brushed his mouth across mine as he pushed off me and rolled over onto his back.

"*Now* you can get ready."

I smiled and rolled my head to the side to look at him. "Best reason for being late . . . ever."

"Let's just not tell your dad."

I laughed and pushed at his arm as I climbed off the bed and walked back into the bathroom to fix my hair and put on a touch of makeup. Hurrying into the closet, I put on a bra and underwear, and was stepping into my shorts as I walked back out. My eyes hit the bed just as I started to put my arms into the shirt, and for the umpteenth time in the hour I'd been awake, my heart melted at what I saw in the center of the bed. I shrugged quickly into my shirt and walked over to run my fingers across the outside of the large frame.

Inside was a large, thick paper with a charcoal-drawn replica of the mass of papers downstairs. In the bottom corner of the frame was the note Jagger had given me on the stairs.

I turned to see Jagger and reached out for him. He grabbed

my hand and kissed my palm before wrapping me in his arms. "Thought you might want to keep it, and what's downstairs is way too big and complicated."

"I do, thank you.

"No need to thank me." Releasing his hold on me, he grabbed my hand and pulled me toward the stairs. "You ready?"

I looked at the man in front of me and wondered what I'd done to deserve anyone like him. I couldn't wait to start my life with him. "I've never been more ready for anything in my life, Jagger Easton."

Chapter 17

Grey
September 27, 2014

I WALKED AROUND the shop part of The Brew, talking with a few customers and seeing if anyone needed a refill, but the entire time, an annoying feeling kept nagging me. It had my neck tingling and a weird chill going through my spine. My eyes were everywhere as I walked, and only stayed on the customers for a few seconds before I was looking somewhere else. Just before I turned to go back behind the counter, I saw her standing at the end of a book aisle.

Mrs. Easton nodded at me once and waved me over, and I took careful steps toward her. I hadn't seen her in the almost month and a half since I'd given her the check, and something about her being here didn't feel right.

"Hey, Mrs. Easton," I said cautiously when I got closer to her. "How are you?"

"I'm okay, but I needed to see you."

I laughed once and gestured around the shop. "Well, you obviously know where to find me." If we'd lived anywhere other than Thatch, it would bother me that she knew where I worked, or when I was working. But this *was* Thatch. Everyone knew pretty much everything about everyone all the time. It was hard to keep a secret here.

"Yeah, well . . ." She trailed off and gave me an odd smile. "Honey, I need more."

"More what?" I knew what she was talking about; I just wanted to avoid the subject and wished I hadn't walked over to her in the first place.

I'd been agonizing over our last encounter, even more now that Jagger and I were engaged. Talking with Graham about it had helped remind me why I'd kept it from Jagger in the first place, but it was hard to remember as days went by, and all I could think about was the fact that I'd kept something so important from the man I was going to marry.

"Money, Grey. Two . . . three thousand, at least."

The air in my lungs rushed out quickly, and I gave her an incredulous look. "I don't have that kind of money . . . I can't afford to give you any money, Mrs. Easton. Didn't you find a job yet? Maybe I can help you look for somewhere to work."

"You're marrying my son, I know you have money," she hissed, and I took a step back, my eyes and mouth widening with shock. I'd never heard her speak in any way other than her signature everything-is-made-of-love tone.

"How did you know?" Mrs. Easton hadn't been at our celebration breakfast last week, and unless Jagger had seen her while I was at work, he hadn't gone to her house while she was there, or even said anything about her this whole time.

"Do you really think I wouldn't find out if one of my children got engaged?" She clucked her tongue and gave me a patronizing look. "Oh, honey, that's cute. Really. But there isn't much about them that I don't know."

"Look, I'm sorry, but I can't help you and I need to finish the rest of my shift."

I'd barely turned when she grabbed my arm and brought me back so I was facing her. "I know you have—"

"Jagger and I don't share accounts, Mrs. Easton! I'm sorry, but I can't help you!"

Her grip tightened like she knew I was preparing to make another attempt to leave. "If you don't want to ruin my son's life, you *will* give me what I need."

"Ruin his life? There's no way I would ever do anything to ruin him. I think you need to leave."

"I wouldn't be so sure of that. I know something that would ensure my son's devastation. Now if you don't want this little secret getting out, I suggest you give me the money."

"I have no secrets from Jagger!" I whispered harshly, and turned my head to see if anyone was watching us. "Other than giving you that money, there is nothing about me that he doesn't already know."

"It has nothing to do with *you*. This is all on my son."

My stomach churned and I stopped breathing for a few seconds. "W-what—" I cleared my throat and looked around again. "What 'little secret' about Jagger are you talking about?"

"That's for me to know; but if he finds out about it, then—"

"Wait, what? What do you know that *he* doesn't? How could you have something on him that he doesn't even know?"

"Like I said, that's for me to know." Her anger was rapidly escalating, and I was still in shock seeing this spiteful and vicious side of her.

"You don't have anything on him. Just like you don't have anything on me. I don't have money for you, and once again, you need to leave."

I hadn't gone more than two steps before she sneered, "It's just great that you're making sure his kid is going to starve."

I came to a stop and stood there staring ahead of me before looking back at her. "What did you just say?"

"If you loved my son the way you say you do, you wouldn't make his son go hungry because *you* refused to give him the money Jagger owes him as a father."

My throat felt thick. I couldn't swallow and I wasn't bringing in air fast enough, or maybe it was too fast. Either way, my body swayed and I grabbed on to the end of another aisle. "What . . . son? What son?"

"Apparently my kid doesn't know the meaning of the word 'protection.' He knocked LeAnn up over two years ago. But by the time LeAnn came to talk to him, Ben was dead and Jagger was never around because he was too busy taking care of you."

This wasn't happening. Jagger couldn't have a son, especially not with LeAnn. "You're lying."

"Oh, am I? Why don't you ask Charlie why I was never pregnant, but I miraculously gave birth to a baby—since she was there the whole time. Why don't you ask LeAnn why she disappeared that summer and didn't come back until a few months after the baby was born? Oh, wait, you can't ask her because you have a restraining order against her. And why is that? Because she's now regretting that she signed over custody of the child to me, and she's doing everything to get her family back together— and that includes Jagger."

"Oh God," I whispered, and swallowed back the bile rising in my throat. "No, he can't—they can't be the parents. Keith looks just like—" I cut off quickly when I remembered exactly who I'd always thought Keith looked like. A little bit of Jagger with the dark hair, and a little bit of Charlie—who happened to look just like LeAnn—with the same blue eyes, and the full lips that all of the Eastons had. Which was exactly why I'd never questioned that Mrs. Easton was the mother.

"Now, I've been getting close to filing bankruptcy way too many times because I've been paying for this child when Jagger should have been, and it's time he paid for it. So give me what I need, and if Jagger finds out about this, I swear to you I will be gone with that child faster than you can destroy another wedding attempt."

My chest ached at her words, and I once again couldn't understand how she could be so evil. She'd fooled everyone, and I wondered if Jagger knew about this side of her. But I was positive he couldn't know, he would've told me if he had, and I knew for sure then that I had been right in not telling him about his mother. Not because she needed help financially, but because of this ugly side of her personality. I knew it would break Jagger's heart if he learned about it.

This was definitely my time to do the protecting. Jagger's mom needed to be stopped, and I needed to figure out a way to save Keith from her. If he was Jagger's son, then Jagger deserved to know, and get the chance to raise him. But that chance would never come if Mrs. Easton took off with Keith, and taking off was what she was best at next to finding husbands.

"I don't have three thou—"

"Then give me two, or I'm gone."

I wanted to say I didn't have two, but I was afraid she'd know I was lying—and I was even more terrified that she would make good on her threat. *I just need to buy myself time with her.* Looking up at her, I tried to compose myself so she wouldn't know how much this conversation was killing me. "Fine. My shift is almost over. I'll give you the check when I leave."

"You're a smart girl, Grey." Without another word, she walked past me and out of the shop. I didn't move until I heard the door shut. Then, in a fog, I made my way back behind the counter.

Thankfully there were only about ten minutes left of my shift, no new customers came in, and none of the customers needed anything else, so I was able to slowly pull myself together before I walked outside to see Mrs. Easton again. I'd written the check before leaving the back room, so all I did was hand it to her and then continue the short walk to my car.

"You did the right thing, honey," she called after me, but I didn't respond. I just got into my car and drove to the lake.

Not getting out of my car, I stared out at our favorite dock and the lake. The sun had turned the water into a sheet of gold, and I stared, mesmerized by it, until the colors began shifting. For the longest time, my only thoughts were of the water, but as I watched the sun set, my mind started drifting to the things I'd been trying so hard to block out.

Jagger had a son; he was a father and he didn't even know it. If it weren't for Mrs. Easton's threats of taking off with Keith,

I didn't think I'd have been able to keep something of this magnitude from him. I'd already known that Mrs. Easton left town on a regular basis, but I also knew that she always came back. But after what I'd found out about her today? After she'd revealed a side of her no one had probably ever seen—a side she'd hidden so perfectly . . . I would never put anything past her again.

Jagger's a father, I thought to myself as my stomach roiled, and *LeAnn's the mom.* The girl who made the last two years of high school a living hell for anyone close to Jagger. The girl who slept with any man willing to give the town whore a few minutes of his time. The girl who'd been breaking into the warehouse, torturing Jagger and me, and hacking into Ben's old Facebook account. The girl we now had a restraining order against.

My head dropped back against the headrest, and I let out a pained cry as I took everything in. The deceit, the tormenting, and the pain. Jagger and I hadn't talked about having kids; it just wasn't something that had come up between us yet. Our focus had been on each other and on a future in which we were always together, and nothing else. But knowing he already had a son with another girl was breaking my heart. I felt like LeAnn had taken something special from Jagger and me, and couldn't help but wonder how Jagger would react . . . *when* he found out.

I felt beaten down. There was always something, and it seemed like life never let us have more than a few seconds to breathe, and just be happy. I had thought my biggest challenge with moving back to Thatch would be finding a way to survive in a town where there were so many memories and heartaches. I'd thought the difficulties would include my family getting used to seeing me and not worrying that they were going to hurt my feelings if they mentioned Ben, and finding something to keep me busy now that school was over; I didn't want to be one of those people who just sat around wallowing in grief.

There was no way I could've imagined all of this, or prepared for it. And I had no idea how to get through it now.

But I knew that for Jagger I would somehow find a way to get through it. I knew I would do everything to find out the truth and figure out a safe way to tell Jagger. And I knew that we would find a way to get past this, just as we had with all the other problems that had come at us. We'd been through too much in the last two and a half years not to.

Jagger
October 18, 2014

"YOU'RE INSANE. BURGERS are the only thing that should be ordered here."

I let the menu fall onto the table between Graham and me, and pushed it toward him. "They have a ton of other food for a reason. You're supposed to try it."

"Their burgers are famous," he argued, and I rolled my eyes.

"Have you ever even tried anything else?"

We were at Bonfire. A restaurant that had started off as a little hole-in-the-wall place, but had changed locations to a bigger space when everyone began to rave about their burgers and people started coming in from surrounding towns. And granted, their burgers were amazing, but they had a handful of different types of food, and the burgers were nowhere near the best thing on the menu. But Graham and I had been having this fight for as long as I could remember, and there was no way to avoid it whenever we were here.

"No need. I know what's good. What are you getting, Grey?" Graham turned his attention to her when she didn't respond and slapped at her menu. "Wake up, kid!"

Grey's gaze slowly slid over to her brother, then moved to me, her eyes wide and unreadable. "What?"

"Food. Menu. Bonfire. What are you getting?" he repeated.

"Oh, uh . . . I'm not sure. I think we . . ." She trailed off and looked around the restaurant, and Graham gave me a strange look just before I turned to see if something was wrong with her.

"We should what?" Graham prompted, and Grey looked back at him.

"What?"

"Are you okay?"

"Of course I am," she said defensively, her gold eyes hardening at her brother's question. "Why wouldn't I be?"

"Because you just stopped talking. You said 'I think we,' and then just stopped."

Grey sat there for a moment before shaking her head like she'd finally remembered what we'd been talking about. "Sorry, I'm spacing out so much today. Um, I think we should wait until Knox and Deacon get here."

Graham once again looked at me with confusion, but I couldn't even begin to figure out what to say. I had no idea what was going on with Grey tonight. "We are waiting for Deacon and Knox, kid," Graham said carefully. "I was just asking what you were going to order."

"Oh, well, I don't know, we just got here."

"We've been here for ten minutes," I informed her, and watched the shock take over her features.

"Well then, I guess I should figure it out," she said on a laugh, but Graham and I were still staring at her like she'd just told us that cows lived on the moon.

After a couple minutes went by with Grey staring at the menu, and Graham and me watching her every move, Graham leaned over the table toward her.

"Is it LeAnn?" he asked, soft enough that his voice wouldn't carry.

Grey's head snapped up, her eyes wide and pinned on her brother. "What did you just say?"

"I asked if it's LeAnn."

"Why would you ask that?" she whispered harshly.

"Why wouldn't he?" I asked before Graham started talking again.

"Because you're being weird as shit and we're out in public. Are you afraid she's gonna walk in here? If she does she'll have to turn right back around and leave because of the restraining order. You're gonna be fine."

"No, I'm not afraid she's going to walk in here, and I'm fine, Graham," she mumbled as she shook her head slowly back and forth, like we were the ones acting weird.

Leaning over, I brushed back her red hair and put my lips to her ear, and bit back a sigh when she moved away. "Do you want to leave?"

"Why would I? What is the deal with you and Graham right now?"

Before I could respond, Knox and Deacon came walking up

to the table, Knox talking loudly. "Don't go putting the moves on my future wife. I don't care if you're engaged, Grey's mine."

"*My* future wife," Deacon added as he sat down next to Grey.

I looked up and smiled as Knox dodged Graham's fist. I knew they were just trying to get a rise out of him. If I'd ever thought they actually wanted Grey, I'd try to keep her from them.

"I'm fucking starving. Let's order some burgers already."

Graham pointed at Knox, but looked at me. "See? At least someone here is sane."

"I never said the burgers weren't good, I just said there's other food on the menu!" I argued, and Deacon snorted.

"No. There's only burgers on this menu," he insisted as he drummed his hands on the table and looked around. "Where's our waiter, we've been here for an hour."

Grey laughed and tossed her menu at Deacon. "You've been here for about two minutes, if that, and it's a waitress, not a waiter."

Knox and Deacon both looked up at Grey, smiles crossing their faces. "Is she hot?" Deacon asked, and Grey just raised an eyebrow in confirmation.

"Mine!" Knox and Deacon shouted at the same time, but just before they could get into an argument, Grey cut in.

"You haven't even seen who it is yet! And if I remember correctly, all three of you have been with her at one point."

"Fuck," Knox groaned.

"And I like how you try to claim a girl you want to hook up with like you're four years old and claiming a toy."

Knox grinned. "You have to lay claim when you have roommates who are always going after the same girl as you." His eyes narrowed on someone who was standing behind me, then his face fell. "Damn it, it's Julia. You can have her."

"I don't want her. I had her once already," Deacon hissed just as she came up to the table.

"This is awkward," she mumbled with a forced smile. "Obviously I don't need an introduction, are you all ready to order?"

"Yes," I said before Knox or Deacon could ask for another waitress—it wouldn't have been the first time. "We are."

"Great, what can I get you?"

"I'M SO EXHAUSTED. I feel like a grandma, and it's barely nine," Grey groaned almost three hours later when we were back home. "I just want to go lie down in bed."

I finished arming the security system and looked over my shoulder to see her walking toward the stairs. "Do you think we could talk?"

"Of course, what do you want to talk about?" she asked without stopping.

"Not in the bedroom. I want to talk down here."

Grey turned to look at me when she heard my tone, her eyebrows rising in surprise. "Is everything okay?"

"With me?" I asked on a disbelieving laugh, and walked over to meet Grey at one of the couches. As soon as we were sitting down, I met her stare and held it. "Everything's fine with me. I want to know what's going on with you."

"What do you mean?"

"Do you really not know what I'm talking about? You've been somewhere else all night. Your brother even noticed something was wrong."

"Jagger, I'm just tired today. Work was overly exhausting, and everything kept going wrong there, so I'm just out of it because all I want to do is sleep. What is so wrong with that?"

"Was Graham right? Are you worried about LeAnn?"

She scoffed and sat back. "Why do you both think that all of a sudden? Of course I worry about what she might do, but I don't focus on her like I did while she was trying to destroy us. I honestly think she'll do anything to avoid jail, like I've told you before."

I studied her for a while, then sighed, feeling defeated. "Fine. If you say there's nothing wrong, then there's nothing wrong."

She looked at me again and shook her head. "I just want to go upstairs, curl up in your arms, and pretend like today never happened as I fall asleep. Okay?"

"Okay, Grey," I said softly. "Let's get you in bed, then."

I followed her up the stairs and watched her as we both got ready for bed. After washing her face and stripping down until she was wearing only a thin tank top and her underwear, she climbed into bed and immediately curled into a ball against my chest. I looked down and couldn't help but notice that she still looked like something was on her mind even with her eyes closed. Almost like her entire body was tight even after she'd relaxed onto the bed. Wrapping my arms tightly around her, I rested my chin against the top of her head, and exhaled heavily when I felt the tightness in her body slowly relax. No matter what she said, I couldn't dismiss the way she'd looked all night and knew I would do everything to find out what was wrong if she was still the same the next day.

Chapter 18

Grey
November 12, 2014

My FACE FELL right along with my heart when Mrs. Easton walked up to the counter at work. She looked around like she was genuinely trying to decide what to get, without ever looking at me. But from the sly smile on her face, I could tell that she knew I was there, and I knew *why* she was there. It had been another month and a half since her last visit to The Brew, and for a second I wondered if this was what I'd have to continue to expect until I figured out what to do. Every six weeks, her showing up at my place of work, asking for money. Because her man took off with everything, because her son wasn't hers at all, but allegedly Jagger's . . . and whatever else she had waiting to dump on me.

"I'll take . . . four," she mused, and then glanced down at me with a coy smile.

"Four what?"

"Oh, now don't go playing stupid with me, Grey. You and I both know *what*."

I ground my jaw for a few seconds before giving her the same smile she was giving me. "Four dollars? Sure, I'll give you that in cash this time."

"Don't try to act smart."

"That's an insane amount of money," I hissed, leaning forward so my voice wouldn't carry. "I don't even make enough to give you what I have already given—"

"I knew you had access to his money," she bit out, cutting me off.

I didn't. But I also didn't want to tell her I was taking the money out of my savings, because then she would think she could get even more from me. "I don't have that kind of money, and the fact that you think you can keep raising the price is ridiculous."

"My grandson had to go the ER, Jagger should be footing that bill. And since you already know what will happen if Jagger finds out the truth about Keith, I guess you know what that means for you, don't you?"

Unfortunately, I did. "I want to see the birth certificate and papers giving you custody."

Without missing a beat, Mrs. Easton shrugged her shoulders. "Fine. Come on over sometime . . . without my son. I'll show you myself. Or you could always just ask Charlie," she added with a wicked smile.

I already had asked Charlie, and it hadn't gone over well at all. She had just given me a shocked look and wanted to know who was asking—but never actually gave me a yes-or-no answer. And judging from the smile she was giving me, Mrs. Easton knew I'd been asking around. I hated that there wasn't any sign that she was lying. "I don't have the money."

"You better figure—"

"I'll give you what I gave you last time. And then I don't want you to come asking me for money again. I'm done after this, understand?"

Mrs. Easton's wicked smile turned triumphant and she took a step away. "Your shift here is almost over, correct?" When I didn't respond, she turned around and called out, "I'll be waiting outside."

My boss, Anne, came up beside me and bumped my shoulder. "Hey."

"Hey!" I said too brightly.

"Did that person not want anything or . . ." She trailed off, leaving me to fill in the blank.

"Oh, no. It's, uh, Jagger's mom. She just came to talk to me about something, sorry about that."

"Oh!" She looked in the direction Mrs. Easton had gone to make sure she'd left before whispering, "Your conversation looked kind of heated. I was trying to figure out if I should step in and save you."

A hard laugh burst past my lips. "Appreciate the thought, but it was fine. Sorry, she brought family stuff here."

Anne snorted. "This is Thatch. When isn't there family business—or everyone else's business—going on everywhere?"

"That's true," I mumbled.

Once again, I wrote out the check before leaving the shop and handed it to Mrs. Easton without a word as I walked to my car. My savings account was quickly disappearing because of her, but I was praying that now that I had most of my answers, I would figure out a way for Jagger to get custody of Keith before Mrs. Easton came back again.

FOUR DAYS LATER I was sitting in Graham's living room going back and forth in my mind about whether or not I should tell him about my problem with Jagger's mother. He hadn't brought up my weird "hypothetical" situation since the day we'd talked about it, and I knew there was no way to keep Jagger's name out of it if I fessed up. He would know the question was too personal, he would do the math and figure it out, and then he'd just be pissed that I hadn't been up front with him in the beginning.

"Are you going to tell me why you told me you wanted to see me alone? Not that I blame you, seeing how I live with Knox and Deacon, but I didn't know why you wouldn't want to talk to me in front of Mom and Dad or Jagger."

I swallowed thickly and started twisting my hands together. "Uh . . ."

"I would ask again if you're pregnant, but I'm pretty sure if you were, Jagger would know." A couple seconds passed before he asked sheepishly, "You're not pregnant . . . right?"

"No, Graham, once again I am not pregnant."

"Okay, well then, what is so bad that you couldn't let Jagger be here with you?"

I can do this. I can do this, and I need Graham's help, I reminded myself. With a shaky breath, I squared my shoulders and looked at my brother. "Do you remember when I asked what you would do in that hypothetical scenario that wasn't so hypothetical?"

"Yes . . ." he said slowly, drawing out the word.

"It has to do with that."

"Did they ask you for money again?"

Twice, I thought lamely, but shook my head. "This isn't about asking me for money, I just need to talk to you, and see if you can help me out."

"Is Jagger asking you for money? Is that why he's marrying you?"

My entire body felt like it fell right along with my face. "Really? *Really?* No, Graham, Jesus! Jagger has money; he makes a lot off his drawings. God, the way you think blows my mind sometimes, and I told you this doesn't have to do with someone asking me for money."

"Okay, fine, what is it, then?"

"LeAnn disappeared for almost a year after Ben died, do you know about that?"

"LeAnn . . . LeAnn you-went-to-high-school-with LeAnn?"

"Yes, her."

"How am I supposed to know? I wouldn't touch that mess with a ten-foot pole. Why? Did she come after you? Because if she did, you can call the cops. That's breaking the protective order and her probation."

"Oh my God, Graham, no! I haven't seen her since before we found out that it was her harassing Jagger and me. But there's someone who's holding something over Jagger—against him really, and it has to do with her, and why she disappeared."

"Just so I don't have to try to figure out what you're thinking by myself," he said drily, "why don't you simply tell me the rest?"

"There is someone with a toddler, and they're saying it's Jagger's and LeAnn's. They said LeAnn got pregnant before Ben died, but didn't try to approach Jagger about it until after Ben died, and then Jagger was never alone for her to talk to. So Jagger doesn't know, but he does know the kid because the person who is holding it against him knows him really well and LeAnn gave her custody. And he definitely looks like he could be Jagger's son."

"Holy shit, Grey. How long have you known about this?"

"The end of September. A week after we got engaged," I said warily, awaiting the reaction I knew was coming, and Graham didn't disappoint.

"You're fucking telling me that you've known for a month and a half that your fiancé has a son with some other chick, and you haven't told him? Are you fucking insane?"

"You don't—"

"What the hell, kid? I told you that I would keep Knox from knowing about his sister, but that was if it was some bullshit like what you told me before! I didn't know it was this."

"I didn't know either! What I told you last time is what I had been told! But now it's changed to this, and I don't know what to do. I found out just *weeks* after we caught LeAnn breaking into the warehouse, and this person is threatening to take off with the baby if I tell Jagger! I don't know what to do."

"Easy! You tell him because he deserves to know!"

"I'm trying to protect him, Graham," I argued, and Graham laughed like what I was saying was ridiculous.

"Do you have any idea how pissed he's going to be when he not only finds out that he has a kid, but that you knew?"

My chest tightened. Graham had just confirmed everything I'd been thinking since Mrs. Easton came to me the second time. "There's so much more to all of this, but I swear I am trying to protect him from what's going on. It would crush him if he found out about this person, and I can't let her take Jagger's son away!"

"You're not fucking protecting him!" Graham shot back, and I stood up to yell at him.

"You have no clue what I have been going through over this! So don't tell me what I'm *not* doing, Graham! I need to find a way for Jagger to get custody of his son before I tell him, because if I don't have a plan, he will go to this woman, and she *will* leave! So will you please just listen to me and help me?"

Graham watched me for a few seconds with his mouth tightly shut then shook his head. "Fine. Talk."

I sat back down on the couch and tried to calm my breathing. "At first, I thought the woman was lying to me. But then I started finding out things, like that LeAnn *had* actually disappeared for that year—which I found out right before we all went out to dinner at Bonfire and why I was so spacey that night—and when I tried to trip the woman up about something, she practically offered the whole story up to me on a gold platter without a second thought."

"Kid, just tell me who—"

"I can't. Just trust me; I can't tell you that right now, but I need your help. I have no idea how to go about finding a way to make sure she either can't take off with the kid, or find a way for Jagger to try to get custody immediately—which would also not allow her to leave with the kid."

Graham shrugged and looked at me helplessly. "How am I supposed to know what to do about that?"

"Don't you have any friends that would know? Or have you slept with a girl that would? Something, anything. Because I just keep hitting a wall."

For a long time, Graham didn't respond. He just sat there staring off into space with a frustrated look on his face. "I don't know. Maybe. There's one girl, but she might not help me—I'm pretty sure she hates me."

"That's fine, I just need you to try."

"One condition. Whether we find out a way or not, you have until the New Year to tell Jagger, or I tell him for you. He deserves to know."

"I can't risk losing his son, Graham."

"Grey. Tell him, or I will."

My stomach churned, and the tightness around my chest increased. Looking Graham directly in the eye, I breathed, "I promise."

Jagger
December 20, 2014

THE PAST TWO months with Grey had passed quickly. There'd been nothing distracting her or keeping her away from me; every day started with her in my arms and ended the same, and my time with her never seemed like enough—but somehow was always perfect.

We'd had Thanksgiving dinner with her family, and the next day she'd gone shopping, and when she came back she turned our home into something that belonged in *Elf.* But I hadn't complained, and I'd helped her decorate everything because it was the first time since Ben had died that she'd even been excited about Christmas. I wasn't about to do anything that made her constant smile leave her face, or dull the way her eyes lit up every time she walked into the warehouse.

I'd been about to send off another shipment of drawings to

the gallery in Seattle, but Grey made me wait so we could bring them ourselves. She said she wanted to see everything on display again, and used it as an excuse to do some wedding stuff while we were there. Charlie had traveled to Seattle earlier and immediately met up with Janie so they could go with Grey to try on their bridesmaid dresses today.

We were going to the gallery in a few hours, and then heading back to Thatch the next day, and I was just waiting for Grey to get back so we could get ready and grab dinner before we took off.

My eyes had been slowly closing as I lay back on the bed, and barely cracked open at the sound of a key card opening the door. Grey walked in and came toward the bed slowly, a come-and-get-me grin on her face as her eyes locked with mine.

"Did you have fun?"

She nodded her head, but didn't say anything as her hands moved to lift her shirt off her body. Once her pants and shoes were forgotten on the floor along with the shirt, she said, "I found my dress for the wedding."

I dragged my eyes away from her almost naked body, and my eyebrows rose. "You did? Where is it?"

Grey made a face. "Not with me. Besides, you can't see it anyway." She crawled onto the bed and slid one leg over my body so she was sitting on me, and ran her hands up my torso and across my chest until she was almost lying on me. "But you know what I was thinking on the drive back here?"

I shook my head and unsnapped her bra then pulled it off her, and pressed her down on me. "Not a clue."

She sat up enough so she could reach between us and pull down the top of my pajama pants, and her eyes widened when she found no other layers beneath.

"Didn't feel like putting much on after my shower," I said, answering her unspoken question and groaning when she slowly stroked me.

"I'm not complaining." Grey moved back to take my pants all the way off, and I sat up to prevent her from lying back down on me.

I ran my hands over her bare breasts and stomach, then made a trail over her hips and down in front of her to tease the inside of her thighs. Every time she tried to sit down so my hands would be where she wanted them, I'd move them away and back up to her hips.

"Are you going to tell me?" I asked huskily before pulling one of her nipples between my teeth.

Grey moaned and tried to rock against me, but I was still holding her up.

Releasing her breast, I looked up at her with a challenging stare as the tips of my fingers ran over the front of her underwear, and barely traced between her thighs. "Is that a no?"

She growled when I moved my hand away, and looked down at me. "I was thinking about how excited I am for you to see me in the dress, but then started thinking about you taking it off me."

I bit back a smile and ran the tip of my nose between her breasts before kissing her there. "And?"

"And what you would do to me," she said on a breath, dropping her head back when I moved her underwear to the side to trail my fingers against her.

"And what's that?"

"Pretty much what you're doing now."

Grabbing her waist, I flipped her over so she was on her back, and quickly pulled her underwear off and spread her legs. Positioning myself at her entrance, I kept my eyes on her while I teased her clit, and pushed slowly inside her when she wrapped her legs around me. A breathy moan escaped her mouth, and her eyes fluttered shut when I began moving inside her, keeping in sync with my fingers.

Her breathing became ragged, and she tightened around me within minutes. The feel of her around me as she got closer and closer to coming had me straining not to go with her. I wasn't ready for this to be over. Grey's chest rose with a heavy inhale and stayed there, and I moved my hand away just before she fell over the edge, judging by her frantic pleas and intense moans.

I slammed my mouth down over hers and gripped the sheets as I moved faster inside her, and soon she was matching me thrust for thrust and clinging to my back. Someone knocked on the door a few minutes later, but I ignored it as I reached between our bodies to run my thumb over Grey's clit again. She tightened painfully against me before her body started shaking between mine and the bed, and her moans broke through our kiss. Just as I started to follow her with my own release, there was a louder knock on the door, and I growled in frustration at whoever was out there. "People have bad timing," Grey managed to mutter through heavy breaths, and moved her head to kiss my chest.

"Jagger, is Grey back yet? She forgot to give me the key to my room."

"Are you kidding me?" My head whipped around to look at the door, then back at Grey.

"She has the worst timing *ever,*" she said as she scrambled away from me before running into the bathroom.

Grinding my teeth, I got off the bed and pulled my pajama

pants back on before stalking over to the door just as Charlie knocked on it again.

"Oh! Hey! Did Grey make it back yet?"

"Charlie. You have the worst. Timing. Ever."

She looked confused for half a second before a look of utter horror crossed her face. "Oh God. Oh my . . . eww. Um, I'm just going to go. I'll go to the lobby and ask for a new key. I'm sorry. Tell Grey I'm sorry. So gross. I'm leaving now."

"Don't," I said when she turned around. "Just stay there." Walking back into the room, I grabbed Grey's purse off a counter and searched through it until I found the only key card it contained, since ours was on the counter next to her purse. Key card in hand, I went back to the door and opened it so Charlie could leave.

"I swear to God I'll call you from now on. Or something."

"Worst timing," I repeated, and she nodded quickly as she took the key.

"Yeah, I know. See you in a few hours for dinner. I mean, if you guys . . . never mind. Bye."

Shutting the door, I locked the dead bolt and turned to go find Grey in the bathroom. I stopped as soon as I saw her, laughing so hard that no noise was coming out.

"How can you be laughing at a time like this? This is the third time she's shown up during something like that!"

Grey nodded and took a staggering breath. "That's why! It's like she knows when *not* to show up, and does it anyway." I just glared at her. "Come on, we have to be able to laugh about it by now."

"No. Now I'm scarred for life. I should never have to hear my sister's voice after getting off."

"Ew, why do you have to make it even worse by saying that?"

I looked at her like she'd lost her mind then gestured to the hotel room. "Because that's what just happened! Like I said, I'm scarred."

I turned on the water in the shower, not caring that I'd just taken one about an hour before, and stepped in. Less than a minute later, Grey was stepping in beside me and wrapping her arms around my waist.

"I'm sorry I laughed, but I couldn't help it because she *always* shows up."

"I'm so disgusted right now."

Grey's lips tilted up in a smile she couldn't hold back, and she nodded. "I know you are. Let's get ready for tonight and try not to think about Charlie's uncanny sense of timing, and then tomorrow when we get home, I'll work at de-scarring you. Sound good?"

I looked over and reluctantly agreed. "As long as she doesn't show up again."

"Deal."

Chapter 19

Jagger
December 21, 2014

As I SET out the food I'd picked up on the counter the next day, I cursed when it hit Grey's purse, knocking it off the counter and spilling the contents on the floor. We'd only been home for a little over an hour, and I was ready to just eat and relax.

"Jag?" she called out from upstairs.

"Yeah. Sorry, I'm just knocking over shit. You ready to eat?"

"Yep! I just got out of the shower, let me throw something on."

I smirked as I bent down to pick everything up. "Or you could leave the clothes off," I suggested, and heard her soft laugh.

Shoving everything back in her purse, I paused when I glanced at what was in my hand. I blinked a few times and shook my head before looking back down, but nothing had changed.

Grey's checkbook sat in my hand. All the duplicates were

folded over and held in place by a rubber band, except for the most recent check Grey had written. Just a month ago.

"What're you doing on the floor?" Grey asked on a laugh as she came down the stairs, but I didn't say anything as she crossed the floor. "Babe?"

"What. Is. This."

"What are you talking about, what is wh—" She cut off suddenly when she knelt down next to me and saw what I was holding. "Oh God."

A harsh laugh burst from my chest. "Oh God? Really, Grey?" Standing up so I was looking down at her, her eyes glued to her knees, I took off the rubber band and flipped back through all of her checks before throwing it on the ground next to her. "Why the fuck have you given my mom five grand, Grey?"

She flinched but didn't move.

"When were you going to tell me about this? That first one was months ago, were there any others?"

"No, just the three times." Looking up at me, her face tightened in what looked like pain as tears filled her eyes. "I'm so sorry, I couldn't—I couldn't tell you."

"And why couldn't you tell me?" I asked, my voice rising even more. "You should've told me my mom was coming after you for money. Shit, Grey, this is what she does; this is why I won't let her in our lives. She's constantly trying to get money from me."

Grey jerked her head back. "W-what?"

"Ever since I got the inheritance money from my grandparents, she has been coming after me trying to get it because she blew through all of hers. This is what she does. Why did you give it to her, and why the fuck would you keep something like this from me? We're getting married and you're hiding the fact that you've given my mom five thousand dollars of what you've earned?"

"She's been coming to you for money?"

"Yes, Grey, for years. Now tell me—"

"Why didn't you tell *me,* Jagger?" she yelled. "That is something I should've known—something I should've been warned about!"

"You're really going to start yelling at me when you've been hiding the fact that you gave my mom money, and all I did was not tell you that my mom did this kind of shit?"

"Yes! Yes, I am! If you would've just told me, none of this would've happened! I wouldn't have gone through this for months—I wouldn't have had this guilt eating at me!"

"That right there should've told you that I needed to know what she was doing!" I yelled back. "I was protecting you; you were keeping something from me that you knew you shouldn't have kept! Why the fuck did you keep it from me?"

"I had to! You don't understand, Jagger, she said I couldn't tell you—I had no choice!"

"You always have a fucking choice, Grey!"

Her eyes looked around wildly as if she could find something to help her explain. "The first time she said she'd been laid off from her job, and that some guy named Mike had taken her car and all her money and left. She said you'd begged her not to date him and that you and Mike had exchanged threats every time you saw each other. Your mom was afraid you'd go after him and get arrested, or give her all your money to help her."

"What? I don't know who Mike is, and my mom has never worked a day in her life. She got her money from her parents, and then from all her husbands. But regardless of what she told you, if you *thought* my mom was in trouble, you should have mentioned it to me!"

Grey flinched back again from the force of my voice, and sat roughly on her ass, her body shaking. I was trying to calm down, but the more she said, the more pissed off I was getting. Only now my anger wasn't only directed at her. Mom was manipulative, and Grey had never known anything bad about her because I'd kept her from this bullshit, just like I'd kept Charlie from it.

"You don't get it," Grey sobbed, her anger quickly fading as some other unreadable emotion covered her face. "It was killing me that I'd kept it from you, but I thought I was helping her and Keith when they needed it—and helping you by not letting you do something stupid when you found out."

"She doesn't need anything for Keith, Grey. I buy him everything he needs, I have since I realized the money I was giving her *for* him wasn't even going to him."

"Wait," she said suddenly, her head jerking back and her eyes pinning me with a stare that was a mix of confusion and doubt. "Why would you give her money and buy things for Keith?"

"Someone had to! He had nothing and Mom wasn't making an effort to give him what he needed, and I didn't want Charlie to waste her money on him. Why, if you thought you were helping them and protecting me, wouldn't you tell me the second time? Or, Christ, the third time at least? How would you feel if I kept something like this from you?"

Grey studied me for a few moments, and I watched as her shoulders sagged in defeat. "There was no sob story the second time she came, she just asked for more money."

"And you just continued to give it to her?" My voice bounced back at us in the room, and I fisted my hands as I tried to keep it together. Kneeling down beside Grey, I cupped her face in my hands and made her look at me. "Baby, I'm sorry. Right now I'm mad at *her,* I swear. I hate that you didn't tell me, but my mom is evil, and I'm the only person to ever have seen that side of her. I hate that she went after you. I hate that she's been near you. I'm so fucking mad I'm just trying to talk myself out of going to her—"

"You're not the only one," she whispered, cutting me off.

"What?"

"I know your mom is evil. I saw it that second and third time. I wasn't going to give her more money, but like I said, she left me with no choice. She—she had something on you, and was threatening to do something that I knew would kill you if I didn't pay her, or if I told you."

Confusion quickly replaced my anger when I realized what she was saying. "What on earth could she possibly have on me?"

Grey lifted a shoulder and shook her head. "When I started walking away from her, she said something along the lines of making sure your kid was going to starve."

My heart skipped a beat, and I shook my head to clear it—knowing I'd heard her wrong. "What did you just say? What kid?"

Grey just looked up at me with the most pained expression, her eyebrows rising as if to answer me.

"Grey, I don't understand."

"*Your* kid—*your* son, Jagger."

Ice flooded my veins and pinned me to the floor. I wasn't even sure if I was breathing anymore as her words echoed over and over in my mind. It took over a minute before I could say anything. "Excuse me?"

"LeAnn's son. Your son." Grey shook her head slowly back and forth before choking out, "Keith is *yours,* Jag."

I felt dizzy . . . I felt sick . . . I was so fucking confused. "No he's not. He can't . . ." I trailed off.

"Your mom said LeAnn got pregnant, but by the time she tried to tell you, Ben had died and you were always with me. She said LeAnn disappeared for a long time to hide her condition, and after Keith was born, she gave over custody to your mom— she even said to ask Charlie if I didn't believe her."

My head swung back to look at Grey, shock covering my face. "You're telling me Charlie knows? My own fucking sister has known for two years that I have a kid and didn't say anything? *You* knew I had a fucking kid, with *LeAnn* of all people, and didn't say something to me? I've been thinking he was my brother all this time, and you've all just kept this from me! Was it some sick joke you were all in on?"

"No, Jagger, please stop yelling at me!"

"Well, Jesus Christ, Grey! How do you expect me to react to what you just told me?"

"I'm *sorry,* you have no idea how sorry I am, but I just found out—and like I said, I couldn't tell you! Not only had we *just* found out that it was LeAnn who was doing all the Ben stuff and breaking into the warehouse, but your mom said what LeAnn had been doing to us was because she'd been trying to get her family back together. And it made sense, Jagger! It. Makes. Sense. And then I found out that your mom wasn't lying about LeAnn disappearing for that time, and your mom was threatening to disappear with Keith if I told you! Do you see why I couldn't tell you? It *killed* me, but I had no choice. I've been doing everything I could to find out what happened, and find a way for us to get Keith from your mom once I realized how horrible she really is. That is why I kept it from you, all I wanted to do was help you and help Keith so your mom couldn't leave with him."

At some point in her explanation, I'd begun pacing, and didn't stop for another couple minutes after Grey had stopped talking. I just listened to her cries as I tried to wrap my mind around everything. That my mom had gone after my fiancée. That Grey had kept the fact of the money from me. That she'd kept the truth about Keith from me. The fact that Keith was actually my son, and not my brother.

I stopped pacing, and without turning to look at her, I asked, "How long were you going to continue giving her money? Because you can't honestly believe that she would've just stopped coming to you. Or that she would've stopped trying to hold this over both our heads."

"I was just trying to buy us some time." Grey sounded like all the life had been drained from her. She sounded exhausted in a way I hadn't seen since right after Ben died.

"What else are you keeping from me?"

She looked up at me, and I knew my question had hurt her. "Nothing! There is nothing else, I promise. But what are you keeping from me? I understand that you didn't know about your son. But I just found out that your mom has been doing this for years, why didn't you tell me that? What else do *I* not know?"

"Nothing. I don't have a relationship with my mom for a reason—or with her boyfriends or husbands. I didn't tell you about her because I wanted to protect you from her."

"And what do you think I was doing!" she yelled back, her voice breaking at the end. "I was trying to protect you."

"By paying off my mom, and keeping the truth about Keith

from me." I nodded a few times and bit the inside of my cheek before turning and walking toward the door.

"Where are you going?"

Just before I hit the door, I turned to look at her, still sitting on the floor. "Whether or not you thought you were protecting me, you have no right to keep something like the fact that I have a child from me."

"Jagger!" she cried out when I opened the door and stepped outside, her voice still calling after me as I got into my car.

I took my phone out of my pocket, shut it off, and tossed it onto the passenger seat as I pulled onto the street and headed toward my mom's house. The more I drove, the more confused I became over the whole thing and realized nothing about LeAnn having a son—*my* son—made sense. LeAnn would've said something when she tried to get me back before Grey and I had gotten together. Shit, she would've said something when she tried to break us up those countless times. With all her games and lies, I knew without a doubt that having my child was something she would've used against me.

Pulling up in front of Mom's, I glared at the Escalade parked behind Charlie's car as I stepped out of the car and walked up to the house. A car pulled up to the house, stopping quickly, and I knew without turning around that Grey had followed me here. But I didn't care to acknowledge or wait for her. My mom, sister, and fiancée had all kept something from me—and I would've never imagined that their betrayal would hurt so bad. Not bothering to knock, I opened the door and let myself in, my eyes immediately hitting Charlie as she stepped out of the kitchen. She turned around when she heard me, and a smile broke across her face.

"Hey!"

"Where's Mom?"

Charlie's eyes widened when she heard my rough tone, and she pointed toward the kitchen. "Are you—"

"Where's Keith?"

"Sleeping, what's—"

"Mom!" I snapped. I couldn't let myself move from the front door. I knew if I got too pissed off, I would need to make myself leave. Just before I heard my mom's voice, Grey came running up behind me, and I jerked away when she touched my shoulder.

"Yes, honey?" she called from the kitchen, her tone making it seem like my coming to her house was the most innocent action in the world.

"Jagger, what's wrong?" Charlie asked before her eyes drifted to my side. "Grey?"

"Oh, Jagger, my sweet boy. Why didn't you tell me you were planning to stop by?" My mom walked into the living room, a gentle smile on her face, like every time she was around anyone other than me.

"How could you?" I growled. "How could you all keep this shit from me! Why did you go after Grey like that when I *told* you to stay away?"

Mom's smile faltered, but her voice was still deceivingly calm. "I don't know what you could possibly be talking about."

"Don't try to act like you don't know what I'm talking about. I *saw* her checkbook; I *saw* the goddamn duplicates of the checks she made out to you!"

"Jagger, you couldn't possibly think I would take money from her." Turning around, she glanced at Charlie. "Go to your room, sweetheart."

Charlie didn't move, and I was past caring. It was time she knew too. "Don't bullshit me just because Charlie is here!" I looked at Charlie as I pointed toward Mom. "She's been trying to force me into giving her money for years. That's why I buy everything for Keith—because what I did give to her went to her, and her alone. This whole I-love-everything-and-am-always-carefree-and-happy attitude is just an act. She's made Grey give her five grand!"

"Don't be ridi—"

"I told you I saw the damn duplicates!" I yelled at my mom, and Grey placed a hand on my back and gripped the hand closest to her with the other. Instead of flinching away again, I squeezed her hand and tried to remind myself that even though I was hurt that Grey had kept this secret from me, in Grey's own mind, Mom really had given her no choice. "Grey told me everything. How at first you told her you'd been laid off and Mike took everything. Whether or not some douche named Mike took all your money, I know you sure as shit didn't get laid off because you don't work, and your SUV is still in the fucking driveway."

"Jag—"

"There was never a Mike," Charlie said softly, her eyes touching on Mom before looking at me. "Mom got married again three months ago to Robby, you met him here when you came to talk to me this summer."

"What a surprise," I growled, my gaze going back to my mom. "But that's not it, is it, Mom? That's not the worst part. You tried to use Keith as a way of getting money, didn't you? You tried to say he was LeAnn's and my son? I don't even need to talk to LeAnn to know that is the biggest bullshit I've ever heard! If it was true, you can be sure she would have been the first person to use it against me."

"Jagger, that girl is lying to you to make you think—"

A harsh huff left Grey, but she didn't say anything as her hitched breathing started again. "Really? You're really going to try to utter that bullshit when she's standing right here? Tell me who Keith's parents are."

"You and LeAnn," Mom said immediately, and Charlie turned quickly to look at her—her eyes wide.

"Tell. Me. Who. Keith's. Parents. Are," I gritted out. As soon as Mom started repeating herself, I yelled, "Stop fucking lying to me! I *know* LeAnn would have said something! Charlie," I barked, and turned my attention to her. "If Keith isn't Mom's, then who are his parents?"

Charlie didn't say anything; she just stood there with a ghost-white face and eyes wider than I'd ever seen.

"Don't try to pull your sister into this," Mom hissed.

"You don't want me to pull her into this? You did that all on your own when you told Grey to ask Charlie about Keith!"

Charlie's eyes flashed to Grey before going back to Mom. "What did you say?" she whispered, her tone full of horror.

"I told Grey the truth," Mom said simply.

"*What* truth?" Charlie asked louder.

"That I've been taking care of LeAnn's son since day one, and it was time Jagger started paying." Mom finally looked over at Charlie with a challenging stare, and immediately I knew she was lying again.

"Bullshit! You think I don't know your manipulative looks by now? *Charlie!* Tell me who Keith's parents are. Now!"

"I can't!" she responded, her answer sounding more like a plea.

"Jagger, let's just go. Please," Grey begged. "She's not going to tell us, this is just going to keep going in circles and getting worse."

"Listen to your whore, son, she's smarter than you are, and maybe this one will actually tell you when she gets pregnant with your child."

"Shut the fuck up!" I roared, and took a step inside, but Grey pulled me back. "If this is how you're going to be, and if Keith really is mine, then I want him."

"You can't have him," Mom shot back, and held up a silencing hand when Charlie started to talk.

"You can't even take care of him! I've been taking care of him since he was born anyway. Now I'm taking him, or I will go to court to get him from you."

"You really think I'll just give up custody of him because you finally decided to acknowledge that he's yours?"

"I still don't even think he's mine! But I can be a better fucking parent than you've ever been!"

"You can't take—" Mom began, but was cut off.

"Keith's *my* son!"

Chapter 20

Grey
December 21, 2014

EVERYONE FROZE AT Charlie's words. The only sounds in the house were Charlie's quiet sobs as we all stared at her. Jagger and me in shock, Mrs. Easton with a look that was beyond my comprehension. She looked like the very incarnation of evil, and all of that evil was directed at her daughter.

"Shut up!" Mrs. Easton hissed, and I watched as Charlie shook her head back and forth.

"I'm so sorry. I'm sorry for more than you could ever imagine," she cried as she looked from Jagger to me. "Keith is my son."

"Charlie, no," Jagger finally said. "Don't do this—don't try to save Mom. She's not the kind of person you think she is."

"I know all about her," Charlie responded with a sad smile.

"We hid the pregnancy from you. It wasn't hard since you were always with Grey that summer, and I just wore loose shirts the more I started to show and stopped leaving the house when it became obvious. Then you didn't even come home that winter break after Keith was born—it wasn't hard to play it off as Mom's son. I'd given up custody before I even gave birth to him because Mom didn't think I could handle being a mother. That's why I never went away to college, and that's why I don't like leaving here. I can't be away from him for long, and Mom refuses to give custody back to me."

"She's lying!" Mrs. Easton cut in. "Don't listen to her. She's just trying to take the blame so you won't have to."

"Just *stop*!" Charlie shouted. "Stop with everything. You are hurting everyone, can't you see that?" She took deep breaths in and out, and we waited long moments for her to continue. "Grey, you know I loved Ben. I'm sorry for loving him when he was yours, just as I know Jagger was sorry for loving you when you were Ben's."

I went still. I wasn't sure if I was breathing. I wasn't moving or blinking. All I could do was think about the couple of times Ben and I had been in Thatch in the months before his death, and that Charlie was now crying about her baby and because she'd been in love with Ben. Jagger turned to look at me when he felt how still I'd gone, but I couldn't look at him.

A choked sob burst from her chest, and she dropped her face into her hands. "Spring break of your sophomore year at Washington State, you all came home. You all had gone to a party that first night you were home, and Jagger didn't come home after, he went to LeAnn's."

"Charlie, where are you going with this?" Jagger demanded.

"Jagger," she pleaded. "Ben came over sometime after the party ended looking for Jag, but he wasn't there. Ben wasn't drunk, but he was definitely tipsy, and I let him in to make him something to eat because I didn't want him driving like that. We started talking about random stuff while I was cooking, and I finally asked him why he'd come looking for Jagger if they'd just been together . . . and that's when he told me he hadn't."

The room went silent again except for Charlie's quiet cries. Jagger had gone just as still as I had at her last few words, and Mrs. Easton had stormed out the side door a couple minutes before. I released Jagger and stumbled past him into the living room, where I sat down roughly on one of the couches, my eyes never leaving Charlie's—and hers never leaving mine.

"He—"

"Don't," Jagger ordered as he sat next to me and gripped one of my hands. "Do not finish whatever you're about to say."

"No, Jagger, let her," I somehow forced out. "I need to know."

"Grey . . ."

Glancing at him for a split second, I tightened my grip on his hand before looking back at Charlie. "It's fine."

After another few seconds, Charlie continued. "Ben said he'd never been more confused in his life, and when I asked him what he was confused about, he said everything. He said he was confused about what he knew others wanted and deserved, what he wanted, and how he didn't know what to do or how to feel about what he wanted. I tried to make a joke about it, saying he thought too much when he drank and that it was probably a bad time to start thinking. He just came up next to me and turned the stove off and said, 'You're right, and that's my problem, I finally start thinking about everything I normally push away. But now I can't stop thinking about it, and now I'm here.' Before I could say anything else, he—uh . . . h-he kissed me."

Jagger stood from the couch and began stalking around the room, but I couldn't look at him, and I could no longer look at Charlie.

"I didn't know he was about to kiss me, because Ben and I had always talked, and I'd always been in love with him, but I never thought—I don't know. But at that moment I just thought I was finally getting what I'd always wanted. He said, 'Why do I want you so bad when I love her? And why do I love her when I know she should be with him?' He asked if I wanted him too, and I told him how I'd always felt." Charlie stopped when it got too hard to speak, and Jagger and I stayed silent waiting for the rest. "I gave him everything that night and the next, and I thought everything was finally going to be how it should be. Me with Ben, and Jagger with you, Grey. The day after that second night . . ."

"We got engaged," I finished for her, and finally looked back up at her.

"Yes," she whispered, her face full of a pain and sorrow I knew so well. "I was—I was heartbroken, I was pissed, I couldn't understand it. I didn't know *why* we were going to a party at your house that night, Grey, only that Jagger said he needed me there. When I heard you'd gotten engaged I knew why he said that. Because it was killing Jagger . . . but he had no idea it was killing me more than anyone could've possibly imagined. Ben came after me that night and I started screaming at him, asking how he could get engaged to you after all that had happened between him and me. He said what we'd done was a mistake."

Her voice broke, and she took shuddering breaths to try to compose herself. "I tried everything, I asked how he could tell me that you and Jagger belonged together and then two days later ask you to marry him. I asked how he could be confused and reminded him that he hadn't been drinking the second night we'd been together . . . I asked him how he could suddenly be so sure. He said if he were selfless, he would let you go, and let you be with the guy who'd always loved only you. But that he still loved you too much to let you go, and after everything the two of you had been through, he couldn't risk losing his life with you for someone he loved, but wasn't *in* love with."

"Oh my God," I whispered, my head dropping into my hands as tears fell quickly down my cheeks.

It felt like I was being suffocated, and I couldn't figure out how to breathe again. My heart was broken, but I didn't understand the feeling. My heart had shattered when Ben died, and Jagger had pieced it back together. Years later, Jagger became my new life, and I knew he was everything I would ever need or want from there on out. To learn years after his death that Ben had cheated on me days before we got engaged was the most confusing kind of heartbreak I'd ever experienced. Like I couldn't be upset enough, because my world had already been rocked by his death. Like I'd been betrayed, but somehow knew that my heart hurt for Charlie too. Confused. Devastated. And somehow whole because of the man behind me.

"I found out I was pregnant a few weeks later, and told Ben before you came home after that semester. I didn't know what I'd thought would happen . . . he'd leave you to be with me? He'd be happy, scared, or *confused* again? I didn't know, but nothing happened. He hung up the phone when I told him, and every day after would send me a text asking how I was feeling, but that was it. He wouldn't answer my calls, never responded to my texts, nothing. I tried to see him when you came back, but he made sure he was never alone if I was around. Then he died, and I didn't know how I would ever move on from him. That's why I was so mad that you were able to, Grey. I'm so sorry for hurting you. You'll never know how sorry I am."

Charlie walked away when neither of us said anything, and Jagger came back to sit next to me on the couch and pull me into his arms.

"I had no idea," he mumbled against my head once I'd stopped crying.

"I know you didn't," I whispered back. "Jagger, I'm so sorry that I kept what your mom was—"

"Don't," he begged, interrupting me. "I'm sorry I left, and I'm sorry I yelled at you." He grabbed the ring on my left hand and began twisting it around my finger. "I'm upset that you felt like you couldn't come to me, but after I calmed down I understood why you felt that way. I should've told you about my mom a long time ago. If I had, we could've avoided all of this."

I didn't respond because while I agreed with him, I also couldn't let him take the blame for something that was both our faults, and I knew he would continue to do just that. "What are we gonna do? About your mom, Charlie, and Keith . . . what do we do?"

"I don't know, Grey. I just don't know."

Jagger
December 23, 2014

"I THINK I should go talk to Charlie," Grey said a couple days later.

I stopped putting the dishes from our breakfast in the dishwasher and turned to look at her. "Are you sure you want to do that?"

"Yeah, I am. There are things I need to tell her, and things I need to make sure she understands." Grey sat down on one of the bar stools and rested her chin in one of her hands—her eyes unfocused.

We hadn't talked much about what Charlie had told us. We hadn't talked much at all. After working a morning shift at The Brew, Grey had come home and pulled me upstairs to our bed. Without a word she shrugged out of her boots and jacket, and curled up on the bed still fully clothed. She'd said all she wanted was to lie down and think, and for me to just hold her.

Hours later and only a few words exchanged between us, I'd gotten dinner and brought it back upstairs to eat with her in bed. She lay between my legs while we ate, and for the rest of the night we only talked about the wedding and another show of my work in Seattle coming up. That is . . . *when* we talked.

She'd seemed better that morning and had sung to herself while she made breakfast for us, and I'd just been waiting for the moment when she was ready to talk. I hadn't expected her to want to go straight to Charlie.

"I can call her—" I started to offer, but Grey stopped me.

"No. I want to go to her, not make her come to us." Grey's eyes looked off into the distance for a second, then she asked, "You know how you've always come to me when I was hurting?" When I nodded, she continued: "Well, right now Charlie is hurting, so I need to be the one to go to her."

My eyebrows rose as I took in her determined expression. "And you're not . . . ?" I asked, trailing off.

"Not like I thought I would be. I feel . . . weird. I just feel weird," she confessed with an unsure smile. "I'm more upset right now for Charlie than for myself. When she told us, it hurt, and I didn't understand it. I kept thinking that what Ben and I'd had was a lie. But I know it wasn't. And somehow everything that happened has kind of given me this awkward form of peace."

"Peace," I stated dully. "You found out Ben cheated on you and that my sister had his son . . . and you feel peace?"

She sat up straighter and put her hands on the counter, her palms lightly slapping against the granite. "I told you I feel weird! Okay, so Ben knew how you felt about me, and even made sure to not throw our relationship in your face because he loved you. Ben told Charlie he knew I was supposed to be with you. For so long I didn't know how to keep moving, and I didn't think I was. But you were always there helping me, taking care of me, making sure that both of us kept moving. Once I knew how you felt, all I could think about was Ben, what we had, and what he would think if he knew how I felt about you. And I know you struggled with your own feelings about it."

I shook my head when she paused, and stuttered out, "I don't— where are you—I don't know how that has made you feel peace."

"You don't?" Grey looked directly at me and a beautiful smile crossed her face. "We've both wondered what Ben would think. We've both struggled with our feelings for each other because of Ben. And now we know. Ben loved me, and I loved him. But he knew I was supposed to be with you, and knowing that, and knowing how he tried to make it easier on you, just tells me that what you and I have together is exactly what Ben would want for both of us. Not just now that he's gone, but even when he was still here. It is the most calming thing knowing that. Yes, it hurt when

Charlie told us. It hurt knowing that he'd cheated on me when I'd been with him for seven years; we'd already talked about getting married so many times, and we came back to Thatch specifically to talk to our parents about moving in together—*knowing* they would say no, and tell us we needed to be married first. But I have you now, and right now the thing that hurts me the most is what Charlie went through, how he treated her, and how she's gone through the last two and a half years with this huge secret."

"So you feel weird," I finished for her, and her smile widened.

"Yes. I feel weird, and I want to go talk to your sister."

"All right, then you should. Do you want me to go with you?"

"I do, but I want to go in and talk to her alone. I want you there if she needs you, and I have a feeling I'm going to need you when it's all over."

Pushing away from the counter, I walked around the bar and turned Grey so she was facing me and I was standing between her legs. "After everything you've gone through, you're still so strong. With Ben's death, and then everything that's happened over the last few months, no one would blame you if you just shut down and wanted to get away from everything. But you've stood strong, you've faced it, and now your main concern is my sister, when everyone would expect you to hate her." Cupping her face in my hands, I brought her closer to me and placed two light kisses on her lips. "You're amazing, and I love you."

She smiled against our next kiss, and wrapped her arms securely around my waist. "I'm really not. If we had found this out any sooner, I probably wouldn't be this calm about it. But I feel like all the hard stuff is behind us. Ben's death. LeAnn trying to keep us apart. Your mom. And the secret that Charlie's had to keep all these years. Everything's done now. We've already been through hell. There isn't much more that can happen, Jagger. Knowing that, and having you here, makes all of this a lot easier."

Grey
December 23, 2014

WITH A CALMING breath, I raised my hand and knocked quickly on the door to Jagger's mom's house. When no one answered, I knocked a little louder and waited when I heard someone running inside. Charlie swung the door open, her face falling when she saw that it was me.

"Grey . . ."

"Can I come in?"

She stared at me for a few seconds before nodding. "Yeah, of course."

I stepped in and glanced around before asking, "Your mom isn't here, is she?"

"No, she went somewhere with her husband yesterday morning, I haven't heard from her since then."

"Did she take Keith?" I asked quickly, my chest tightening at the thought.

"No, I'd just put him down for a nap when you started knocking. Are you here to . . . if you're going to yell at me, then just start."

Turning to fully face her, I threw my arms around her and pulled her close. After a few seconds of hesitation, she wrapped her arms around me and started sobbing into my chest. "I'm sorry for everything you went through, Charlie. I was hurt the night you told Jagger and me, but now I hurt for you. If I had known what had happened all along, things would've been different. How different? I don't know, because to be honest, I probably would've been a lot more pissed off then than I was the other night. But at least you wouldn't have had to go through all the suffering alone."

I stood there holding her until she finished crying, and then walked over to a couch, waiting for her to join me.

"Why aren't you screaming at me?"

"Because I forgive you, and I forgive Ben for what he did to me . . . but not what he did to you. I now have Jagger, and apparently I was really the only one who didn't see what I was supposed to see for a long time. But my friends saw it, Jagger saw it, my family saw it, and apparently so did you and Ben. Even the man who I thought was the love of my life knew who I was supposed to be with."

"But you did love him," she argued.

"I did, and I still do. I will always love Ben. But after what you told me, and after thinking about my entire life with Jagger, I'm not sure that Ben really was the love of my life. I loved him for such a long time, and that love grew, but thinking back— even before I found out what he'd done—I knew something was different in what I have with Jagger now from what I had with Ben. So now I'm wondering if it was the thought of it all that I wanted so much. I'd been with Ben since I was thirteen; getting married felt natural; and since we wanted to move in together, it kind of became necessary. And getting married to my childhood sweetheart was something of a fairy tale for me—or at least that's how it seemed. I remember thinking that it was all perfect, that my life was playing out exactly how it should, because not many people get to have the type of story Ben and I would've had.

"I loved Ben, and I would've married him and been happy for the rest of my life. But the way I was seeing that life was what made it seem so perfect. I was living in a fantasy and blinding myself to everything else around me. If I hadn't, I would've noticed what I felt for Jagger earlier. Because I still can't think of when I changed from loving Jagger to being in love with him, I just knew one day that I was in love with him and had been for a long time. And if I hadn't been in my fantasy, I would've noticed that Ben was confused. I would've seen how he stayed away from me when we were around Jagger, for Jagger's benefit. I would've seen that he had feelings for you in all those times we were around you. I would've seen that something was going on with him in the weeks leading up to his death. I would have seen that we were only getting married right then because we wanted to live together and I wanted my fairy tale to move forward, and not because we were ready. But I didn't see any of those things, and because of that you had to live through years of pain. And I'm sorry."

By the time I finished, Charlie was sobbing again. "You shouldn't apologize to me. I made him be unfaithful to you. I was mad at you for being happy with Jagger."

"You didn't make him do anything. It was his choice, his decision, his acting on something he was confused about. And I understand why you were mad. I understand it completely and don't judge you for that at all."

She was shaking her head back and forth, her eyes looking down as she continued to whisper "I'm sorry" over and over again.

Scooting closer to her, I grabbed her hand and waited until she looked up at me. I sent her a sad smile as tears filled my own eyes. "Stop apologizing, Charlie. We all, unfortunately, know how short and unpredictable life is. It took me a long time to realize what I was doing to the people around me and myself by clinging to what had been and what could've been. That's why I'm treasuring every second of my life with your brother, and that's why I want for you to heal and move on with yours. I learned very recently how to let go of the past, and it was the most freeing feeling when I did. Letting go doesn't mean forgetting. It's accepting, forgiving, and being emotionally ready to keep moving."

"I don't think I can do that," she admitted. The pain in her voice was the same pain that had echoed through my own mind just months ago.

"I know it's so much easier to get trapped in the past because you *want* to stay there, but it's also dangerous, and you have to be the one to decide you're ready to move on. I love you, Charlie, I've known you most of my life, and you've always been like a sister to me. I'm not letting Keith or what happened come between us. It's in the past, and I'm willing to let it stay there if you are."

She didn't say anything, just stared off into space as she quietly nodded her head; so I hugged her tightly, and then stood up. When I got to the door, I turned around to look at her.

"Do you ever go to the cemetery?"

She slowly looked up at me, her eyes red and puffy. "No."

"Maybe you should. Go talk to Ben . . . about anything. Yell at him, tell him everything that's happened, whatever you want. But it might be good for you."

"O-okay."

"Jagger's worried about you, and so am I. Come talk to us

whenever, and bring Keith with you." With a smile in her direction, I stepped outside and walked to Jagger's car.

He stepped out as I got closer, and rounded the hood to pull me into his arms. "How'd it go?"

"Good, I think. I gave her a lot to think about."

"You think she'll be okay?"

"I do." Pressing my mouth to his, I leaned back and tightened my arms around him. "And she'll let us know when she is."

"All right." He glanced up at the house and took a deep breath; then he nodded and repeated, "All right. Let's go home."

Epilogue

Grey
December 24, 2015

MY FOREHEAD PINCHED together and I looked back into the bathroom I'd just walked out of before glancing at the empty bed again. I'd only been in there for a max of twenty minutes as I took a shower and got ready for bed; and when I'd gone in, I'd left a sleeping Jagger.

Making sure to make my steps as silent as possible on the stairs, I walked down to the first floor and rounded the walls of the room we'd added on to the warehouse about six months ago. I loved this room. It was large and broke up the space of the warehouse perfectly, all while hiding the stairs leading up to our loft.

I opened the door to the room and rested my body against the door frame as my chest warmed and a smile crossed my face. This was the best part of the room. It held our three-month-old daughter, Aly, and currently a sleeping husband on the chair with our sleeping daughter on his chest.

Stepping into the room, I brushed my hand against Jagger's shoulder and carefully took Aly from him. Breathing her scent, I held her close for a few minutes before putting her back in her crib. I turned around to my half-awake husband and held my hand out to help him get out of the chair.

"She started crying," he mumbled as he pulled the door until it was barely cracked open and followed me toward the stairs.

"I figured, since when I left you, you were out."

"Liar."

I looked over my shoulder at him and lifted one eyebrow. "You sure about that? You fell asleep midconversation."

"No, I—" His barely open eyes glared up at me, then he nodded and put his hands on my waist to push me up the stairs. "Maybe."

"Yeah," I whispered on a laugh. "Maybe."

Putting my hands over his, I gripped them tightly when we reached the loft and he released my waist, and led him to the bed. He crawled in after me and automatically wrapped his arms around me, pulling me against his chest. Sliding one of his legs between mine, he tightened his arms and kissed the back of my neck before murmuring something about crying babies and needing to make bottles of milk for all of them because there was a breast-milk shortage in the world.

I bit back a laugh and sighed as I got comfortable in his arms, wondering how much of everything he'd done over the last twenty-five minutes had been done while he was actually conscious. Hazards that came from having a toddler and infant in the house.

Jagger and I had found out I was pregnant a month after Charlie told us everything about her and Ben's short time together, and the reactions from everyone had been mixed, to say the least. After getting over the initial shock, Jagger and I were beyond excited. We hadn't been using protection anyway, so it was something we both knew could happen; and just like with everything else that had happened in our lives since we finally got together, it didn't seem rushed. It was perfect—nothing else could describe the pace at which our lives were going.

Charlie had taken it hard at first because she had still been at a point where she was starting to openly grieve what had happened to Ben, and because she had never been able to be excited about having Keith. But ultimately she'd been happy for us, and after a few months had wanted to be involved with everything even when she was away at school.

Graham had glared at Jagger every time he saw him for a solid three months until we'd gotten married, and then refused to acknowledge that the baby I was carrying was mine and Jagger's for a few more months—chalking it up to my somehow managing to get pregnant all by myself. Whatever. He didn't attempt to kill Jagger, so whatever ridiculousness he came up with had been fine by me.

My mom continued to ask if we were using protection even after she found out that she was going to be a grandma, and still gets a little flustered whenever she sees Jagger. It's weird and somewhat disturbing, but Jagger and I have just learned to roll our eyes and ignore her. Dad on the other hand was a little bit harder to get through to. After already having tried to prevent my moving in with Jagger, he was livid that we'd gotten pregnant before we were married. He was still my loving dad, and was as nice to Jagger as he'd always been, but it wasn't until Aly was born that he finally broke down and was excited about her.

We hadn't seen Jagger's mom in a year—actually, no one had seen her in almost a year—so she didn't even know about Aly. Charlie and Keith had moved in with us once Charlie realized her mom wasn't coming back, and had started going to a school only a couple hours away this past fall. Now that it was winter break, she was with us and staying in the back room with Keith. A few months after Charlie and Keith moved in, we found the rest of their belongings in front of the warehouse door. Jagger's mom had cleared out the house and moved away with her latest husband, Robby. No one knew if they were actually still married or not, but we all doubted she would return to Thatch even if they divorced, since she knew she wasn't well liked around here.

Since she'd more or less abandoned Keith, and Jagger and Charlie could prove that she wasn't a fit mother, Jagger and I began the process of getting legal custody of Keith. It was easier for us since we were older than Charlie, had money coming in, and had been about to get married—and the agreement stated we would raise him until Charlie was done with school and financially capable of taking him. It was crazy becoming parents to a toddler and infant all within a year, but we'd learned quickly what we needed to know, and now things were better than ever.

Things were great here. Our lives weren't perfect. We had our moments, but it was as close to perfect as anyone could get. I was married to my best friend, my protector, and the love of my life . . . and I couldn't be happier. I had just started back at The Brew after taking time off for Aly, and Jagger was still selling his drawings to his guy in Seattle—which gave us an excuse to see Janie every few months. Keith was a riot and had quickly captured both our hearts, and Aly was the most precious baby. Even when she was screaming her head off, it was impossible not to be completely enraptured by our little girl. And we still visited Ben's grave every now and then just to give him an update on everyone—including Charlie.

Like I said: not perfect, but as close to perfect as we could be.

Hands tightened against me for a second, then Jagger mumbled against the back of my neck, "Grey?"

"Yeah?"

"Merry Christmas, baby."

I opened my eyes to see the clock on my nightstand reading 12:04 A.M., and smiled as I squeezed his arms. "Merry Christmas, Jag."

The End

Acknowledgments

As always, thank you to my amazing husband, Cory. I really could not do any of this without you, thank you for everything you do for our girls and me so I can get the stories written. Love you!

My amazing agent, Kevan Lyon, and my wonderful editor, Tessa Woodward: Thank you from the bottom of my heart! You two are incredible and I am so so thankful to have you both on my side. Right now you are both at RT14 and I'm pretty sure I sobbed because I didn't get to be there with y'all again!

AL Jackson, words cannot express how thankful I am for you! Thank you for the sprints, thank you for the long phone calls so we could talk out our stories, and thank you for being an amazing friend! Love you, BB!

Amanda Stone, what can be said that hasn't already been said? I love you, my days would be dull without you, and I honestly don't know how we went so long without each other! You're my best friend and Sef, and what would I do if you weren't there to listen to the craziness that is my street caught on camera? ;)

To all the readers and bloggers who helped promote this story: THANK YOU, THANK YOU, THANK YOU! You all make my heart so happy, and I am beyond blessed to have your support with these novels. You're all wonderful and I love communicating with you on social media whether it's about randomness in my life, my stories, or someone else's . . . I love it, and I love y'all!

Want more? Keep reading for a sneak peek at Molly McAdams's next heart-wrenching and heart-warming story, *Trusting Liam*.

Kennedy

CRACKING AN EYE open, I immediately shut it against the harsh light coming into the room and bit back a groan from the pounding in my head. Making another attempt—this time with both eyes—I squinted at the unfamiliar hotel room and blinked a few times before letting my eyes open all the way as I took in my surroundings. Well, as much of them as I could without moving.

There was a heavy arm draped uncomfortably over my waist, a forehead pressed to the back of my head, a nose to the back of my neck, and an erection to my butt. What. The. Hell. I was naked; he was naked. *Why are we naked, and who is behind me?!* If I wasn't seconds from screaming for someone to help me, I might have snorted. The *why* was obvious, there was a familiar ache between my legs, and my lips felt puffy from kissing and where he'd bitten down on them.

I inhaled softly. *He. Him.* Oh God.

Flashes from last night took turns assaulting me with the pounding in my head. Impromptu trip to Vegas with the girls after finals ended. Dancing. Club. Drinks. Arctic blue eyes captivating me. More drinks and dancing. *Him* holding me close, and not close enough. Lips against mine. Stumbling into a room. Hands searching. *His* tall, hard body pressing mine against the bed—still not close enough.

My eyes immediately went to my left hand, and I exhaled slowly in relief when I didn't find a ring there. *Thank God, the last thing I need is a marriage as result of a drunken night in Vegas.* I rolled my eyes. The last thing I needed was a man in my life, period. And if my family wouldn't kill me for it, I would have died from embarrassment if I had ended up with a ring on my finger after last night. Because unlike what everyone loves to believe so they can feel better about their dirty deeds while in Sin City, what happens in Vegas doesn't always stay in Vegas.

Trying not to wake him, I slowly slid out from under his arm and off the bed to search for my clothes. Once I was dressed, I told myself to just leave, but I couldn't help it—I turned to look at him in the light. I needed to be sure I hadn't made *him* up.

The images from last night tore through my mind again when I saw the large, tattooed arm resting where my body had just been. The muscles were well defined, even relaxed, and the face had a boyish charm now that *he* was asleep. Such a difference from the predatory stare and knowing smirk I kept seeing in my mind. Before I could stop myself, I gently ran my fingers through his dirty-blond hair that, now in the sunlight, I could see had a red tint to it. And I knew if he opened them, those arctic blue eyes would once again captivate me.

But I couldn't risk that.

I'd already stayed too long; I'd already made a mistake with him. Drunken one-night stands weren't my thing. Drunken one-night stands with strangers in Vegas were even worse.

Straightening, I turned and walked quietly from the room.

Chapter 1

One year later . . .

Kennedy

"WHY ARE YOU trying to doing this to me?" Kira yelled as she stood from where she'd been sitting on the couch.

I looked over at my identical twin to see a look of horror on her face, and waited for the freak-out that I knew was only seconds away. Shifting my attention back to our parents, I mumbled, "Told you it wouldn't go over well."

"But—you can't—Kennedy, why . . . Zander's in Florida," Kira sputtered out, and I rolled my eyes at the same time as my dad.

"Is that supposed to mean something to me?" Dad asked as he crossed his large tattooed arms over his chest.

Not willing to give Kira time to respond to that kind of question, I started talking over Dad before he could finish. "Did you ever think that maybe a little distance might be a good thing for the two of you? And did you *not* hear Dad? These guys are out of prison, Kira!" I shouted and punctuated the last few words, just in case she'd missed the memo the first time around.

"Maybe Zander will go with you," Mom offered, a sympathetic look on her face that I knew was as well practiced as it was a lie. The worry was still there in her eyes, as was the eagerness to get us away from Florida . . . and it wasn't exactly a secret that we all wanted Kira to get space from Zander.

They'd been together since we were fifteen, and the more time went on, the more Kira's world revolved around only him. It was annoying.

"And leave his job?" Kira countered.

"Well, then maybe this will be good for you, like Kennedy said. Get a break from Zander so you can see other options. You girls are only twenty-two, you just graduated from college, and you're too young to be getting serious anyway, Kira. You'll regret not enjoying life first."

Dad's head jerked back and he sent Mom a look. "What the hell is that supposed to mean? You were twenty-one when we got engaged."

"Seriously, Kash? That was different. *We* were different. She's *only* dated Zander."

"Can we get back to the more important discussion?" I cut in before Dad could respond. "*I'm* going to California. *You're* going with me. *Zander* can deal with it."

"You can't do this! I'm not going!" Kira shrieked as the tears started.

"You act like I'm giving either of you a choice. Both of you need to start accepting this."

My eyes widened at my dad's dark tone, and I shot right back, "You act like you still have a say in our lives. You haven't for four years. And if you remember, I'm going along with what you want without complaint. So don't throw me into the same category as Kira when she's the only one fighting you on this."

One dark eyebrow rose, and I saw Kira sink back onto the couch from the look he was giving. Too bad I was just like him: hardheaded and stubborn. I may be my sister's mirror image, but I was nothing like her. I raised one eyebrow back at him, and Mom sighed.

"I don't know how I put up with you two sometimes," she groaned, rubbing her hand over her forehead. Looking at Kira, she said, "You're going to California, no more discussion. This is for your safety, why can't you see that?"

"I'm not going!" Kira sobbed. "Who cares if some guys Dad put away *years* ago are out of prison?"

I snorted, but before I could respond, Uncle Mason's deep voice sounded directly behind us. "The men do."

I turned quickly to look at him, and tried not to laugh when he gave Dad a questioning look and mouthed, "Zander?"

"Is there any other reason she would be freaking out like this?" I asked as I stood to go give him a hug.

"Are you both packed?" he asked.

"Packed?" Kira yelled again. "They just told us! I haven't even called Zander!"

"Oh my God, no one cares."

"Kennedy," Mom chastised, but I knew she was thinking the same thing.

As soon as Kira was out of the room, I sighed and turned and headed to my room to pack as much as I could. Kira was already packing and sobbing into her phone when I passed her room, and I somehow managed to hold back an eye roll. Never mind that our parents had just told us that our family was being threatened by members of a gang our dad and uncle Mason had put away before we were born. A gang whose members had kidnapped our mom and held her for over a month in an attempt to free their main members from prison. Or that the majority of them were getting out of prison within the next handful of months. Or that Kira and I were the main targets in their threats. Nope . . . none of that mattered to Kira right now. What mattered was that we were going to be living in California for the time being—close to our mom's side of the family—and Zander wouldn't be going with us. No Zander meant devastation in Kira's world. She couldn't even get dressed without telling everyone about a memory with Zander in that outfit, or that it was one of his many favorites.

Snatching a hairband off my desk, I pulled my thick, black hair into a messy bun on the top of my head and started packing. I didn't turn to face Kira when she came into my room ten minutes later, but I knew she was there.

"How could you do this to me?" she asked quietly, her words breaking with emotion. "You're supposed to be on my side, you're *always* supposed to be on my side. And you went behind my back and planned this with Mom and Dad without even warning me?"

I glanced over my shoulder, my eyebrows rising at her assumption. "I didn't plan shit, Kira. They told me while you were talking to Zander right before they asked you to get off the phone. They just wanted me to know because they thought you would freak out and they needed me to be able to try to talk you into it calmly—rather than hitting us both with the news at the same time. The only difference between you and me, is I have no problem with this move because I'm not stupid enough to think that the gang won't actually make good on their threats. Or try to."

I went back to packing, and there was a couple minutes of silence before she said, "I know why you're all really doing this. Don't think for a second that *I'm* stupid enough not to realize this is about Zander."

I released a heavy breath, and shook my head. "Despite what you think, this has nothing to do with you and your boyfriend. But I *do* think that this is something we need to do, and I think it will be good for us."

"I won't forgive you for this. You of all people should realize how much this is going to kill me."

My breath caught, but I didn't reply. I knew I couldn't without lashing out at her. Without another word, she left my room. The only sounds were her soft cries and her feet on the hardwood as she did.

"So now that you have us on a private jet—which just makes this all the more weird, by the way—do you mind telling us details about where we'll be spending the next however long?" I asked Uncle Mason a few hours later.

"Didn't your mom and dad tell you everything?"

I gave him a look that he immediately laughed at.

"Okay, tell me what you know, and I'll fill in the blanks."

"Basically, all I know is that Juarez and a handful of others from his crew are getting out within a few months of each other starting next week. They're somehow threatening us—but more specifically, Kira and me. I don't know the *hows* or *whats* though. And we're going to be in California for an undetermined amount of time, close to Mom's family."

"I wasn't told most of that," Kira muttered from where she was sulking across the aisle.

"You *were* told that," I shot back. "All of that. You just couldn't get past the California-equals-no-Zander part, and flipped while they told you the rest!"

Before we could start on another war, Uncle Mason spoke up. "You'll be just North of San Diego, near your Uncle Eli. He's already been looking into places for you live, and your parents are working something out with them for a car."

"Lovely. Sounds like everyone is already completely filled in," Kira sneered.

Uncle Mason didn't respond for a long time, just sat there staring at Kira with a somber expression. It was so unlike him. "I don't want you two to have to do this any more than you do, trust me. Your dad and I know better than anyone what it's like to pick up and move at a moment's notice, not being able to have a say in it, so we know what you're going through."

Kira mumbled something too low for me to hear, but it was obvious in her expression that she didn't agree with him.

After a subtle shake of my head, I looked back at Uncle Mason and tapped his leg with my foot to get his attention again. "Okay, so we've heard about Juarez's gang, and what happened with Mom being taken. But here's what I don't understand and am having a little bit of trouble with. Why, after so much time has passed, do you think it's them threatening us? Wouldn't they be over it by now? I mean, couldn't it just as easily be someone you've arrested recently, and you're just jumping ahead and thinking its Juarez?"

Uncle Mason was already shaking his head before I even finished asking my questions. "No. It may have been twenty-three years ago, but we haven't forgotten what happened, and we know for a fact they haven't and are still holding a grudge because there have been letters delivered to your dad."

"What did they say?"

"It doesn't matter."

"What did they say?" I asked louder, and Kira leaned toward us in her seat to hear what he would say.

"I said it doesn't—"

"We deserve to know!" I snapped.

"They said, 'Can't wait to meet the rest of your family', and 'How are those daughters of yours?'" Uncle Mason sighed heavily and looked out the window for a few seconds.

"That's it?" I asked when he didn't continue. "I mean, that's really creepy but it doesn't really prove much of anything."

"It does, because at the bottom it had the gang's symbol. A symbol your dad and I used to have tattooed on us when we were undercover. A symbol they left spray-painted on your parents' wall after kidnapping your mom."

"Oh," I breathed, and Uncle Mason sent me a look.

"Yeah. 'Oh.'"